VIRTUOUS VOWS

USA TODAY BESTSELLING AUTHOR

T.L. SMITH
KIA CARRINGTON-RUSSELL

Did you tell him about me? How you stroke those pages when you think of me.
Sincerely,
Your book boyfriend

 Created with Vellum

Warning

This book contains sexually explicit scenes and adult language and may be considered offensive to some readers. This book is intended for adults ONLY. Please store your books wisely, where they cannot be accessed by under-aged readers.

Honey

I was destined to marry another man when I first met Dawson.
He was charming, deadly, and everything my father hated.
And I lived by my father's rule, which happens when he's a king of the underworld.
That was until I managed to escape and somehow straight into the arms of the man who sells your desires for a living.
But did I have a price?
Or was he willing to share me for free?

Dawson

Innocent and breathtakingly beautiful, she was as her name described.
Honey suited her perfectly in all senses of the word— soft, sweet, and a little sticky.
My world and hers should not have mixed.
But something as sweet as honey is meant to be enjoyed.

CHAPTER 1
Honey

Be a good girl and don't think about dick.
Stop thinking about his dick.
Dick.

Dick.

Dick.

Argh. How is that all I can think about?

My sister dances with Crue, the hem of her ankle-length white dress flowing across the floor. And if I'm being candid, I think it's the first time I've ever seen her in white. Dawson and I are dancing together in slow motion. And I can feel him.

"Did you just say..." He shakes his head.

"Huh?" I reply, confused. Looking up at his bluer-than-blue eyes, I'm almost taken aback. Not only with his eyes, but Dawson is beautiful., charming, and he has everything. The perfect jawbone, straight and faultless, to his long lashes fanning those blue eyes. Jealous really. His hair, mocha in colour is slicked back, but not in a bad way. It's more like, I want to run my hands through it to mess it up, badly.

"You said dick."

Well, shit.

Knowing there's no way I can dig myself out of that one, I lean in and sheepishly whisper, "Yes, I'm pretty sure I can feel your dick."

He stops moving and stares at me, his magnificent jaw locks. I can't believe I said that to a man I hardly know, and I instantly feel the heat flushing my cheeks. I look away, but his hand cups my chin and pulls me back to meet his gaze.

"Does that bother you?"

Dick.

Dick.

Dick.

"Yes," I say, and I can't tell if it's a lie.

Does it really bother me? Not really, but it's all I can think about because this man is beyond ridiculously attractive. How could it not be my focus? And on the middle of a dance floor surrounded by family and strangers, it's the last thing I should be thinking about.

With the façade of a gentleman, he pulls away and walks off the dance floor. And I'm left standing here, dumbfounded and wondering how the change of events happened so quickly these last two weeks.

Obviously, I know...

I was engaged to my sister's husband.

Today is their wedding day.

Weird, some might say.

But I never once kissed or even touched Crue in any way. It was an arranged marriage, and being the good girl I am, I was going to go through with it since my sister refused.

Rya left the country to get away from marrying him. Yet here we are, dancing at her wedding as she looks up at her husband with such love, and now I am left wondering if I will ever have what she has. I mean, I thought it was what I wanted because I was told the position was mine.

I've always been watched, told how to act, and praised for my submission. Because if Rya wasn't here to do her duty as the eldest daughter, I had to be the backup. But now, with the marriage contract complete, I don't know what I'm supposed to do or what I'm even good for.

I've played the good girl for so long that I don't know who I am outside of this role. No longer obligated by a looming contract with the families, I still have no idea who I am.

I'm still a goddamn virgin, for God's sake.

I don't want to be a twenty-seven-year-old virgin.

And it's not like I haven't done other intimate things, but I planned to keep my virginity for my husband. I want to give him that because I was told, virginity is to be cherished and special.

I mean, I'm not a complete saint—I have sucked

some cocks in my life. I even had a man go down on me. However, I didn't quite enjoy that.

But the cock sucking part? Well, I liked the power I held. I wasn't giving them everything, but I could still dabble in being what might be considered naughty.

"Honey, are you okay?" my sister asks, snapping me out of my thoughts. I don't particularly appreciate how Dawson arouses these feelings and curiosity. It's like I want to explore and find myself through him because why the fuck not?

He's so attractive.

But he's completely off-limits.

And probably the fantasy of every other woman here.

And if I told others I'm a virgin, they'd probably laugh at me.

"Honey," my sister repeats worriedly.

"Did I tell you that I'm still a virgin?" I ask her.

Crue coughs from behind her. I know he heard me, but I don't care. The man's now basically my brother, right? But he's the type you'd never want to get on the wrong side of because you know he'll bury you six feet under if you piss him off, family or not.

"Father said I don't have to marry now that you've completed the contract between the families, and to be honest, I don't know what to do—" I stop abruptly, realizing I've disclosed *way* too much, especially on what is meant to be her special day. "I'm sorry. I'm being super insensitive." I change the subject. "The champagne's nice. Maybe I should get another glass." *Shut up,*

Honey, and stop nervously blubbering. You look like a damn idiot.

She touches my shoulder and says, "I have to go back home in a week. Do you want to come with me? To get away?"

"Princess?" Crue says quietly from behind her. "We will be fucking on every surface of our home. Are you sure you want your sister to come and stay with us?" His words are supposed to be a whisper, but I hear him clearly.

Rya turns, her expression somehow reprimanding as she kisses his cheek reassuringly. Crue huffs, and I know she's gotten her way. It baffles me how she has this powerful and deadly man wrapped around her finger. And yet, I wouldn't expect anything less of my sister. Hell, even I wouldn't screw with her.

"You can at least come two days after," he says to me as if it is his thought and agreement before he walks away.

My sister looks over to our father. "Do you want him to organize an arranged marriage for you? Because you know he will if that's what you want."

No, that is *not* what I want at all. But when it's implied your whole life that you're to be wedded on someone else's whim and then suddenly set free, it definitely fucks with you. I consider her offer. Despite my sister living in New York for the last fourteen years, I'd never visited her as I continued to study and kept my parents happy. But if Rya was able to find herself there, then maybe I could have the same luck too.

What do I have to lose, right?

"I'll come," I tell her.

Her expression asks if I'm sure, but she doesn't say anything at first. Then she nods, kisses my cheek, and says, "Okay, good. It will be really nice to have you there, and we can figure out the rest I'll start your visa process so you can work. Maybe you can try for a job? It's usually a good way to make friends in a new city."

I've never worked a day in my life, but the thought seems almost exhilarating, so I answer immediately. "That sounds really good, thank you." Maybe I could become a new me. I could have a try at my own income and support myself instead of everything being taken care of for me.

Almost simultaneously, we feel Crue's gaze focused in our direction as he stands near the bar, ignoring those who approach him. His attention is on only one person in this room.

"Maybe we should talk more about this later," I say, taking the obvious hint.

Rya chuckles. "Excuse me while I attend to my husband and let him fondle me." But then she quickly adds, "Don't stress about being a virgin, Honey. You'll know when the time is right."

It still shocks me that I'd blurted that out. But worse, I've always thought the same, and now I don't want it to feel special. I'd held on for too long, and for what?

I make my way to the opposite self-serve bar. Grabbing a bottle of champagne, I pour myself a glass and look at the dance floor.

"Are you still thinking about my dick?" I jump and almost spill my drink. I didn't even hear Dawson sneak up beside me. My hand presses against my chest over my rapidly beating heart.

"I wasn't..." I trail off.

He smirks, reaches for the bottle I put down, and pours himself a glass.

This man should not be this attractive. It's almost a crime.

"But you are now?" His blue eyes pin me as he takes a sip of champagne. I can't look away.

"Well, since you brought it up..." I say courageously. I haven't been this daring with most men. But for some reason, with Dawson, it's easy. Maybe because I know I won't see him again.

He puts the drink down and smirks. "I know of an unused closet back there if you want to—"

"Okay," I blurt abruptly, and he seems almost surprised. I don't know why someone this attractive is shocked. I bet all types of women agree to whatever he wants with little hesitation. His head drops to the side, then he places my glass on the bar counter behind us. He reaches for my hand and pulls me toward the back of the room. We leave the reception, and my gaze is glued to his hand holding mine and how casually yet possessively he leads me. I'm too nervous to look in any other direction and at who might have seen us.

I can hear my heart pounding.

Am I really about to do this?

No, surely not.

Losing my virginity at my sister's wedding? Is that really what I'm signing up to do? But then, once it's done, it's done, right? A new me. A decision I've finally made for myself.

We stop before a door, and he pulls it open to reveal a supply closet. Dawson ushers me in, then steps inside behind me, filling up most of the space, he closes the door. The light is on, and before I can nervously say anything or convince myself this is a bad idea and flee, he pushes me up against the door with a small thud. His hands are on my hips before his lips touch mine.

And I immediately melt into him.

An onslaught of desire, of heat and burning want, overtakes me.

And fuck me, does he know how to kiss. His tongue is demanding yet lazy. Possessive yet offers me space to explore as well. Definitely the best kiss I've ever had, but my mind is racing.

What do I know of this man?

He's funny.

He's very good-looking.

And he makes my girl parts sing.

He's also friends with my sister's new husband, who just so happens to be incredibly dangerous. Does that make Dawson just as dangerous? Most of the people at this wedding are criminals in one way or another. *Is Dawson?* Most likely.

All those thoughts leave my head when I feel his hard dick push against my inner thigh.

Dick.

Dick.

Dick.

There's no room for thought...

... only Dawson.

I want more.

Need more.

Shamelessly and thoughtlessly, I take everything this man is willing to offer.

I lift my hands, which have been rigidly hanging at my sides this entire time, and grab hold of his shirt, pulling him even closer, if that's possible. My hips naturally grind against him, thirsty for the friction of his dick. I let my body take over with its own form of desire since I have no idea what I'm doing.

"Hold up!" Dawson pants and pulls back.

I feel the loss of his lips instantly. *Did I do something weird?* My arms fall to my sides, and I know lipstick is probably smeared across both of our faces, but I can't meet his gaze.

"I don't have anything," he says.

Oh! Right, a condom... of course. I can feel the energy in the room changing, but I don't want this to end. I finally lift my gaze, and when I meet his, it's hooded and filled with heat. I suck in a sharp breath. I want this so fucking badly.

Him. I want *him*.

I find some form of courage and act before I can reconsider.

I'm here now, so I'll make the most of it.

Grabbing a handful of my dress, I lift it slightly, taking a step closer to Dawson. I drop down to my knees in front of him. He studies me, those stormy blue eyes glued to me. He doesn't ask me what I'm doing because he already knows.

I reach for his belt and start unbuckling. When I get the belt undone, it's easy to free his cock, and the second I do, I start comparing. The last cock I had in my mouth was a lot smaller. Will this one even be able to fit my other hole if we had sex?

Shit.

I kiss him just above his penis, and he grunts as my mouth moves lower. I dart my tongue across his tip, having my first taste.

I think I'm good at giving head. I learned a lot from girl talk, and the men I've sucked off before always came, so I am fairly certain I'm doing it right. And I really want to make Dawson come. I want to know that I can make a man like Dawson weak at the knees.

"Fuck, Honey." He grunts, and I lean forward and cover his tip with my lips, wrapping around it.

A knock sounds on the door, and I freeze. The doorknob rattles as someone tries to open it. Startled, my teeth close around his cock, and I bite down on accident.

Dawson grunts loudly and pushes me away from his cock. "Fuck," he hisses.

I fall onto my ass as we both stare at his cock. I'm terrified. How could I have bitten him? I almost expect it to no longer be attached. Before I can give his dick a good inspection, I still at the use of my name.

"Honey, are you in there?" It's my father's voice.

Oh shiiit! I panic. As I get off the floor, my head smacks into something hard.

"Oh my fucking God." Holding my head, I look up to find Dawson bleeding from his nose.

Well, that didn't go as planned.

"Honey?" my father calls again. The doorknob rattles once more, and Dawson huffs.

"It's just me. No Honey." And as he says the words, his eyes pin me. One hand is still on his cock, and the other is attending to his slightly bleeding nose.

"Okay, thanks." I hear my father say and stay quiet until I hear footsteps disappearing down the hall.

"I'm so sorry." I reach for him, but he steps back.

"Let's not," Dawson says, shaking his head.

I look down to his exposed cock and see painful red bite marks circling the girth. "I didn't mean to," I whisper, biting my bottom lip, utterly embarrassed. He carefully tucks himself away and grunts when his trousers brush against the raw skin. I watch as he slips a hand into his pocket for a napkin and wipes his nose, removing the traces of blood.

"It's time I head home for the night. This was..." Dawson seems lost for words and doesn't finish as he steps around me and opens the door without a backward glance.

Then he's gone.

Fuck.

CHAPTER 2
Dawson

I'm back from Italy for two weeks now. And I'm pleased to state my cock has healed.

My ego, though?

Well, I think that has a bit to go.

I didn't speak another word to Honey before I left, and that was probably shitty of me because that little vixen is the prettiest pot of honey I have ever seen. Which also is part of the problem.

But despite how fast she was to get on her hands and knees for me, I know women as much as I know men. It's my business to know. And Honey is innocent and inexperienced. To what extent, I'm not entirely sure. But it's best I walked away when I did before I traumatized her by showing her shit she'd never thought possible.

"Dawson." I turn to find my right-hand woman, Lesley, next to me. She helps me with all my businesses' ins and outs and daily workings.

I am in the business of pleasure, of need, of desire and lust.

You need a date? I have the person for you.

You need a companion? I have that for you as well.

Some would call us an escort service. I prefer to simply say that we'll meet any and all of your *needs* because no two people have the same tastes.

And we don't hire our staff to just anyone.

No. You are vetted and tested to the best of our ability before you're even allowed near our staff.

We are not a company you can simply call and book. To even get our number, you must know someone who has used our services. And if you ever fuck us over, your access to our services is terminated. And that someone who told you about us is also severed from our services.

We take our work seriously, and we respect all staff in our industry.

Even if you want to hire someone to disrespect— believe me, we've had husbands hire women to dress like and act like their wives simply so they can punish them— that's okay, but we need to be told in advance so we can pair them with the right staff member.

We are here to fulfill desires.

And desires for some people are taboo.

Unless you're rich.

I'm looking over the invitation Lesley has handed me. It's a black calling card with gold foil lettering suggesting the time, date, and location of our upcoming event. Some might call it a mixer of sorts, where clients and escorts can mingle for a personal touch before services are purchased.

Lesley then hands me a list of guests to whom invitations will be sent. I skim through the regulars. I know all of my clients, but there's one name I tell her to remove.

"And here's a recent complaint about one of the clients and an accusation about abusing the contract," Lesley says as she hands me a profile image and official complaint. Every face and complaint is passed through me because I handle every incident personally. We might do lucrative work, but I never ask my staff to get their hands dirty. If I want a message delivered, I'll often do it myself.

I raise my eyebrow at the accusation detailed in the complaint. It looks like I'll be visiting a certain someone tonight.

CHAPTER 3

Honey

"No, I'm not changing my mind about staying with Rya," I tell my father as I pack my bag. He shakes his head as he watches me.

It's been two weeks since the wedding.

I figure that's enough time for Crue and Rya to settle back in at home—although I imagine Crue would argue with that—and say my goodbyes to everyone here.

My mother has already cried twice, begging me not to go. But I need to.

For as long as I can remember, I have done everything required of me, mostly because my father was so upset about Rya running away, and I never wanted to disappoint him. I'm not saying she was, but her choosing to live with her mother in the States instead of staying here and marrying put the responsibility squarely on me.

And now, for the first time in my life, I feel like I can explore who I am or who I want to be rather than who I was told I *had* to be. A Ricci woman, daughter to one of Italy's most powerful and dangerous men. Now, even if for a short time in the States, I can try to be Honey, whatever that entails.

And it's not like I'll be completely free of my family's influence. My father is forcing my personal bodyguard, Marco, to accompany me. He's practically an uncle to me and has been Rya's and my bodyguard for as far back as I can remember. The good part is he's honored to follow me. Or so he says. It was a burden at first when Rya left, so I started to rebel. I dabbled with men, the few who were brave enough to even let me touch their cock, but it never went past that. They all feared my father's wrath because he'd no doubt kill them if he disapproved. But now, I am free of that obligation, and to be honest, if I choose to, I can fuck whoever I want. *Maybe.*

"I'll be back. And I will bring Rya for more visits," I assure him. At least he cracks a smile at those words. Rya is one thing I can never compete with, even with his disappointment in her. She is his firstborn and headstrong, exactly as our father is. It's one of the reasons my sister is a top criminal attorney. Rya has never lost a case and always seems to get what she wants. So I want some of the life she has created. I don't want to live under my father's roof any longer. I'll turn thirty in a few years, so I'm sure it's not healthy living with your parents at that age. Even if my father and mother try to convince me, I have everything I need here with them.

"Good. Your mother is still probably in her room,

crying. Be sure to say goodbye again." He wraps his arms around me in a tight hug. For someone with a reputation for being fearless and ruthless in the mafia world, he sure has a soft spot for his girls, and it's why I love him so much. I doubt any man can truly live up to my expectations as I watched how my father treated my mother. But there's one thing I am certain—no one will meet his expectations of what's good enough for me.

THE FLIGHT IS LONG, arduous, and grueling but also exciting.

My sister is waiting for me upon arrival, and she isn't alone. Crue stands next to her, his arm possessively around her waist. It would never have worked between us, and I knew from the minute Crue and I got engaged he wasn't in it with me. Even though it was an arranged marriage, there was a greater distance than there should have been, but I couldn't quite put my finger on why.

It turns out that distance was my sister.

He was in love with her.

Granted, she is worth every bit of his love. And by the looks of it, Crue doesn't plan to ever let her go. The ring on her finger is a testament to that fact. And I'm certain if anyone looked at her twice, he'd probably shoot them dead.

"Father let you escape," Rya says, bringing me in for a cuddle.

Marco remains quietly standing behind me.

"He did. Although, I did bargain with him to bring you with me when I decide to go back." I smile at Rya.

She raises a brow. "You're planning your return already?"

"Not yet. But I don't know how long I'll be staying. I'll figure it out as I go." I politely smile. Because as exhilarating as it is to land in New York, I don't know if it will fit me like it does my sister. She's been here for fourteen years. Maybe I won't like it. Or at least not permanently. But I won't know until I try.

"Hi, Honey," Crue says, reaching for my bag but keeping his hand on his wife.

"Hi." I nod to him and look back at my sister. It seems strange to see this mafia boss so domesticated. People still step cautiously around him. The atmosphere surrounding him makes it incredibly obvious he's dangerous. Or maybe it's the two guards he has not so discreetly flanking them.

I take in the intimacy between Rya and Crue. They have a life here, and I instantly think, *Maybe she feels sorry for me.* So I say, "Should I look for somewhere else to stay?"

"Yes," Crue says at the same time Rya says, "No."

She glares at him and shakes her head, then turns back to me with an eye roll. "We have a spare room in our home. In fact, we have multiple spare rooms," she makes a point of adding. I know it was originally Crue's home, and she moved in as soon as they returned from Italy.

Though she told me she still has her apartment for safe-keeping for the times when Crue pisses her off. And she has no doubt his controlling nature will piss her off frequently.

Crue says nothing, though I know he wants to. But he must have learned my sister can win any argument. But the truth is—for at least the first few days—I want to spend time with my sister to get to know her again and see where and how she lives. After fourteen years, I want to know what's so great about America and why she never returned home.

"Okay, well, I'm excited to be here," is all I can think to say. "Cheers to new beginnings and all."

CHAPTER 4

Dawson

"Why are you here?" I ask Crue as he reaches for a bottle of whiskey.

"My house has been invaded. All week, any time I fuck my wife, I'm told to be quiet," he complains.

I sigh. I don't know how the fuck that's *my problem*. But also, I know when Crue imposes himself, the only way to get rid of him is to wait it out until he leaves of his own accord.

We sit in my office, paperwork on potential client-escort matches piled in front of me as Crue sits on the other side of my desk.

"Okay, why?"

"Her little sister currently lives with us."

I don't let my surprise show as I organize my pile.

Honey.

Memories immediately come to mind—how she felt

beneath my hands, the taste of champagne on her lips and tongue. So sickly sweet and so damn innocent. That little thing has crossed my mind more times than I can count, not only because of what happened at the wedding but because she made an impression on me in spite of it.

And I can't seem to get her out of my head.

And now she's here.

Trying to act unaffected, I say, "Tell her to move out."

"My wife said I can't say that," he grumbles.

I want to laugh at him being told what to do.

This man is *never* told what to do.

Except by her.

It was a shitshow when he involved Honey. Getting engaged to Honey when Rya said no to meeting their families' arrangements was messy, but it was only ever Rya who could handle Crue.

And the thought of Honey and Crue...

"What did she say exactly?" I ask, reaching for the bottle of whiskey that he just seems to be playing with and not pouring. I grab a glass and pour myself one.

The thought of Honey and Crue is unbearable.

It unnerves me further by how much she's gotten under my skin.

"She said, and I quote, 'If you even mention kicking my sister out, I will not let you touch me for a week.' " He groans. "That's a long time when I can't even go a few hours without her."

I laugh, and his furious gaze snaps to me.

I roll my eyes and take a sip of whiskey. The soft, smooth, and silky feel as it glides down my throat helps the burn and annoyance I'm feeling as I suggest, "Why not send her to Rya's old apartment?"

He grumbles. "You think I didn't suggest that already? But their father won't permit her being so far away from us."

Sounds about right. Where Rya might have had a slightly longer leash, Honey was their delicate, precious flower, and the give on her lead was evidently minimal.

"Then buy an apartment and offer it to Honey." He goes to speak, his mouth opening and then shutting. "In the same building you're in," I offer. "That way, Honey is close to Rya, and you have your space."

Something dark dances across his features before he reaches for his phone, and after a few moments of typing, he smiles. "I'll be back."

I watch as he puts the phone to his ear and strides out of my office.

Looking back through my paperwork, I wonder how long it will take to finish the pile. This shit is the worst part of running a business. All the potential escort candidates are attractive, but we don't only accept attractive. There has to be something special and defining about each one. I've struggled to find that allure in anyone since Italy. And I figure a certain little honeypot has to do with that. And now the temptation is too great, knowing she's in the same city as me. My cock twitches at the thought of her painful bite. The image of that woman on her knees in front of me, lashing her tongue against my cock...

I'd been reckless.

But it's stuck with me ever since.

"Done. I owe you." Crue snaps me out of my brooding thoughts and taps my desk. "Come. You're going to help her move."

"I can't."

"Oh, but you can. Because if I recall, you left a supply closet with her at my wedding." His gaze pins me. *Fuck! I hate how much he sees.* We're the same in so many ways. But I don't want him imposing on my business.

"Since when do you fuck women who haven't been heavily vetted by you?" Crue raises a brow.

This is true. When I want to fuck, I make sure NDAs are signed, and no one can come back to me or go after anything that's mine.

I built this business from the ground up, and I would never let any fucker take it from me. Not a chance in hell.

Honey had been that one moment of impulsiveness.

But I'm not playing into Crue's insinuation, either.

"And here I thought you only had eyes for your newly wedded wife that day. I'm flattered," I say. "Nothing happened."

"Bullshit."

I shrug nonchalantly and look back at my paperwork. "Hire a company to move furniture. It's not my expertise," I reply casually, then take a sip of whiskey. The temptation is too great, and I have to stay away, or I'll risk all the boundaries and rules I've put into place to protect myself and my empire from blowing up in my face.

Crue throws back his drink and leaves without so much as another word. I adjust my uncomfortably stiff cock, the earlier thoughts of Honey have put my body into complete disarray.

CHAPTER 5

Honey

R ya and I sit around her kitchen counter, polishing off the last of the Tiramisu I made while Marco enjoys a coffee and reads a paper at the circular coffee table closest to the windows. It blows my mind that despite how massive the kitchen is in this place, neither Crue nor Rya use it. And although, at first, I thought I'd been encroaching the last week, I've spent much of my time in the kitchen with their personal chef. We gave each other cooking tips, and it was the one thing that made me feel at home. I always cooked at home, and it simply made me happy.

"Damn, Honey, that was good." Rya pats her stomach.

I sheepishly smile. "I saved one last piece for Lawson and want to know what his critique on it is," I say thoughtfully, referring to their chef. Besides my deceased

Nonna, no one in my family cooks, so it's nice to share with someone who loves cooking as much as I do.

"How's the job hunting going?" Rya asks me.

My father's allowance is more than enough that I don't need a job while I'm here, but I've never had to work, and I want to give it a go, so I've been applying for jobs since I arrived. It's hard when you're twenty-seven and have no real experience. So, I've applied for various roles, but I'm not entirely sure what I want.

"I've been applying. I just don't know what I want to do."

My life has been laid out for me until now, and I never thought about what I might want for myself. I envy Rya for paving her own path, but I'm not her.

"Take your time. You've only just moved here. I know they're looking for a receptionist at my hot yoga studio."

"Maybe," I say, considering it.

The elevator doors to the penthouse open, Crue waltzes in, and his usual fitted black attire looks pristine. He presses a kiss to Rya's cheek in greeting and drops a set of keys in front of me.

Rya pins him with a stare, but he pays her no mind.

"To your place," he tells me.

"Sorry, what?" I ask, confused.

"Two floors down. You"—he points to me—"move now."

"Crue," Rya scolds, and he turns to her.

"I want to tie you to the bed and have you scream.

Do you really want me to do that while your sister is here?" Crue asks her.

I try not to choke as I throw back the rest of my coffee.

And that is definitely my cue to leave.

And I don't take it personally.

"Okay, I'll pack my things," I state, standing.

To be honest, I'm grateful he's given me a place to live. I love spending time with Rya when she's home, but listening to my sister and her husband have sex every single night is painful. And even noise-cancelling head-phones only block out so much. I haven't told Rya I've been looking at apartments, but this makes it much easier. Although, when I looked this morning, there wasn't one available in this building, so it must have recently been listed.

"You don't have to go," Rya says, pinning Crue with a glare as she follows me into the spare room.

Happily, I throw my clothes into the suitcase and smile at her. "Rya, it's fine. I was already looking at getting my own place, so this works out. I love you, but shit, you two are loud." She doesn't even blush. "You're newlyweds, and you need your own space, so it's good for me to have my own. I can't remember the last time I was alone."

Pretty sure the answer to that is never.

I'm excited to have a place to myself. It will most likely be quiet, but it might give me the space to figure out who I am and what I want. "This was meant to be a fresh start for me, but it is for you two as well. I'm fine with it. I'm twenty-seven... this is a normal step."

Rya seems hesitant but nods, seeming to understand. "Do you need money?"

I laugh. "You've met our overprotective father, right? He sends me a weekly allowance."

My phone pings, and I pull it out of my pocket. I read the message, and my stomach swirls with anticipation. "Oh my God! I have a job interview tomorrow."

"Really? Where?" she asks, leaning over my shoulder.

"There's a lingerie shop not far from here, so within walking distance, that's looking for staff. I dropped by yesterday and asked the manager about the job. Wow." I feel almost shocked by how serendipitous this all is and how quickly it's taking shape right before me.

"I think I know the one you're talking about," Rya says. "If you want to come work for me, I can maybe try to work out something as well."

Laughing, I shake my head. "No, I will leave all that stuff to you. I could think of nothing worse," I tell her, not as an insult, which she gets. All my life I've had people control me. I almost feel like the lingerie shop is completely out of my wheelhouse in every way possible, and I'm excited by that.

"Well, the offer stands."

"Not to live here anymore, I hope," Crue states, walking in and lifting my suitcase. I try not to laugh because I know Crue Monti does not take kindly to being laughed at, but his eagerness is humorous.

"Is there at least a bed?" I ask him.

"Yes. And a couch and TV. Everything is sorted, and you're welcome." He strides out of the bedroom, and as we reach the door, he looks back to Rya and growls, "Be naked when I return."

"I did not need to hear that," I tell them, shaking my head.

Crue and I go down a few floors in the elevator, and at the end of the hallway, Crue stops at a black wooden door. I'm amazed by how chic the style is when he opens it. This apartment is not as big as the penthouse, but the two-bedroom is still massive, which is perfect for me.

Butterflies dance in my stomach as I take in the living room on my left and the kitchen on my right with an island bench. Past the entertainment area are floor-to-ceiling glass windows with a stunning view.

"I had the TV delivered today, and all the other bull-shit. Don't bother your sister for a good twenty-four hours," Crue demands, placing my things down and then walking out, shutting the door behind him.

Crue also slammed the door closed on Marco, preventing him from entering. No doubt he wants to come in and inspect the safety of everything, but I want a few minutes alone to inspect it myself.

I bite my bottom lip, and a little squeal escapes. *This is actually all mine?* I run my hand along the kitchen counter, admiring its space and imagining everything I can cook . I peek into the bedroom. Seeing the dusky pink duvet on the bed, I jump on it, feeling like a big kid, and look to my right at the view through the windows. *Maybe New York will look good on me.* Slowly, all the expectations that have weighed me down slip away.

No one knows who I am here—not even me—and I feel like I'm taking my first deep breath for the first time in a long time.

A small spark of rebellion ignites within me.

Maybe I should try to have as much fun as possible while here.

And with that thought, the excitement is overwhelming.

CHAPTER 6
Dawson

I t's not often I interfere with who my store managers hire and fire, but I do see all the names that come along my desk regarding payroll sign-ups. And when *her* name pops up, I'm surprised and recognize it immediately. Part of me almost considers whether Crue put her up to this, but he isn't the type to waste time playing games on something trivial. That and no one else knows how much this little honeypot has gotten under my skin.

Honey Ricci.

How has she wound up so innocently stepping into my world?

This particular store hires only on looks, employing only those who can sell the products and understand the garments. Without even looking at her resume, which I doubt has very much, if any, work history, it's obvious why the manager hired her. She reeks of innocence and wild fantasies, and the incredible part of that is she doesn't realize it.

"Dawson." I look up as Daphne confidently strolls into my office. Daphne and I have an on-again, off-again relationship. Contractual, of course. She once worked for me as a private escort until we progressed further. With boundaries, contracts, and expectations in place, we're both protected. I look after her financially, and she abides by my regular catch-ups to please me. This is a catch-up I haven't organized since I got back from Italy because of a certain slip-up I had with Honey. I can't believe I almost gave her something for free, leaving myself open to liability—the woman could have taken everything I've built if we went there.

My jaw tightens as Daphne sits on the corner of my desk, my mind still raging on Honey. Something about her drew me in, and I lost all my senses. I would have fucked her in that supply closet without protection, and that little rendezvous could have cost me everything.

Which is very unlike me.

"So, I need new lingerie..." Daphne smiles at me. Her long brunette hair falls over her shoulder as she looks at me pointedly with her forest-green eyes. I know she's probably unsure why I haven't called her in the last few weeks, and curiosity has gotten the better of me regarding the store.

"Great, I was just heading to the store. You can come with me."

Pleased with my answer, Daphne hops off the desk

and adjusts her skirt. Usually, I would give her my credit card or tell the store she's coming. I would never personally take her there.

My stores cater to a particular level of clientele—those who can splurge at around the cost of a new car.

"I'm auditioning for a lingerie model role and want to walk in your brand. You know... to showcase it."

One thing I have always liked about Daphne is that she isn't someone who takes. She never really asks for too much, and, to be honest, she sucked at being an escort. She's too soft and became too attached to the clients. She's also too kind, but that's what made her appealing to most. She would reel them in with her sincerity of companionship but was well-equipped and open-minded to the different forms of pleasure.

Nothing like Honey, who reeks of innocence. She seems like the type who only wants a ring on her finger and would perform marital duties in the same position every fucking time. And I don't know why that pisses me off. I have nothing to do with her, and yet I've become obsessed. I never thought she'd come to New York and work in one of *my* stores.

I'm not even sure she knows I own the store.

"I want you to know how much I appreciate you." Daphne reaches over and touches my leg. "You have this hard exterior, and I get it. You hang with the mafia, and you've done bad shit. You probably still do. But you also care for those you consider close to you."

I say nothing, perplexed as to why she's bringing this

up—most likely because I haven't called on her as of late —but I know she doesn't really care about me. Although, I know she does in her own way. But it doesn't impact me.

"I know you only give me a small part of you and never let anyone in, but I thank you for allowing me to even be here."

I curl her hair around my knuckles and yank her head back. She waits almost expectantly. But as I look at her, her open mouth and the way her tongue flicks over her lips in anticipation of what she knows I can offer her, I feel...

... nothing.

Fuck!

"Noted," is all I say before letting her go and striding for the door.

She seems almost confused but says nothing as she follows me, updating me on her personal endeavors as a model, as if nothing has changed between us. But truthfully, she doesn't do it for me anymore, and that's a concern in and of itself. And I wonder if it has to do with the sweet little mafia daughter I'm about to corner.

BY THE TIME we arrive at the store it is dark. The lights are on, and a few customers are browsing before closing time.

Daphne gets out of the car without another word

from me.

I don't bother telling her the only reason she's here right now is because I can fuck her and trust she won't run her mouth. I don't see Daphne as anything more than someone I use to meet my needs. And that's not meant to be cruel. It's just how it is, and she knows it. I've never given her reason to think otherwise.

Daphne doesn't wait for me before she heads into the store, and I already know my innocent Miss Ricci is in there because her bodyguard, Marco, stands outside, casually smoking a cigar as he thumbs through his phone. That's definitely a problem. She already sticks out too much. But I doubt Mr. Ricci will let his baby daughter go anywhere unprotected.

I pull open the door and instantly spot Honey, who stands behind the counter with her back to me, reaching for something on the wall. Her hair is down and longer than I remember. She's wearing a tight black shirt that clings to all the right places.

Daphne is handed a flute of champagne by our greeter who can't make eye contact with me. She offers me one, but I'm quick to deny it as I watch Daphne walk over to Honey and ask for her help. She smiles, bright and welcoming, as Daphne points to a piece she likes in the size she needs. Honey steps out from behind the counter and rises on her tippytoes to grab the item, but she fails. She huffs and tries again. I step up behind her and reach above her head, grabbing the bra she's after and handing it to her.

Her back is to me, so she doesn't know it's me, that is, until she turns around and her eyes go wide.

"Hello, Honey." I smile as she quickly cradles the bra to her chest.

Daphne looks between us, and as if suddenly jolted out of her shock, Honey smiles tightly and hands Daphne the bra for her to try on. Daphne walks to the changing rooms, but not without looking over her shoulder suspiciously one more time.

"You're here," Honey says, confused. And I like the hot flush that runs across her cheeks. It's different from how most people look at me—like I'm a prize of sorts. They either stare or avert their gaze. But not this woman, who is so confident in herself and yet has such a peculiar innocence about her that she sometimes looks like a lost doe. I lean in close to her ear, inhaling her scent—definitely smells like bad choices.

"I've been having honey every day. I wonder if you taste as sweet as your namesake." She sucks in a breath, and her cheeks redden further.

When I pull back, she can't seem to find words.

My cock twitches at the sight.

I shouldn't have come here.

I should have stayed in the dark.

But now I'm wondering if I should let her bite my cock again. How her lips would taste if I took her against this wall.

I can't stay away.

CHAPTER 7
Honey

I'm confused, unsure of what exactly is happening, not with the situation but with my body. I can feel every part of me on fire.

All because *he* is here.

And almost touching me.

He shouldn't touch me.

"Y-you're at m-my place of work," I stutter.

I see Marco peering through the glass doors, watching us intently. Dawson is recognizable, and considering my father isn't a fan of him from the wedding, that, by default, means Marco doesn't want us talking.

"It appears so." He smirks.

I look him up and down, and he impresses me, as usual. That was one of the first things I noticed about Dawson when I first met him. He has style and can pull off almost anything.

It's totally unfair to the rest of the population.

But then he made me laugh, and soon all I wanted to do with him was unspeakable things.

And I still do.

I've never wanted another human to touch me as badly as I do him.

And that's a problem.

Dawson shouldn't be here.

"Why?" I manage to ask. "This is a lingerie shop." Oh God, please don't tell me he has a girlfriend or even a wife. Surely, he doesn't, especially after what we did in the closet. My mind goes into overdrive at the thought of him already being someone else's.

"I'm very well aware."

"Miss, do you like cats?" I turn around at the question and find the beautiful brunette who I served earlier standing behind me.

"Um, sure?" I reply.

She is gorgeous. Her body is long and lean as she turns in a slow circle. The woman looks like a model with beautiful, tanned skin and forest-green eyes.

"Question, do you think a cat would like this?" she asks.

What? I hesitate, not sure if I've heard her right. "I—"

"I have an audition tomorrow, and I must hold a cat wearing it. The lingerie is for cat food advertising, and they want me to dress sexy, to show that not all people who own cats are old and lonely."

I try not to laugh. "Cats are great. And I think the cat will like the outfit," I tell her. She smiles, happy with my answer, and sashays back to the change rooms.

"You don't like cats, do you?" I jump at Dawson's question as he leans over my shoulder, smirking.

Instantly, I try to put some distance between us. "Not at all. I hate cats. I'm more of a snake person," I say, crossing my arms over my chest.

"Why is that, Honey? You don't like their claws?" Before I can answer, he holds up a finger. "Because if I recall correctly, you certainly like to bite. Your teeth definitely left an impression on my cock."

Heat flushes over my skin as I glance around to ensure no one can hear our conversation.

"I..." Dammit! He's teasing me and taking great pleasure in it.

"Just gathering a list of things you like. Noted... dislike for cats."

"Why does it matter what I like?"

Dawson reaches out for the gold necklace around my throat, inspecting the pot of honey pendant. It's lame, but it's my nonna's last gift, and I've worn it ever since. His fingers feather against my skin, and his touch freezes me in place. He then beams a sinful smile at me.

"Want to see something, Honey?" he asks.

I want to shake my head in answer, but instead, I nod submissively. It's stupid, really. I bet everyone falls under his spell. Before I can resist, he grabs my hand and pulls me toward the back of the shop. He steps into the employees-only area, turns on the light, and then undoes his pants.

"I'm at work, Dawson," I hiss out the words, more shocked than anything. Does he really think I will drop to my knees for him at work? I might have done it once, but that was different, and I never actually thought I'd see him again. He doesn't listen to the worry in my voice. "I could get fired for you being back here," I say, but my eyes don't have conviction because they haven't moved from his pants. Dawson pulls them down to where I can see the start of his shaft, and that's when I notice a bit of redness. I lean in because I can't possibly be seeing what I think I am. "Is that..."

"Your lips? Yes." My hands fly to my mouth.

"Did you really get my lips tattooed on your cock? You do remember I bit it, right?" I ask, embarrassed. And shocked. Why would anyone do that? And yet, I can't help but be flattered in a weird, twisted way. Does that make him messed up or me? Or both of us?

"Oh, I do." He pulls his pants back up as my manager walks in. She stops in the doorway, and her gaze locks on us. I go to explain, but she smiles at Dawson.

"Hi, Dawson."

"Hello, Alana," he replies, letting her pass.

"You checking out the new employee? Honey has been amazing and the customers love her," Alana says.

"I'm confused. Why would he care?" I ask Alana, but it's Dawson who answers, "You are in my shop, Honey."

What?

No.

What the fuck?

"But I thought..."

"Alana runs it for me, and she does a great job," he states.

I blanch. *Shit.* Am I really working at his store?

"Dawson, I got what I need. Let's go," the beautiful brunette asking weird cat questions shouts from the front.

He leans in with a suggestive smile. "Now, if you will excuse me." I feel his breath hot and heavy against my cheek, and all I can think about is *his cock* and *that tattoo.* Of *my lips.* My body floods with irrational need and heat like it had on that day at the wedding.

Fuck.

Fuck.

Fuck.

I watch as they walk out together, unsure if that woman is his girlfriend, a friend, or his receptionist. But surely you wouldn't bring a receptionist to buy lingerie? Then again, I know nothing of Dawson Taylor.

But more importantly, I'm left wondering if I should quit.

CHAPTER 8

Dawson

I feel Daphne watching me.

She was silent while in the car as if expecting me to talk, which I didn't.

"She was nice. Who is she?" Daphne asks.

"No one."

"Must be a pretty amazing no one from the way you were eye fucking her." She laughs.

"I was not," I say under my breath as we walk back into my office.

"Oh, you totally were. So, do you know her well?"

I sigh, realizing she isn't going to let it go.

"If you must know, I met her in Italy," I grit out.

"Ohhh... that explains a lot."

"How?" I ask.

She takes a seat on my office chair and kicks her feet up under her as she rummages through her bag. "Since you've been back, you haven't wanted sex, and if I'm not mistaken, you also got a tattoo." She eyes me.

"Feeling lonely, Daphne? I'm surprised you're keeping track of our sex. And how do you know about the tattoo?"

She gives me her best eye roll.

"When you came back and I visited you, you got out of bed naked, like you usually do, before you told me to go home. I saw it then." She shrugs. "I didn't really understand it until I saw you eye fucking the innocent little Italian flavor now working at your store. Pretty special to have her lips on you, huh?"

Tension ripples through my jaw at her calling my little honeypot a flavor. She is more than that.

The tattoo had been an irrational choice. I wasn't entirely drunk when I got it and I don't understand why I did it. I just know what happened in that closet left a mark. *She* left a mark. Something I didn't want to forget. But I can't figure out its significance or depth.

"You can leave now, Daphne."

"Do you think she needs friends? I mean, she's from Italy, right? She probably doesn't have many friends if she's new in town. She could easily be a model herself." She's speaking absentmindedly as she finally finds the lip gloss she's apparently been fishing for this whole time. "And I'm curious by anything that gains your attention," she adds before swiping a layer of thick gloss on her lips and checking it in a small mirror, satisfied with the red sheen.

"You plan to be her friend, and what? Tell her you fuck me but can't talk about it because it could get you sued or killed?"

She chuckles and kicks out from the chair. "Please. She knows we fuck. I saw the way she watched us walk out. That woman was mad. And if you want to pursue a contract with her, you might want to clarify that our relationship is purely mutually beneficial." She snaps her clutch shut.

I never intended to make her mad.

My little honeypot is mad.

Interesting. And I look for these signs—it's part of my job. But when it comes to her, everything is different.

"Dawson, are we going to fuck or not?" Daphne asks.

I step to the side. "You can leave."

She giggles. "Okay. But you're not fooling me, Dawson. You've got a hot little number under your skin" —she leans in and presses a kiss on my cheek, and I feel her smile—"and I hope she gives you hell."

CHAPTER 9
Honey

"Dawson owns the shop I work at," I tell Rya the following week as I'm kneading dough in her kitchen. All I've been able to do is cook since finding out that tidbit of information. I haven't seen her due to her crazy work schedule, and when she's free, I'm usually at work, so this is the first opportunity I've had to talk to discuss it with her.

She's casually reading paperwork, but I've caught her attention and she lifts her head. "Come again?" she asks. "Crue!" She screams for her husband.

Marco stands behind me, almost bemused, as we hear Crue grumble down the hallway before he comes out dressed in a towel. I avert my eyes as she turns to him. "Did you know Dawson owns Peche?"

"Yes. He owns that and many other businesses," Crue says matter-of-factly as he picks up Rya's coffee and sips. He glances at Marco but doesn't say anything. He's made it clear he's offended my bodyguard thinks I'm not safe in his home. But Marco's always been diligent in his role, perhaps too much at times, but I get it, so I say nothing.

"What else does he own?" Rya asks.

"You said no business talk at home." He raises a brow at her.

Rya puts her hand on her hip.

I don't think it's such a big deal that I'm working at Dawson's store, but I'm too curious for the answer to stop her questioning Crue.

"Dawson owns multiple businesses, both legal and illegal, including escort companies, lingerie stores... fuck, he even auctions off virgins. And that's just a small part of his reach." He takes one of the cookies I baked from the tray and walks away.

"Did he just say *virgins*?" I ask, baffled. She looks away, and I ask her again. "Rya, did he just say Dawson auctions off virgins?"

Well shit! Who is Dawson, really?

I knew being connected with Crue, Dawson must have been some type of trouble. The suits and his aura scream danger, power, and mystery. *But auctioning virgins?*

I absentmindedly offer Marco a cookie as I stare down my sister. I know he'll decline; he always does. I always make far too much, and back home, I offered them to the servants to take to their families. At least then, I knew they were being enjoyed.

"Crue doesn't lie," Rya states, and I can tell there's a hint of concern in her tone as she looks back at her papers.

"How much?" I ask.

"What?" She looks up at me.

"What does a virgin go for?"

"I don't know, Honey! But don't you even think for a second about doing that."

I continue kneading the dough and shrug. "I wasn't. I'm just curious. Seems pretty crazy, huh?"

Rya huffs out a laugh. "Tell me about it. I married one of the crazies." And I know Crue is dangerous, but I've never had the guts to ask how bad. If I can just accept him as my brother-in-law, I'm fine with that. It's enough that I know my dad is one of the "bad guys." But never to us, not his girls. I understand I was sheltered from that part of our life.

Rya is different in the way she pursued her job and wouldn't back down from anyone.

And I envy her for that.

I wonder if I could ever be that strong.

Or if I'll only ever be a coddled woman.

That is, after all, what I was raised to be—the perfect daughter and housewife.

As if picking up on my subtle mood change, Marco leans over, picks up a cookie, and takes a bite. I offer him a small smile, guilt still driving me hard. He should be with his family. It should have never been Marco who came with me, but I am grateful and selfish that he is. He is a piece of the famiglia and home I knew.

"Maybe you should wait until you're married, like you planned," Rya suggests, noticing the mood change.

I want to smile and brush it off, but I simply can't. I'm sick of keeping my wants and feelings inside to please others. And if I can't talk to my sister, then who can I talk to? "What if I don't want marriage?"

"That's fine. You don't have to marry anyone any longer." Because she did it for both of us, and our families' contract is now fulfilled. The Monti got their Ricci. Rya was always meant to marry Crue, but she refused. So, as the contract stated, a Monti had to marry a Ricci daughter, and I was next in line. And I was going to do it. Not because I wanted to but because I *had* to. I couldn't risk my father being killed. But, thankfully, Rya realized how much she loves Crue despite the contract.

And here we are.

I'm a free woman.

But I'm still figuring out exactly what that means. Especially as I was always told I had to marry, but did I want that myself?

I now live freely in a whole new country and earn my own money. And that's a big thing, considering I grew up with the idea that I would never be free and that a man would always control me.

"It's just all new here, you know? I really want to figure out what I want for myself. And I know that sounds stupid because I'm twenty-seven, but it wasn't easy for me after you left."

A somber atmosphere takes over the room. Feeling almost silly, I divert my gaze as I focus on kneading the dough, grateful for the distraction. I love my sister, I've always been envious of her courage, but in truth, I felt left behind. Now I see her almost daily, as if time hasn't affected us. But she's established, and I'm... well, I don't know.

She puts her hand over mine. I look at her. My sister isn't overly affectionate, and it brings tears to my eyes.

"I never wanted to leave you behind," she says earnestly. "But I had to do it for me, and I'm sorry it left you with that responsibility."

I nod. "I already know that," I say as I wipe a tear with the back of my hand. *Oh my God, why am I crying?* This is embarrassing. "It's just a stark realization that I've only ever pleased others. I love our father and don't hold it against him, but it's a lot being here too. And it seems crazy with the new apartment and job. It's happening so fast, but in a good way, I guess." I smile brightly because I'm certain I am happy about how things are progressing.

She considers me briefly before saying, "Do you want me to call Dawson and tell him to stay away from you? I can make my husband do it." She winks.

I choke out a laugh, grateful for her lightening the mood. And Dawson is certainly not the issue here. Although, he does take up far too much of my attention.

"I will do no such thing," Crue says, re-entering the kitchen.

Rya glares at him as she taps her nails on the counter. "Oh, you think you can just say no to me?" She scoffs.

He stops and thinks about his answer. "If I say yes, does that mean I don't get to fuck you tonight?"

"Hm," is all the response she gives before she turns back to her papers, hiding a smile.

"What do you want me to ask him?" Crue questions as he steps up behind Rya and wraps his arms around her waist. "I want it stated that Dawson is a very clever man and will know it's not a threatening message from me."

"And dangerous, don't forget that," Rya adds.

"I think everyone in our world is dangerous, princess. Even you." Crue leans in and kisses her cheek.

She seems satisfied by his answer.

"No, don't say anything. He's my boss, and I can respect those boundaries. I'm sure he can too," I reply. Again, that isn't my main concern. However, I immediately think of his tattoo, which screams complications and something next level.

"Are you sure?" Rya asks. "I can get Crue to kick his ass."

He grumbles something in her ear, and she ignores him.

I wave her off with a laugh and add more flour to the dough.

I can totally deal with my boss.

I think.

CHAPTER 10

Dawson

"I must confess, for someone who says he's a happily married man who is fucking every second of the day, you seem to be demanding my time and attention a lot lately. Are you sure you're not lonely?" I say to Crue.

He flashes a smile that doesn't meet his eyes, and I know if any other fucker in this place said that to him, they'd be dead. We sit in his establishment around midday, which is also strange for Crue, almost always meeting in the early morning hours.

Various men and business partners surround us, snorting coke from the table. He takes a sip of his whiskey. And though often it's business with Crue and me, we're also friends.

"I didn't realize a certain little Ricci is working at your store. What a small world," he deadpans.

I shrug. "You know I don't hire staff in the stores. I

have competent managers to deal with that." It goes without saying for my legal businesses, but my attention is always on illegal businesses and clientele. "But, surely, you didn't call me all the way out here to talk about your new little sister-in-law?"

He considers me. "I've been made acutely aware that were anything to happen to her, I'd have to involve myself."

I can't help but offer a suave smile over the edge of my glass, and this seems to piss him off. "Wifey's orders?" I taunt.

He grunts in reply.

I hold in my desire to laugh. Who would've thought a woman could control Crue Monti? Nor did I ever think he would actually settle down. But then again, I've met Rya and can see why it works. Contractually, yes. But to be so smitten? It's a weakness. And yet, I'm genuinely happy for him. I wrote off any type of fairytale for myself a long time ago.

"Do you really want to discuss how Honey is settling in?" I ask as I want to know. Fuck, do I want to know what she's up to, but I push away my interest. Because curiosity is not healthy... ever. The most I could offer was tattooing a part of her next to my cock. And I thought maybe that'd be satisfying enough, but she's haunted my thoughts ever since.

"Just an observation, but you seem more on edge since Italy. Are your needs being met? Sex is just sex, right?" Crue says.

I don't like his observation.

Or his insinuation.

I'd given him shit about this months ago when he started blue balling because he only wanted to fuck Rya. But when it's on the flip side, I won't go into detail. Because the truth is, I haven't fucked Daphne, or anyone else, since I got back from Italy. But he doesn't need to know that. At my silence, he continues, evidently having enjoyed his dig. Fair, considering I had done the same to him.

"I just wanted to check up on how my 'security' is performing for your staff." I almost laugh at his coy use of "security." Which tells me that there's either someone here who can't be trusted or there's an underlying question.

This shit is all for show—him inviting partners to drink on the house—but also to remind them who is in charge. If he didn't trust them, they wouldn't be here. But then again, I know Crue doesn't trust anyone.

We'd come to an agreement years ago when I first met Crue. My services and business were in high demand, and I needed protection for my staff when the clients' demands became more specific. And rich fuckers always think they can push or do what they want, even if it isn't contracted. I know because I'd dealt with them myself. Having Crue's men stand as guards in the room during the "dates" as said pleasures were played out reduced the danger to my women and men. And if I were to find out anything happened before or after, I'd deal with it personally. And in exchange, I offer services and entertainment for such occasions.

"As usual," I say, watching two of my girls work the men in the room. Entertainment, of course. Both of them can defend themselves if something were to ever go down.

These men are dangerous.

But they also pay a lot.

Crue considers this. "I've received some intel that I don't think you'll like."

I furrow my brows. "Such as?"

Crue lets out a sigh. He's not one to pull punches, but if it affects my business, he knows better than the next how *unyielding* I can be.

"One of the girls at my bar was approached by a man. We don't have clear footage because he was wearing darkened shades. I only have two security guys at the bar, who pretend to be regulars, and even they can't make an accurate description of him. He propositioned my bartender."

I take another sip of the whisky, my jaw clenching. "So what does this have to do with me?"

Crue places his empty glass down and waves for one of my girls, who immediately fills it back up. "He told the bartender that he works for Dawson Escorting."

I almost shatter the glass in my hand. "What?" I ask, unsure I've heard him right.

Crue eyes me and dips his gaze to my strangled glass. I retract my hand and smooth over my white jacket. "I thought your security was top-notch at your establishments. How can no one identify him?"

"Don't offend me, Dawson," Crue warns.

I throw back my whisky, then hold the empty glass out to be refilled. I've had little fires pop up here and there as people try to take what is mine. But no one had blatantly tried to use my company name and services.

"Whoever it was, they wanted to go undetected. Unfortunately for them, they probably didn't realize it was one of my establishments and that I would report the incident to you."

I think on this for a while. "Or they knew exactly what they were doing and saying. And who you were and your operations in my business," I state.

Either way, I'll have to deal with it immediately and make visits and calls to find out anything and everything I can about this mystery man.

"A calling card, you think?" Crue considers. "Either way, friend, it looks like you have a stray or an enemy brazen enough to grab your attention."

CHAPTER 11
Honey

For a few weeks I don't see Dawson, and I'm fine with that. Although part of me expects him to walk through the door every day. But that leaves a bitter taste since the last time he came here, it was with an outrageously beautiful woman. And I was too embarrassed to ask Crue if that beautiful woman was his girlfriend. Because that would make it sound like I'm interested in Dawson, and I shouldn't be.

No! I mean... I'm not.

That is until I'm closing the store, and a car pulls up. I recognize it immediately. I'm attempting to lock the front door as he slides his sunglasses onto the top of his head while strolling toward me. My heart rate picks up a notch as he gets closer, and I wonder if I should shut the door in his face and hide inside.

Probably not the best of ideas.

He is my boss, after all.

Marco pushes off the pole that he's leaning against. It's the same place he waits for me every day because he refuses to let me walk to and from work alone.

Dawson raises his hand to stop him. "I have business here with my employee, and you are not to interrupt, or I'll consider it trespassing."

"You can't speak to him like that," I say, angrily. *How dare he speak to Marco like that.* But then I turn to Marco and say, "Dawson won't hurt me, Marco."

"Your father doesn't like him. Therefore, I don't trust him," Marco states. And I know he'd do anything to get to me if he had to.

Dawson is oozing with that no-fucks-given power shit, but there's something else. He also seems tense and slightly off. "I'll be fine, Marco. Just wait out here for a little longer, please."

He doesn't lean back against the pole but remains where he is, alert.

I step to the side to allow Dawson in. He walks past me, and I catch a hint of his scent. He smells good. *Really good.* But there's an undertone of whisky. He's not drunk, but he's definitely been drinking. Shutting the door behind him, I lock it so no late shoppers think we're still open and walk in.

He's watching me. The store is dark, and he makes his way silently through the racks and out the back. I follow him with a huff, feeling like an obedient, devoted worker. But then again, he is my boss, and I should do as he says.

When I finally step into Alana's office, he's leaning against the table, waiting for me expectantly.

"Honey," Dawson says, with that smile that would drop women to their knees and break them.

I can't help the gulp I take as I drink him in. He's so imposing in size, taking up most of the space in the small office. And I know he's imposing in size elsewhere too. *Stop thinking about that.*

"Dawson," I say, crossing my arms angrily over my chest, still mad at how he spoke to Marco. At least he didn't call him a lapdog or something like that. Marco has been called all manner of things over the years because of his dedication to his role in shadowing me. But I suppose someone like Dawson respects the role, understanding the life-binding contract my father had forced Marco to take to protect me.

"I had a visit the other day from Crue," he states.

"Okay." I'm confused what that has to do with me.

His gaze never leaves me. But the harshness that was there when he walked in seems to be vanishing. Little by little, I see the tension in him dissipate. I don't even know if he realizes he has his own tells. Or maybe no one has looked close enough before.

"You were asking about me?" Dawson says.

"No," I lie.

"Hm..." He pushes off the table and steps toward me. I want to step back, but I don't, and I stand my ground. I've grown up with powerful men all my life and know not to back down. But with Dawson, it's different. It's not intimidation, it's temptation, and that's a more powerful thing. I fell for his game once. Stopping, he stands directly in front of me. "You were asking about me," he states again.

"I..." I pause.

"If you lie, I will remove my clothing."

My mind goes blank. "Sorry, what?"

"For every lie you tell, a piece of clothing will come off," he says playfully.

"I'm not lying," I tell him, then he reaches for his jacket. He pulls it off and drops it to the floor. I look around, shocked that he's actually doing this. No one else is in the store, but I can't help but think about the cameras, though I know there aren't any in this room. *What would people think?* I stop at that thought. I told myself I need to stop caring what people think.

But this is...

... not normal, right?

Damn! It does feel good to be standing in this man's compelling presence. I could breathe him in all day.

"Do you wear anything from here?" Dawson asks.

"Yes," I breathe out because I can't stop looking at him. I can only imagine what's beneath his fitted white button-up. Surely, he's only teasing me, like he did that time before he walked out on me. The truth is, I love the products in this store—the material feels amazing on my skin. But I wonder what he'd feel like against it instead.

"Good." He pauses. "Now, show me."

A heated flush runs through me, and I immediately shake my head.

I can't be left heated, flushed, and alone again. I know the last time was a disaster. Can I risk that with this man twice? Considering he's my boss now.

"If I remember correctly, you were eager to drop to your knees once before. Would you prefer me to remove more items?" Dawson questions, touching his belt.

"No," I say, and I can taste the lie as it leaves my mouth.

"Lie." He undoes his belt and holds the end of it in his hands. "Show me," he demands, nodding to my dress.

"No."

"Show me," he says again as he stalks toward me, his belt held loosely in his hand. I don't even notice I'm backing away from him.

"I-I have to g-go," I stutter.

"Lie." His other hand lifts to the buttons on his shirt. *Fuck, is this really happening?* And I can't help but watch, transfixed, as his fingers flick open each button. It's a mistake, a bad idea. But, surely, he's not going to leave me again like last time if he's literally the one taking all his clothes off in front of me.

Oh God.

"I can't do this," I insist, waving a hand between us. "This is wrong."

"How?" he asks, continuing to undo his buttons. "We are consenting adults, and there is nothing wrong with this. Some might even feel satisfied by the fantasy of *doing their boss.*"

A shaky laugh escapes me, and he seems surprised by that. Because him being my boss isn't my main objection. "You're with someone."

"I'm not with anyone," he states.

"The beautiful brunette you came in with the other day. The cat lady." I hate that he's making me spell it out for him because it makes me feel stupid, but I will not be a sidepiece.

Understanding crosses his expression. "Would you like me to cut my contract with her so we can fuck instead?"

"Contract?" Every time I speak to this man, I become more confused.

Honestly, it makes me feel sheltered and stupid.

"Yes, a contract. You are the only person I haven't asked to sign one yet," he discloses. And although I have no idea what the fuck that means, he seems more perplexed by it than me right now. "But we should sign one."

"Sign a contract?" I scoff. "I'm never agreeing to another contract in my life. The last one almost had me married to my sister's husband."

His shirt is now completely undone and hanging open as he stares at me. I can't help but let my gaze roam over him. I can peek at what looks like a chestpiece tattoo. His tanned skin glows under the lights. *Is that an eight-pack?* He has ridges and dips I haven't seen on any other man. And I thought his cock was impressive. I shouldn't have expected anything less. And now all I can think about is his dick again.

Dick.

Dick.

Dick.

Shit! I'm back to that again.

"You need to leave."

"No." He drops to his knees and then taps his shoulder. "Hook a leg over and hike up that dress."

I should run far, far away, but my breath comes out in short pants. This man is opposite to the world I know. He doesn't make sense, but I feel his demanding tone.

He wants me.

And I want him.

But I can't help thinking there's more than just this. He isn't acting like himself. Something's upset him. And I want to be that distraction for him.

But I need to understand precisely what I'm getting myself into when it comes to Dawson.

CHAPTER 12

Dawson

"Get up," she says, shaking her head and stepping back. "Please get up and get dressed."

"Can't say I've had any woman turn me down," I tell her, standing but not bothering to do up my shirt or let go of my belt. I don't know why, but since sending out feelers and speaking to numerous people after my conversation with Crue, I came here. To her. And I don't understand that. But for the first time in a long time, I'm acting on impulse—just like with the tattoo—and it all has to do with her. I need to get her out of my system.

"I'm not turning you down," she says, hugging herself. I know she wants this just as much as I do. I can read all the signs. "But I don't want to do it here."

"So you would rather go to a hotel?"

"Why do you have a contract with that woman?" Her hands fall to her waist as she asks me. *Insecurity.* Something I imagine very few see from this confident, beautiful woman.

"I have contracts with everyone I fuck. Almost everyone in my life has a contract of some kind."

"Even your family?" She raises a brow.

"Yes, even them." I try to hide the tone that always resonates when speaking about my fucked-up family, as it sounds so brusque.

"Why?"

I don't know why she cares or has to know. It's not something I often talk about, and I never go into depth. But being a Ricci daughter, she must understand this much. "Because everyone wants something from me. If I can stop them taking it, I will." I imagine her father has a similar outlook on life. We might be in different businesses, but that doesn't change the outcome. There is a reason why men like us stay on top because breaking a contract is as good as a death sentence.

She nods in understanding and then steps past me. Her eyes are glued to my stomach, and part of me wishes she'd rake her nails over me as she walks past, simply to give me something... physical. I've never been in a position where I've been denied touch. If anything, too many touched what they do not have the right to.

But her? I want her touch.

Fuck, I even sought it out tonight.

Honey opens her locker and grabs her purse before moving to the door where I stand. She looks me up and down again, biting her bottom lip. I don't even think she's aware that she does it. Then her almost silver eyes find mine. Fuck me, she has no right to be this beautiful.

She leans over and I can't help but rake an appreciative glance down her enticing body. This woman is making me crazy. She offers me my jacket from the floor and says, "I'm hungry. You should feed me."

I take the jacket, almost dumbfounded, and blink a few times. I've never been rejected before. And God fucking knows I need a release because this little honeypot has had me twisted for weeks. She flicks off the light and walks toward the office door, waiting for me. "Where to?"

"Well, I already know what I want to eat," I tell her with a lustful grin as I button up my shirt. This did not go the way I thought it would. And yet, I find it almost amusing.

"What?" she asks.

This woman's genuinely innocent, I know that much. But to what extent?

Fuck! Would I break her? Do I want to break her?

"You, but you just told me no." Her gaze finds the floor before her cheeks redden. "So I guess food will do, for now."

I slide my belt back on and buckle it before I slip into my jacket. "And how do you think your bodyguard is going to take you going out on a date with me?"

She pauses at my words. "It's not a date. Can't two friends have dinner together?"

"I'm not your friend, Honey," I all but growl. I don't do friends. Crue is a very loose exception.

"Yet," she says with a smile that lights up a room.

Does she even know that she has that effect? That despite all the shit I carried with me today, that fucking smile ripples the tension out of me. And I hate it. I hate how effective it is. She's like a bright fucking sun to my darkness and sins.

Her father has good reason to be wary of me. And yet, selfishly, I want to revel in that light, if only for one night.

The bodyguard is a problem, though.

"Come here," I instruct and offer my hand.

Honey eyes me cautiously but slowly steps toward me. Her hands are soft and small in comparison to mine. And I roll my thumb over her knuckles appreciatively.

"Let's sneak out through the back and walk instead of taking my car. Let's see how long it takes your bodyguard to find you."

She pouts. "I don't want to get Marco in trouble."

There it is, the good girl. Does as she told. But she's so much more than that.

I sense her desire to break free.

Isn't that why she came to New York after all? No contracts? No rules?

I lean in and whisper seductively, "Don't you want to break the rules just once?"

It's foolish, but I sense that this girl has never snuck

out, partied too hard, or stepped out of her role. And now she thirsts for it.

Her gaze locks with mine, and I know I've hit the mark.

New York is big, and I realize Marco will find her eventually. I can't help but feel satisfaction in knowing that this will piss her father off. Perhaps I'm playing with the devil a little, but it was him who smothered her. And she will always be safe with me.

Honey bites her bottom lip, and a small, uncertain smile lights her face. I was right coming here. She has been the perfect distraction. Usually, I wouldn't seek out a distraction with how serious the situation at hand is, but I had to see her. It definitely wasn't what I expected.

"Any suggestions on where to go?" I ask.

"I'll eat anywhere. I forgot lunch today. We were busy, so I didn't get anything. You pick," she says as I grab a leather jacket from our dominatrix apparel in her size off one of the racks and offer it to her. I know it will be cold out tonight.

She looks at the jacket and then stops dead in her tracks as I lead her to the bathroom.

"What?" I ask.

She wraps herself in the jacket and flicks her hair over the collar. "We don't have a back door."

I laugh—an actual legitimate laugh escaping—at the fact she only now realizes that as I open the bathroom door and walk to the back of the powder room. I step up on the red leather couch and prop open the window.

Her eyes go wide. "You want me to jump out the window?" She scoffs.

"Come here," I order. I hear her mumble how ridiculous this is, and she's going to hurt herself. "I'll help you up."

I take her hand and lead her to stand on the couch, then I grab her waist. The moment I do, she sucks in a breath, and her gaze meets mine. My cock twitches as the tension runs between us, and I lift her high enough where she can hook a leg over the windowsill.

"This is so stupid," she hisses under her breath. "I feel like a damn teenager."

She carefully wiggles herself out, and I follow her lead, jumping out the window. My polished shoe slides across the gravel, and I freeze.

She chuckles at my unimpressive landing. "Did you ever do anything like this as a teenager?" I ask. I don't know why I care, but I'm curious. I assume I know her upbringing, but I know better than anyone that what lies on the surface isn't always the truth.

I lift her again, and she reaches to close the bathroom window from the outside. It locks shut.

"Once," she replies as I set her down. "But Marco caught me before I even got off the premises."

I cock a smile. "You didn't sneak out with the right person."

Reaching out, I grab her hand and sneak down the back alleyway.

She's quiet, not saying a word.

A few blocks later, we're in the heart of New York, near Times Square. There's no way Marco will find us here any time soon. I wonder if he's realized we're not coming out.

"Why do you think you can just waltz in, and I will say yes to doing things with you?" Honey asks.

I wrap my arm around her shoulders and pull her into me as someone almost shoves past her. She smells floral and sweet, and I'm pleased to note she's wearing one of the perfumes from my store.

Honey's question is easy to answer. "You want me, I want you. That attraction has been evident since the first time we met."

From the very moment Crue introduced me to the younger Ricci sister, who was supposed to substitute for Rya, I felt it.

"Yes," she says. "But..."

"But nothing. Even if you'd married Crue, I would have found a way to have you."

And I mean those words. Fuck, it would have created a war. But I knew from the moment I laid eyes on Honey I would have her one way or another to get her out of my system, even at the risk of my friendship with Crue. And that makes no logical sense. I am a man of contracts, of discipline. But Honey? She has me walking through Times Square, sneaking around for dinner.

Almost hesitantly, she says, "You can't have me. You get that, right?"

I turn to look at her and raise a brow. "Are you so sure about that?"

Those cheeks go red again, but she doesn't look away this time. "I had a lapse of judgment at my sister's wedding."

"Seems we both did, but I was the one who walked out injured," I point out.

"I didn't mean to."

"No? Are you sure? I never said I didn't like it."

She huffs out a breath. "What? Is that like an actual kink or something?"

"Are you kink-shaming?"

"What? No, of course not." She shakes her head animatedly, worried that she might have offended me. So innocent. And I can't help but think of all the ways I can corrupt her—to open her mind to my world—but it almost goes against every boundary and restriction I've put on myself.

"Good, I hope not. Considering my business is sex."

I stop us outside an old storefront. It's been easily a decade since I last came here. I am not even sure if they are still in business.

"Where are we?"

"Best pizza in New York," I reply.

"You know I'm from Italy, right? We have the best pizza."

"If you say so, Honey."

CHAPTER 13

Honey

"You don't have to walk me to my door," I tell him.

"I know," Dawson says as he walks into the elevator with me. I press the button for my floor, and the doors close behind us.

Dinner was good, unexpected, but good.

Dawson definitely stood out, as his entire wardrobe screams "I am only used to fine dining." So, watching him hold an oversized slice of pizza and casually ask me questions seemed somewhat strange. He never created a space where I could ask him questions in return. And I realized after we each had two slices that it was intentional. Dawson knows how to control a conversation, a room, and hell... he probably also knows how to control people.

But it wasn't unpleasant. Just a strange turn of events

since only two hours ago, I thought I'd come just home and cook a risotto.

"The pizza is still better at home in Italy," I state as I fish out my keys and walk down the hallway.

"Whatever you say, Honey."

I smile, shaking my head. I'm slightly nervous about bringing him to my apartment. If he asks to come in, that means he wants more, right? More often than not, I end up giving head to any guy I spend more than a brief exchange with. And Dawson has been straightforward all night about what he wants.

I harden my resolve.

But if I don't have my virginity anymore, then it can be done with, and I don't have to worry about it, and I can break the chains of waiting for marriage. I can use Dawson to help me with that. It's not like it would be a hardship because I'm definitely attracted to him.

"So, this is me," I chirp nervously, then focus on unlocking the door, unsure if he'll stay or go.

"Show me around."

My heart races as I spin around to face him. I want Dawson, but I don't want to seem easy. Is it dangerous to get involved with him? There's still so much I don't know about this man.

I bite my bottom lip. "Look, you can't do what you did last time. No stripping and trying to seduce me. If you come in here, do *not* attempt anything."

"Noted." I wait for him to say something else or even object, but he doesn't.

Does that mean he isn't interested in me anymore?

I'm not sure how I feel about that.

And I hate how much my mind bounces to so many conclusions.

This is not normal for a twenty-seven-year-old, I'm certain. But I simply don't understand how this works. This leads me to consider something I've wanted to ask for the last week.

I take a deep breath and straighten my back as I close the door behind him. "I want to ask you something," I tell him. I turn on the light, and he glances around before he looks back at me.

"No sex is what you said."

I roll my eyes. "Presumptuous much?" I joke as I place my keys on the kitchen counter and pull out some ingredients. I need to do something with my hands.

He wanders around the apartment and picks up small pieces I've purchased over the last week. He only picks up the things I've added to the furnished apartment. Maybe it's obvious that they don't belong here.

"Do you want a drink or something?"

Dawson shakes his head.

Okay. I begin to make a salad for tomorrow's lunch.

"But I do want to ask you something," I say, my heart racing.

"What?" He sits down on the opposite side of the island and watches me cut vegetables for the salad.

"You sell virgins?" I blurt, not looking up as I start slicing the onion.

He's quiet. And I chance a glance in his direction. He doesn't seem all too pleased that I know, and I hope I haven't broken his trust with Crue and Rya or something of the sort.

"Yes," he replies hesitantly.

I release a breath. At least he's not avoiding the conversation.

"Why?"

"You can look at me when you ask these things," he says.

I raise my gaze to his, the knife blade hovering over an onion. I want to look away because I feel silly for asking, but there's no judgment in Dawson's expression. The tension flows out of me immediately. "Because men pay a lot of money for things that are hard to come by."

"You don't offer up underage girls, do you?" I might not know much about this business, but I draw a line at that. And if that is the type of man Dawson is—

"Absolutely not. Not fucking ever. All our women, and men, for that matter, are consenting adults."

"Okay, good." I nod and go back to chopping the onion.

"Why are you asking?"

I bite my bottom lip and scrape the onion into the bowl. "How much does a woman get for her part of the service?"

He eyes me quietly, and I look away, waiting for him to answer. I pretend to be busy searching for the oil in my pantry.

"Why are you asking me this? Are you recording our conversation?" he questions, looking around suspiciously.

I whirl on him, almost dropping the oil. "What? No!"

He seems amused by my reaction. "This is why I make people sign NDAs and contracts." Okay, I guess I get it now because it's not exactly legal.

Maybe Dawson is the answer I've been looking for.

"I'm curious," I add. "How much?"

"All are above one million. The highest someone paid was ten."

My eyes go wide.

Holy shit.

That's life-changing money.

Don't get me wrong, my father has money. And one day, I will inherit a part of that money, more so than the allowance I already get, but I want to earn my own way. Since being here and seeing how successful Rya is in her career, I know that if anything ever happens, she will be secure and could truly fend for herself, and I can't say the same for myself.

I put the oil down. "There is a reason I said no to you earlier."

"Earlier?" he asks, confused.

"Yes, when you wanted to have sex."

"I wanted to eat you, but yes, after that, I planned to fuck you."

"Yes, so, um..." How do I say this? I've never

confessed this to a guy. My sister is the one and only person I've told.

"Do you not want me to fuck you?" Dawson asks, leaning over the counter. "Because your body says otherwise. You unknowingly lean into my touch every time."

I'm suddenly aware that I do exactly that. *Fuck*. And I slightly pull back away.

"It's not that I don't find you appealing. And if we hadn't gotten interrupted on my sister's wedding day, I may have gone further than I thought possible."

"What do you mean?"

I give him my back as I grab the balsamic vinegar and mozzarella. I can't be facing him for what I have to say next. "I'm a virgin," I confess. I wait for him to say something. But when I don't hear anything, I turn back to find him staring at me. "Dawson?"

"Is this some type of sick joke?"

"Sick joke?" I choke out.

"I don't fuck virgins, I sell them."

"Well, you almost did," I tell him, my anger rising.

"Thank fuck I didn't," he bites back as he stands and heads for the door.

"Wait, Dawson," I call after him.

He doesn't turn back, and when he opens the door, there's a seriously pissed-off Marco on the other side.

"I don't appreciate you taking Mr. Ricci's daughter out unattended," he grits out.

Dawson ignores him as he pushes past, and I'm left standing there wondering what the hell just happened.

CHAPTER 14

Dawson

Did she drop that on me like it isn't a big deal?

I'm not sure what she expected the outcome to be, but I sure as shit do not fuck virgins. I never have, and I never intend to. I need a clean break—this infatuation I have with Honey comes to a stop. *Now.*

I get it that it's some people's fetish. And it's how I make a lot of fucking money, but that has never interested me. I like to fuck hard and fast, and you can't fuck a virgin hard because it would scar them for life. And I would never inflict the same kind of pain that was forced on me time and time again. No. Fucking. Way.

No matter how much I want her, I will never take her as a virgin. I'm not even sure how it's possible for someone who looks like her to be a virgin. I surround myself with beautiful women and men daily, and she is by far the prettiest of them all. It's her natural charm and glow that draw others to her.

But how had I become susceptible to that?

Fuck, that must have been it.

This would have never happened if I'd had her sign an NDA because my contract states that they are not to lie about being a virgin. Not that she ever lied to me. I just never thought to ask. *Why would I when she was so good at getting down on her knees and taking me in her mouth?* I mean, until she imprinted her teeth on my cock. But my cock twitches at the thought, still wanting her to finish what she started.

I shut that thought out. I am *not* fucking a virgin.

"You're late," Lesley declares as I enter the room for our meeting.

I want to see Honey.

I want to fuck her.

And all this tension that comes with her out of my system. I'm about to break. I have an appetite, and it's been weeks. *Fuck.*

"I was preoccupied," I grit out.

"Let me guess, by the hot little piece with honey-colored hair who works at the lingerie store."

I throw her a glare. Daphne is playing a dangerous game by disclosing anything we do privately, even if it is to Lesley. I trust Lesley with some of my most intimate secrets. She is the only person I trust in this business because she's been there every step to help me grow my empire. Making her a very wealthy woman in the process.

"No."

She scoffs at me, knowing full well I'm lying. And she's one of only a few I will allow to speak to me so casually.

"Have you received more information about the person claiming to work for us?" I ask to keep her from prying any further.

She quickly sobers.

"No, but we're working on it. I still can't believe it, to be honest. He's someone with a death wish, using your name and trying to make money from it."

My jaw ticks at the fact that we're no closer to finding this guy. Granted, it's only been half a day, but I don't care. I want results.

"We have client interviews. I've already completed two while you were... preoccupied," she taunts. I give her an unimpressed look, and she bites back a grin. "Despite what's happening with the mystery man, business must go on." *Naturally.* And we only vet new clients once a month, which happens tonight. "The first two were awful." She slides their profile images and background checks toward me. "They would have to sell a portion of their business or their house to have one experience with our escorts. And their desires are basic at best."

I sigh. "How the fuck did they get our details if they're not even worth considering?"

She crosses her arms over her chest. Often she does that when I take a tone with her.

"You know it can be hit or miss. But I think the next

one will have the funds, and perhaps the network you'd like in your back pocket. Which is why I've asked them to wait until you returned."

This piques my interest. Lesley knows I like those who can offer me power and sway. I love money. But I prefer power and security more.

She places the profile down and smiles sweetly. "Perhaps this will make you happier today, even if you can't get laid."

My gaze snaps to her, but she's already laughing and heading for the door. When she opens it, a man is waiting on the other side.

I recognize him instantly—a powerful and prominent judge. Young, only forty, reasonably good-looking, and wealthy. Most men in his position can get anything they want. We deal with many powerful people because discretion is what we're known for. They know we use ironclad NDAs so none of their information will ever be shared unless they break the contract first. It's also made abundantly clear that if our agreement is broken, there are consequences.

He walks into the room as if he owns it, running his hand down his suit jacket before taking a seat across from me and studying me in the same way I do him.

I smile and offer my hand in greeting. The difference between us is that he's only ever tiptoed in lucrative business- this is new and exciting for him. However, I was raised in it. And I can tell already he is willing to pay handsomely for the desire that led him here.

People with money always want to buy what they can't ordinarily get.

"I appreciate you taking the time to meet with me," he says.

"The pleasure is mine," I reply and pull out a bottle of whisky. He seems uncertain but agrees to a glass.

"I'm sure Lesley has gone over the finer details with you. Contracts and all. Considering your background, I'm positive you went over it with a close eye."

His chest rises pridefully. I always find it interesting how people act when they step into this type of world. Because what I offer isn't simply an escort business you could walk into off the street.

"A very thorough ironclad contract," he admits as he takes the glass of whisky.

"So, tell me, what brings you here tonight?"

He licks his lips and takes a small sip of his whiskey. I can tell he's trying not to cough at the burn.

"I'm under the impression you have specific auctions," he says.

I clasp my hands together and lean back in my chair.

There are two types of auctions in New York that are known by those who can afford them.

The Ivanov Auctions cater to almost any black-market needs.

And my auctions.

The Ivanov Auctions have been around long before my time, so I made a deal with them. I auction virgins under my name and give them a cut without infringing on their business. And I only auction virgins. But what they get out of the deal is nothing compared to the money that is passed through for the service of those involved. And, of course, my cut.

"And what do you hope to gain from this particular auction?" I ask pointedly. No one has ever gotten their wires crossed with the two auctions. And only a chosen few know of both. He probably has no idea that the Ivanov siblings exist, but I'm always cautious.

He licks his lips. "I want..." He pauses.

I open my arms. "You have stepped into the world of pleasure. There is no judgment here. Only fair business and provision of services. I doubt you went through the vetting process only to choke on your demand here in my office."

If people can't be honest about their desires, I won't draw it out of them. With the contract in place, my business is safe whether they satisfy their needs or not. But they always do. Because desire is strange, it can haunt you daily until you can satisfy the need.

He nods and rounds his shoulders. "I want a virgin."

CHAPTER 15

Honey

I'm in Rya's kitchen again. This time, I'm busy working alongside their chef, Lawson, with whom I've enjoyed cooking in the past weeks. We're due for a family dinner. Something Rya's made a point of every Friday night, and Crue begrudgingly joins us.

It's also become a habit now that I cook while she looks over a few work things. She's in the process of opening her law firm, and I can only imagine the stress it's causing her. It's also very Rya, to return from her wedding and open a business almost immediately. But she always takes the time to listen when I need her.

I feel like my stuff is so small compared to hers, but it's also nice to talk because I missed out on these conversations when she left Italy all those years ago. So weirdly, I feel like I'm catching up on that sisterly bonding we missed back then.

I'm chopping fresh fruit as Lawson works behind me, preparing the entree. Marco is sitting behind Rya, reading a paper with a coffee in front of him. I know he doesn't like it here. He bitterly grumbles "So American" under his breath at almost everything we do or see. I know he misses his family, and I feel guilty the longer I stay here because of that. And despite his lack of enthusiasm for being here, I've noticed that he reads the paper daily, and at times, I've seen him gawking at the drama-filled magazines. It wouldn't surprise me if he watches drama-filled soap operas in his room at night. The thought is almost laughable.

"I signed up to Bumble," I tell her, popping a grape into my mouth.

She opens her hand expectantly, so I throw her one. I can tell Lawson is still trying to get used to us invading his space. I think he enjoys it, although he often remains obediently quiet especially if Crue is home.

"Okay..." Rya says around the grape in her mouth.

"I have a few dates lined up already."

She leans over and takes another grape. She then steps back and says to Marco, "Did you know about this."

His hands clench around the paper, creasing it. "We have discussed it thoroughly. I made it clear I do *not* approve."

Rya chuckles and looks back to me expectantly.

"And to that, I said I need space and can go on a

normal date without a brooding, threatening figure leaning over my shoulder."

Rya chuckles. Despite Crue's controlling nature, she's forced him to promise no guards for her. And if she can do that, surely, I can too. Even if for a few hours.

"I am here to protect you," he reminds me.

I roll my eyes. "Do you know that some of the girls at work ask if he's my boyfriend because he's always waiting to pick me up?" They both inadvertently shudder at the preposterous notion. I had a similar reaction when it was first brought up.

"Perhaps I wouldn't have to be so imposing if someone wasn't sneaking out," he says as he licks his finger and turns to the next page.

I shut my mouth.

Rya raises her eyebrows. "Oh no, not sneaking away from the diligent Marco," she teases. She goes to steal another grape, but I slap her hand.

"Considering the person she snuck off with is someone your father isn't particularly fond of, I'm lucky I still have all my fingers attached."

Rya and I both laugh. And although Marco doesn't crack a smile, I know he's also amused. He's been with us since we were kids and is like an uncle. An overbearing one at that.

"Wait," Rya says. "Was Dawson the person you snuck off with?"

I place the knife down. "Is it that obvious father

doesn't like him?" I ask. I didn't see them talking at the wedding, but apparently, it's well-known how much my father hates him.

Rya studies me carefully before speaking, directing her request to Lawson and Marco. "Can you two give us just a few moments."

Lawson is hesitant to leave his food prep but does so after turning it twice.

"Is there something I should know about you and Dawson?" she asks. And I know she's not the slightest bit impressed. Okay, I get it. He's a dangerous man. But she, of all people, can't reprimand me since she married one.

"No, there's not." I shrug. And I think back on the other night, how he walked out on me, which made me feel like something was wrong with me. The anger rises again. I haven't been able to talk to anyone about it so now is the time. "Actually, I don't know. But what I do know is, he seriously pisses me off."

Rya arches her eyebrow and scoots off the chair. "Perhaps we need a drink for this one."

I lean against the back of the counter with my arms crossed as she pours each of us a drink.

"Look, the guy's hot, all right? And, sure, I know he's going to be great in bed, and I really want to give it a go. Like really, *really* give it a go."

Rya's trying not to laugh and has her hand at her mouth.

"It's different for me, Rya. Don't laugh."

"I'm not laughing at you," she says. "It's just this is what Dawson does. He brings out people's desires. And I won't tell you how much you should avoid Dawson. I like him. But Honey, he can never give you what you want. He's not the relationship type."

"I might not be a relationship type," I say defiantly. She hands me a glass, her brow lifted in question. Okay, maybe. But I don't know yet. That's why I'm trying to find myself here.

"I told Dawson I'm a virgin," I admit, and she swallows her wine slowly. "When he came back to my place after we snuck out after work."

She sits across from me again. "And how did he take it? Was he pressing you for something?" There's an edge to her tone. I can't help but adore her and want to swat away her protectiveness at the same time.

"No, he didn't." I continue chopping the fruit. "But I kind of hooked up with him at your wedding in the supply closet. Not sex, but, you know... stuff."

"I figured something happened between you there," she admits, and I'm grateful that she's not calling me silly or out of my mind. I'm happy that she's listening and letting me vent. "So how did he take it when you told him you were a virgin?"

"He left. And I haven't seen him since."

She doesn't seem surprised.

Oh my God. Is it really that repulsive to be a virgin at my age?

"Okay, so the real question is, do you want to lose your virginity to him? Because from my impression, I don't think he's the right person for you, Honey."

And as furious as I am with Dawson, it still hurts a little to hear. I know it doesn't make sense. And I know what she speaks is the truth. But I can't help how attracted I am to the man.

"What do you mean?"

"He sells virgins, Honey. Dawson would have specific expectations. I've never seen him so much as show interest in a woman unless it's work-related. I wonder if he's doing you a favor by not taking your virginity. I know you don't want to wait until marriage anymore, and that's fine, but it doesn't mean it shouldn't be with someone special."

I sigh. Because Rya is completely the opposite of that. She and Crue fuck all day, every day. And how she dealt with men in the past was to use them for sex. So why can't I have that? Even Rya still sees me as sweet and innocent. And it's frustrating, even though she means nothing by it.

"He kind of alluded to that," I say, somewhat disheartened. *Damn, how did I get here?* There are literally thousands of men in New York. Normal men. I only have to dip my toe into the dating world with one of them.

"So what do you plan to do about it?" she asks.

"Nothing. Nothing at all." I smile. I don't want a

man who doesn't want me because of one simple thing. No, I haven't had sex, but so what? Why is that such a big deal? I mean, I've probably already broken my hymen. I've done a lot of other things and just because I haven't had a penis in me, does that make it more taboo?

Well, fuck him.

CHAPTER 16
Honey

I t probably wasn't the smartest move to tell a stranger where I work. I realized that when he walked into the store earlier than expected and straight up to me while my manager was there.

That was awkward.

Thankfully, Alana is amazing and let me go early since we weren't overly busy. But she'd been surprised when I'd clarified that Marco was far from any type of lover, and this would be my first date here in New York. And now, if anything, she was shoving me into it because she wanted to live vicariously through me.

So now, I sit across from him with him looking at me like he's about to have me for dinner. *Eww.* No, thank you.

I mean, he isn't bad-looking. This man obviously works out. His clothes are tight on him, and he has a nice smile, but the longer I sit here with him smiling at me, the creepier it becomes. My impression of how my first date would go is crumbling fast. Does any vetting happen in dating apps? I'm certain I downloaded the most popular app. But how did it produce... well, this?

"So, do you wear items from the shop under your clothes?" He nods to my dress.

"Excuse me?" I ask indignantly.

"Yeah, I saw a blue piece that would look so good on you."

My skin crawls. "No, I do not."

I do, but he doesn't need to know that because he will *never* get the chance to find out. *Ever.*

Fuck. How did it end up like this? Now, I wish Marco was looming over my shoulder so I could at least find the situation laughable.

"I can always buy you something. You get a discount, right? I know that place is expensive."

"I think I'll be all right," I reply, lifting a glass of wine to my lips.

"You seem almost done with that drink. Would you like to head to my place after this for a nightcap?"

"No," I tell him straight up. I don't intend to lead him on. I can see this will go nowhere. And I want this over... like an hour ago.

"No? So what? You think you'll get a free meal and not have to put out?" he asks. "That's cocky of you."

I'm almost shocked. But not really. He appears the type. *Asshole!*

"I'll pay for my half," I offer. I've been around my share of men, but what sits before me isn't that... that thing is a boy. A man-child at best. I finally understand why my friends at home complained about their dating life. Suddenly, I don't feel like I'm missing out on much.

"I have to go to the bathroom," the ass announces, then stands and weaves his way around the other tables. I sit there with my glass of wine, look at his empty plate, and back to my pasta, which I hardly touched. A meal is only as good as the company you share it with.

"Miss, the bill." I glance up at the waiter.

"I'm waiting for my date to return," I tell him.

"Miss, he left and told me to send the bill over."

Anger bubbles in my blood and I do everything to remain composed, especially in public. *That fucking asshole.*

I politely smile, take the bill, and slide my credit card into the folder before handing it back to the waiter.

When he comes back, he offers me an apologetic grimace. "I just want to let you know he's done this to two other ladies before you. Sorry again, miss."

Two other ladies.

What a fuckhead.

I bet it's because they didn't want to sleep with him, either. I collect my things and stand. When I slide my chair in, I glance to the back of the room and feel eyes on me. It's then I see him—not my runaway date, but Dawson. He's sitting with three women and one man.

Of course, he is. Because why wouldn't Dawson be here?
I raise my chin, turn around, and walk out.

I don't care if that's humiliating.

He can also fuck himself.

Men suck.

CHAPTER 17
Dawson

"Who was that?" Lesley asks.

"No one," I reply, watching Honey leave the restaurant.

"That is the woman from the store, is it not?" Daphne inquires.

Lesley smirks as she puts two and two together.

"She's beautiful," Lesley adds. "Unlike you to fuck your staff. I hope she's signed a contract."

I don't bother telling her that she hasn't. And she doesn't push me on it either. Besides, there is nothing between Honey and me. Couldn't be.

"Find out about that man she had dinner with," I tell Henry.

We're here to discuss the problem of the stranger using my name and company, and Henry does a lot of digging for me. Like Crue stated, it's been hard to find his identity. Even the street cameras didn't get a clear vision of him, and he'd used public transport, so there was no license plate to track either.

But Henry is good at what he does—he's young and eager to make himself useful. He nods and opens his phone, and I know he's hacking into the restaurant's reservation system.

"Why do you care who she had dinner with?" Lesley asks, smirking.

"Even my contract isn't exclusive to just Dawson," Daphne says under her breath to Lesley. They both laugh.

"Lesley"—I turn, facing her—"you may get a lot of things from me, and I find you very useful, but I can always replace you."

"You can't, and you know it," she says, reaching for her drink and offering a cheers to Daphne.

I could, but damn, it would be hard to find someone as good as she is.

"Found him," Henry announces and shows me a picture of a man who looks exactly like the man Honey was sitting with. I'd been watching her since she came in, and she was all smiles at first, but it didn't take long for that to change. It took all my restraint not to interfere. Honey means nothing to me, but when he left her with the bill? That is *not* how any woman should be treated, and he's about to learn a painful lesson.

"Come on, Henry, let's go for a drive."

"Dawson," Lesley warns. I ignore her as I toss my credit card onto the table.

"Ladies, enjoy your evening. I heard the fishbowl margarita is a particular favorite here."

Daphne squeals and hangs off Lesley, and I know she's doing it purposefully to try and pull Lesley's attention away from me. I feel Lesley's gaze on my back as Henry and I leave the restaurant.

THE MAN WAS easy to track down because he keeps his social media profile public and tags himself wherever he goes.

Like a real dick.

He didn't go far, just down the road to a bar. I find him straight away, talking to a woman who I can tell by her body language wants him far away from her. But he seems to be stupid enough that he can't read the signs.

Walking up to the woman, I step in front of him and offer her a smile. "Your friend asked me to save you," I tell her. Her eyes go wide, and she nods. Then she leans in and whispers, "Thank you," before she hurries off.

"Man, that was so uncool. I could have had her if you hadn't interrupted," he grumbles.

"You think?" I turn around to face him.

He nods. This idiot is obviously a dickhead who never outgrew being the star quarterback in high school and thought every person wanted him.

How wrong he is.

"Yes, she was into me. Then you came along." He shakes his head. "Fucking hell, two down tonight."

"Two? That's a bad night for you," I comment.

He runs his hand through his hair. "You're telling me. The first one was a bitch and wouldn't even consider coming back to my place after dinner."

I maintain my smile and try to keep the anger that dances along my skin at bay. "Then you might be interested in what I have to offer. I have a bunch of women outside, ready to fuck, if that's what you're after. Not these fidgety bitches." I look around the room as if to include all the women here, and my insides crawl at my words.

He clearly missed the lesson on respecting women.

But that's okay.

I'm here to teach him.

Some people learn the hard way.

"For real? Hell yeah, man. You are awesome." He slaps my back, and it takes everything in me not to punch him in the face. He follows me when I stand and start through the crowd.

"You had a date earlier?" I ask.

"Yeah, she was hot. But she wasn't eager, you know? She needs a lesson on how to please and respect men." He doesn't question it as we walk through to the bar's back exit, and the door shuts behind us. Just us two in a rundown, trash-littered alleyway.

I stop and face him. "Some women are just bitches.

Do they not get we're only here to get our cocks wet? Like, fuck."

He shakes his head, and that's when he finally looks around. When his gaze returns to me, he asks, "Where are the hoes at?"

And before I can stop myself, my fist connects with his face. He stumbles back, and I punch him again, watching as he spits out one of his front teeth.

He screams and grips his mouth as it pools with blood.

"You think it's okay to disrespect women, and what? Leave them with the bill?" I ask angrily.

"Fuck you," he yells and charges at me.

I quickly sidestep him, his anger propels him forward, and it's too late for him to pull back as I put my foot out and trip him. He falls face-first to the ground. The crack is loud as his face connects with the concrete. At first, I think he's been knocked out, that is, until he groans and rolls over.

Bad move. I lift my foot and glare down at him.

"If I find out you ever disrespect a woman like that again, you'll have a bullet in your head." I bring my foot down hard between his legs. I wince as I hear a pop, knowing that is the worst type of pain, but I'm sure he's inflicted worse. Men like him don't listen when a woman says no.

He sobs, tears falling from his eyes as I reach down and grab his wallet. I pull out a wad of fifties and his credit card. Taking them, I walk away, dropping his wallet to the ground, and head back into the bar. I slap his card down on the counter and look at the bartender.

"Charge everyone's drinks to this card." The bartender nods as if he knows what happened in the alley but says nothing as he takes it. I walk out without another word. I give Henry the stack of fifties and tell him, "Send this to Honey." He knows who she is. He's looking over my shoulder as if he expects the other guy to return. When he realizes he isn't coming back any time soon, he nods and walks off without further questions.

CHAPTER 18
Honey

Some young kid is standing at my door.

"How old are you?" I ask.

"Twenty-one," he answers, still trying to hand me money.

"So why are you trying to give me that?" I ask, nodding to the money.

"You're owed it from your date. He's repaying you."

"Why?" My arms are folded over my chest.

"Please take it, miss. I want to go to bed." I look at it again.

"You take it. Buy yourself some alcohol and get drunk," I tell him.

"I earn good money, I don't need this."

"Okay, give it to someone who does need it. There is a homeless man—"

"Yes, we know. You make him food most days."

"Who did you say you were again?" I ask. No one

knows that except for Marco. And I don't make the man food. If I have leftovers—which is almost always because I cook way more than I can eat on my own—I give them to him. He's always so nice to me when I see him.

"Please take it." He shoves the money at me almost desperately.

Then, it dawns on me who this kid is.

"You were with him, weren't you?" I ask. "Dawson. I remember now. You had your back to me, but it was you at the restaurant. Do you work with him?" I'm getting mad now because this is humiliating. I don't need Dawson trying to swoop in and be chivalrous when he's made it abundantly clear he wants nothing to do with me.

"Yes, but—"

I lean in close, and the boy steps back, as I interrupt him with, "Tell him to shove it up his ass." Then I shut the door in his face.

Silence.

"I'll give it to the homeless man, then," he says through the door.

Argh.

A FEW DAYS LATER, my date that ran out on me, sends me a message apologizing for what he'd done, and it also says he hopes I don't hate him.

Like, what the fuck?

I blocked him.

I'm at work now. We're closing the store so we can finish unpacking new stock.

I fish out a matching yellow silk set. *Oooh, I like it. No, I love it.* I hold the material against my skin, and it's a perfect contrast.

"Ooof, we love!" Alana, my manager, says as she walks out with another box.

"I swear I'm going broke here, Alana," I whine. I love all of it. Discount or not, I've begun an unhealthy relationship with lingerie because it makes me feel sexy.

"And the new toys," Alana adds as she pulls out a pink vibrator from the next box. She admires it before returning it to the box and looking at me again. "I still can't believe that douchebag made you pay for the meal." She scoffs in disbelief.

I sigh. "Is online dating always like this? I mean, honestly. I might stay single forever."

She laughs and then throws me one of the boxed vibrators. "Then maybe you need this."

I flip it over, appreciating it in the same way Alana did. It's cute. And a girl can never have too many toys, right?

"Put it on my tab," I say in a sing-song voice. And although I love it and have only ever had dildos and vibrators, I'm wondering if I'm missing out on anything at all when it comes to men. I mean, this basically does the same thing, right? And most women have told me it's even better. But then I wonder if the person you're with makes the experience different.

"Dawson asked for your work schedule," she mentions, peeking in my direction. When I look at her, she returns her focus back to emptying the box. "Is there something going on with you and the boss that you should tell me about?"

Fucking Dawson... *again.*

I'm still too mad about him handling my date to have anything nice to say, but I try anyway. "He's friends with my sister and her husband," I tell her. I certainly don't need to tell her that I almost bit his penis off. Or that he came in here to seduce me, and the whole time, I sat there wondering if I should let him. Or about the tattoo. Or about anything because there is nothing between us.

"Okay, because work relationships can be messy. But I get it. He's hot." Her eyes bulge as she says it. "Don't tell my husband I said that." She laughs. "Also, if you're not doing anything tonight, a few friends of mine are going out to celebrate my birthday. Want to come?"

Using a hanger, I arrange the yellow set on the rack. It reminds me of the color of honey.

I haven't really hung out with anyone from work, and making friends has been hard. Despite how many people live in New York, I haven't met many people.

"Sure, sounds fun. And if it's your birthday, it's my treat."

"No, my husband is going to meet us later. So he can treat. The goal is always to rack the bill as high as we can until he gets there, then he pays and gets a drunk, crazy, sex-driven me as a thank-you." She winks.

"Husband!" Alana shrieks and wraps her arm around the attractive man in the well-fitted suit. They seem perfectly matched. She's beautiful and charming. He's handsome in an accountant-possibly-a-secret-spy way. But maybe it's the glasses.

"Hi, Husband!" we all say in unison.

He shakes his head as he puts down two large fish-bowl drinks. "I figured if I came with these, I'd be most welcome," he says. Alana smooches an appreciative kiss on his cheek. "But you ladies have been managing an impressive job on my tab, huh?"

"Shouldn't have been two hours late," one of the girls teases as she happily drags the fishbowls toward us.

We're sitting in a large booth in a club. It's private enough but still loud, as we have to yell at each other to be heard.

I told Marco not to follow me and not raise suspicions. He wouldn't leave me, and I know he's here some-where. But for once, I don't care. I want to make friends. I want to let my hair down. And fuck it, after my shitty date this week, I deserve it.

"Emit, I don't think you've met Honey Ricci yet. She's the new girl I work with."

He takes a seat, and Alana sits on his lap. He offers

me his hand in greeting. "Ricci?" he says. "The name rings a bell."

"Her sister is that famous criminal lawyer you see on the news," one of the other girls I work with says as she splashes her drink on herself.

"Oh, that must be it," he says as he shakes my hand.

Three men approach the table with more drinks in hand.

"Scoot in ladies," the guy with short blond hair says.

Talia, my coworker leans in. "Partying with Alana is the best. Her husband always brings his hot colleagues."

I mean, they're okay, hot even. But men are not on my mind tonight. That is, until everyone squishes so closely together that I'm awkwardly squeezed between Talia and one of them.

He smells nice and is well-dressed. I'm pressed between them as she attempts small talk, and I purposefully try to shrink back, taking my drink with me as I sip through a straw.

This group is fun, but it's so different from the partying I did back home with my friends there. Then again, it was always more superficial as well.

"My name's Kit," he shouts over the music to Talia but in the process eyes me. His proximity suddenly bothers me. Not in a bad way, but those small brown curls and dimples have cute fuckboy written all over him.

"Talia, let's dance!" One of the other girls grows impatient and yanks her out of the booth.

"Honey, are you going to join us?" Talia asks.

I shake my head and try not to laugh. "I'm not drunk enough for that yet."

They shrug and run off to the dance floor.

"Is that actually your name?" Kit asks me, and I'm grateful for the space that has now opened between us.

"Yep," I reply and take another sip. *Is this going to be the same type of guy who will leave me with the bill?* I can't help but feel annoyed by all of the male species after this weekend, and my disinterest is probably obvious. I thought it'd only be us girls.

A woman comes over with a tray of shots. "Do I even want to know who ordered these?" Emit grumbles. But I can tell money is not a concern for him as he nips at Alana's neck playfully.

I'm almost envious. It's like watching Crue and Rya. Reminding me that there can be functional relationships. Hell, even happy marriages.

Everyone picks up a shot and raises it. They look at me expectantly, so I oblige. Fuck it! I came to let down my hair. So I will. American style.

"Cheers to my beautiful wife. Twenty-one again," Emit announces. We clink our shot glasses, and I notice Kit's gaze on me before we throw them back. I swallow the shot, a mild buzz running through me.

I mean, I suppose he'll do, right? It doesn't matter who I give my virginity to. As long as I get rid of it, right?

"So, are you new to town?" Kit asks.

"She came over from Italy only a month ago," Alana replys on my behalf. "And she is, like, the best!"

She encourages everyone to grab another shotglass.

"I don't know if I'm still going to be the best tomorrow at work if you keep feeding me these shots," I joke. But I oblige and throw back another drink.

Kit offers me his hand. "Are you drunk enough now to dance?"

I consider him.

I mean, he is cute.

Fuck it!

I take his hand.

CHAPTER 19

Dawson

"So you tried to fuck my virgin sister-in-law?" Crue asks as he sits back in the chair on the other side of my desk. His unannounced visits are becoming quite the habit.

"Remind me, when is your brother coming back?" I ask because he needs to come back soon. Crue and I are friends, good ones at that. He is a powerful man, no doubt about that, but since his right-hand man is off with his wife, who just had a baby, I'm left to entertain him on the days Rya is working late.

"Hopefully soon. And stop avoiding the question because I got an earful for you... I don't even know... not fucking her?" he complains.

Flattered that I've become a household discussion, I think bitterly.

"She's a nice young woman but not my type."

A dark chuckle leaves him.

"What?" I ask, narrowing my gaze.

"Nice young woman. What is that even supposed to mean? Like, nice enough you want to fuck her, or nice enough that you think you shouldn't?"

"Neither." *Both.* And I don't like that Honey has become a discussion topic for us twice now. *Perhaps Crue has become a lonely househusband, trying to entertain himself with gossip.* I smirk into my glass at the thought.

I would rather do bad things to her, but I won't fuck a virgin. And I don't think it's fair to her because I *only* want to fuck her, and Honey seems more like the relationship type.

I sell sex for a living, for fuck's sake.

How would a virgin work into that?

"Well, from what I hear, she has been enjoying the dating world, and tonight, she is on her third date with the same guy. She likes him, so I hear her telling Rya."

He has definitely turned into a gossiping househusband.

This news shouldn't bother me. I shouldn't care that Honey's dating someone else, but for some reason, it makes my skin crawl to know that someone else's hands will be all over that body.

"Why did you just look mad? For someone who doesn't care, you suck at acting like it." Crue gives me a curious look.

"Is there a reason you're here?"

"I was bored. Want to go and watch me kill someone?"

"Who?"

"Just a shop owner who thinks he can keep putting off payment and has been talking shit about us to all the neighbors."

"I'll let you deal with your own shit."

"Unless there is someone you want me to kill for you. I know you don't like to get your hands dirty." He smirks.

"I can take care of my own dirty work," I tell him, and he nods.

"Yes. I saw evidence of a guy in an alley you let live. That was kind of you."

And suddenly, I understand why he's provoking me about Honey because Crue is nothing but intentional.

"How did you..." I shake my head. "It's one of your bars." I guess, to which he nods. Crue doesn't technically own it, but he provides security for it. *Fuck*. Is there a place in this city he doesn't have a piece of?

"The owner called me with photos of the guy and told me he had to personally carry him into the ambulance. He asked if I could handle it. Handle *you*." He motions to me.

"Consider me handled." I roll my eyes.

"Good. Because no matter how much I like you, you and I have much in common. When it comes to business, we don't let others fuck with it, friends or no friends."

I nod in agreement.

He stands, preparing to leave. "And just an observation as your friend... I am sure this guy might be right for her, so make up your mind before she does it for you."

I lean back in my chair. "Marriage seems to have made you soft."

He shrugs. "At least I'm honest. And I am most certainly not a coward."

My jaw tics as my patience nears snapping. He says nothing else before striding to the door and closing it behind him.

We both know how bad I am for Honey. So why is he encouraging me to pursue her? I sure as hell know his wife wouldn't be pleased. But it always comes back to Honey. And the thought of her with another guy...

I look at the paperwork on my desk, which is Daphne's contract. I canceled it, and she didn't seem all that upset about it. Though I guess paying her a nice hefty amount of money helps soften the blow. She asked if we could still be friends, even if we aren't fucking anymore, and I agreed. I've had Daphne under contract for many years, and she has been loyal and incredibly good in the bedroom. And I think she's lonely. I guess we all are in some way.

But that isn't the pressing matter that led me to cancel her contract. It's all due to a certain little honeypot that I can't stop thinking about every fucking day.

I've made it a point not to fuck virgins, so I've stayed away from her.

But fuck me, nothing makes sense when it comes to her.

CHAPTER 20
Honey

I'm not sure it's the right thing to do, but I'm going to do it. Kit, who I have been seeing, has been good to me. Even that first night, no matter how drunk I was, he walked me to my cab, asked for my number, and said he would reach out for a date. Nothing more. I actually think I like him. But we've had three dates now, and it's time.

I've been wondering about my little problem for a while.

Wondering what to do about it.

And if what I'm considering is the right thing to do.

But I don't want it hanging over my head anymore. I want to do this for myself.

I've made up my mind.

Alana messaged me Dawson's office address, where I currently stand, outside his door. It's late, and I should be home in bed. That's sure as hell where Marco probably thinks I am. But instead, I stand here, wondering if I should knock or walk in. Just as I go to lift my hand, the door opens, and a man I don't recognize stands in front of me.

"Miss Ricci, please come in." He steps back and waves me in.

The office is nice, with a fireplace that crackles even this time of year. There are multiple white couches and small tables around the room, but no one to occupy them. There's even a white marble reception desk. It's not at all what I expected of Dawson's office. I genuinely thought it might be two levels deep under a club or something. That was my understanding of most lucrative mafia-related businesses. But Dawson's office looks like a high-end... I don't know, cigar bar or something.

The man leads me to another room at the back. I follow him, and as he pushes open a door, I see Dawson sitting behind a desk. He seems to be expecting me and waves for me to take a seat.

"I'd rather stand," I tell him, fidgeting with my hands. Dawson notices but doesn't comment on it. The man who escorted me in walks out and shuts the door behind him. I'm still unsure if this is the right thing to do. It's been two weeks since I last saw him, and he made it abundantly clear that my "situation" wasn't appealing to him, which is what brings me here today, not for him, but for me.

"What brings you here?" Dawson drawls.

"I want to ask you something," I say, suddenly

finding my confidence.

It's only Dawson.

I can talk to Dawson.

"Okay, ask."

Fuck, my sister would kill me if she knew.

"I want you to sell my virginity," I state with a steady voice. I have been thinking on this for quite some time. I wasn't sure exactly how to tell Dawson I want to sell my virginity, but I figure now is the time to do it.

I want to sleep with Kit. I'm attracted to him, but I'm afraid he'll think less of me because I'm a virgin. And I know there is one way to solve that problem and earn some money from it at the same time.

He stares at me silently, leaving me standing in the heavy atmosphere. I know he won't tell Crue. He's all about keeping people's secrets. But it doesn't make it any less uncomfortable to ask.

"And how much do you take from that? I imagine the women earn a lot of money, and I want to know your commission on it."

"You want to know my commission?" he questions, sitting back in his chair and flashing that cocky smile as if he finds this situation amusing.

"Don't tease me, Dawson. I'm serious."

"Why didn't you ask me to take it?" he asks, curious.

I roll my eyes. I can't believe Dawson's even asking, so I say pointedly, "Because I know you won't, and I want the money."

"You have money, Honey. You are far from being

poor."

"I want to earn my own money. And if I can earn it with my body, I will."

"So you want to sell yourself to the highest bidder?"

"Yes."

He remains silent for a moment and it kills me. *Fuck.* Surely, I'm not that repulsive that he doesn't think he can even sell me. I fidget with my hands. I mean, I'm certain I'm attractive, but maybe it's not enough. *What if he really does laugh at me?*

"Okay," he says simply. "But there are vows you must take before selling yourself."

"Vows?"

"Yes. You vow to not speak about this, to embrace the experience, and to trust in me completely that you will be kept safe. That this is of your choosing and nothing is being taken from you. That you are giving it freely."

"And the man?" I ask. "Does he make vows?"

"No, he signs an ironclad NDA. It's the woman's body, and if she chooses to discuss how she loses her virginity, that's up to her. However, the woman also signs an NDA, as well as a contract regarding my part in the sale. Everything else is left up to the woman and the buyer."

I bite my bottom lip. That's more involved than I thought. Maybe I should've just begged Dawson to take it from me. I furrow my eyebrows. Fuck that. I shouldn't have to beg anyone for anything.

"Okay, I accept those terms and will make the vows."

"Virtuous vows," he says as he stands. "Drop to your knees for me." He steps around his desk and nods to the floor. "Knees."

"Are you serious?"

"I take my business very seriously, Honey. It's a form of conditioning and submission. If you're uncomfortable with this, I don't know if you can handle what will come next."

I do as he says and bow my head as I mumble, "Jesus, you make it sound like a cult."

He raises my chin so I'm forced to look at him, and I'm met with those wild green eyes. "You came to me," he reminds me.

I blow out a breath, my gaze landing on his crotch. I lick my lips, annoyed by the jolt of desire that warms my body.

"You're right." I don't want to admit to him that I'm nervous. I don't think Dawson would outright laugh at me, but the room has a tender balance of give and take.

"Repeat after me." I nod as he speaks. "I vow..."

"I vow..."

"To never speak of or disclose any information regarding my purpose here."

I look up at him to see him watching me intently. This means no one in my family will know either. No more good-girl Ricci. No more being told what to do because I've finally done something for myself. And I'll finally be free of these shackles.

"I vow to never speak of or disclose any information regarding my purpose here."

He nods and steps back, leaning against his desk.

I look up at him. "Can I stand?"

"I'm not sure. I like you down on your knees, though I do get a little PTSD."

"Funny," I deadpan and then stand.

He chuckles, and it heats my insides. *Fuck*. I hate how responsive I am to this man. It's all sorts of wrong, especially when I can't have him and most certainly shouldn't want him.

"So, do we have a deal? Will you sell my virginity?"

"As long as it doesn't get me killed."

"Killed?" I ask. *Oh, right. My family.*

I'll definitely have to get better at sneaking out so Marco doesn't clue in on or ever find out about this. "I won't tell anyone."

I'm hesitant to ask my next question but fuck it, this is a business transaction, isn't it? "How much do you think it will go for?"

He's still considering me, his knuckles going white along the desk's edge. Is he always this reluctant? This is his expertise, isn't it?

"Aren't you dating someone? Why not ask him to fuck you?"

"How do you—" I snap my mouth shut. I'm used to powerful men finding out what they want to know.

I hate how he's looking at me. There's a spark of pity in his eye. Or is it something else? But I won't be tormented by him any further. "Because I'd rather he not be scared off like you were," I throw back at him.

His demeanor changes. "I wasn't scared. I just don't fuck virgins, Honey."

"Noted. But someone will pay to fuck me, and then I won't have to worry about it again. A win-win, isn't it?"

"You could just fuck yourself, you know." I gape at him, almost shocked at how brazen he is to speak to me like that. "Get a vibrator, lube it up, and insert it nice and slow. That pink little number you ordered from the shop should do the trick." He takes a step forward and I meet his stare. I'm sick of him thinking he has the control and can play with me like this. His fingers lightly trail down my stomach and come to a stop, where he cups his hand between my legs. I suck in a breath, my eyes widening.

I hate him.

Hate how much he thinks he can have this.

Hate how much my body leans into him for more.

"It's not enough," I say, and my words come out shakier than I'd like them to. All of me is on fire. My core is pounding with heat.

He leans in again, and I can smell him. My body goes into desperate overdrive as I try to place a hand between us. But instead of pushing him away, it explores his hard pecs through his shirt.

"You could just fuck a stranger instead," he says.

I want him. Not a stranger.

"You screen all these people, don't you? All these potential buyers?" My hand trails down the eight-pack abs I know are beneath the shirt and rests on his belt buckle. "It's not like I would be given to some dirty old man?" *What the fuck am I doing?* I step back, trying to reel in whatever self-respect I can muster.

Dawson looks like he's gasping for air in my absence. And he clears his throat as if he were under the same bizarre spell I'd been under.

I wrap my arms around myself. Dawson's off-limits. I'm not going down that route. *Again.*

"You want to put an age limit on those who can bid?" he asks.

"Yes, very much so," I confirm. I can't imagine being in bed with someone my father's age. Each to their own, but for me, no.

"Done." He walks around to his chair. "Any other questions or requirements?"

I exhale what feels like my first breath since walking in here. "No."

"Okay." He presses a few buttons and the door opens, and the man who assisted me before appears. "Lance will take you to the photo room."

"What for?"

His head drops to the side as he eyes me. "Do you expect people to buy you without seeing you first?"

I kind of hoped so.

"The answer is no. So go and get changed. The photographer is already waiting." He waves me off and doesn't look back up.

I feel like I've got whiplash. This mindfuckery with

Dawson has to end. Once I get what I want from him, I can go on my merry way and try for something normal with Kit.

I walk out with Lance and am taken to a white room. There are cameras and racks of familiar lingerie. A small lady approaches me, grabs my hand, and studies me from all angles. When she's done, she drops my hand to my side and looks up at me.

"White. Innocent." She nods, then points to the lingerie. "Go and get changed. Hair and makeup are in the back." She waves me off, and suddenly, nerves flutter throughout my body.

Am I really doing this?

Should I be doing this?

But I do as she says.

I can't back down.

If I do, Dawson will never let me try again. I promised I would do this for myself. And if I have to get on my knees and take some fucking vows for it, that's what I'll do. Nerves be damned.

Walking into the back room, a lady hands me a robe and tells me to undress and to come back and sit down. I do as requested and try not to show my nervousness with everything happening. I honestly thought I would have time to process the decision and not be thrown straight into it. But I guess that's how Dawson rolls. And it may be a way to ensure I don't back out.

Dressed in my robe, I sit in a chair as the two ladies do my hair and makeup. One of them undoes my robe and puts shimmer all over my upper breasts. I feel naked, which I guess is the point. I don't say anything, even after it's done, I just sit there like a deer in headlights.

As I'm left to stare at myself in the mirror, I can't help but think back to what happened in his office. This thing between us fucking sucks. I hate him, and I want him. And I just feel like a yo-yo in his presence. But I know I'm not what he wants. And I sure as hell will not change myself to fit what he wants. I'm done with that shit. But, damn, does my body betray me when I'm near him.

I'm handed a set of lingerie and told to put it on. After I do so, I secure the robe around me once again before the photographer walks me out so I'm standing in front of the cameras.

"Remove the robe," she orders.

I'm hesitant at first. I mean, come on, I've spent my fair share of time in Europe, clubbing, beaching, and yachting, wearing nothing but bikinis. But this is different. The intent is different, and I must find a way to make it mine.

I do as she says and listen to how she wants me to move my body and how I should be positioned. She tells me not to smile and to keep my mouth slightly open, showing just a hint of teeth. I awkwardly try a few positions, reminded of my younger years and my mother's pressure to follow in her footsteps to become a model just like her. But it never felt right. I always felt awkward with that type of attention.

However, no one will bid on me if I don't do it right this time. Dawson walks in and takes the attention off me as if my saving grace. The photographer watches him expectantly.

I should cover up. Dawson hasn't seen me dressed like this before. But as he walks over to the photographer, his gaze never lands on me.

He looks through the photographs that have already been taken, then, finally, his gaze locks with mine. It fuels me with flutters and heated need. I don't feel judged by him. Only desired. Or maybe that's because I want Dawson to desire me.

And here we go again—mindfuck.

He whispers into the photographer's ear and then leaves the room, dragging his eyes away from me.

"On your hands and knees," the photographer commands.

I'm reluctant at first, watching as the door closes behind him.

Fuck him! I don't want to be seen as a sweet and innocent girl. Just the virgin. And if he wants me on my hands and knees like a fucking good girl, I'll make him regret not being in the same room.

It feels wrong, though, like I shouldn't be doing this.

But I chase that thought away.

I'm going to do it anyway.

CHAPTER 21
Dawson

I'm going to hell.

And it might very well be Crue or Mr. Ricci who send me there if they find out what I've done. I watch her on the video screen as she gets on her hands and knees. It makes my cock hard seeing her in that position, dressed in all white, a picture of innocence. I can't stop uncomfortably shifting. A not so pleasant reminder that I haven't had a release in a month. And right now, the honeypot I want so desperately is in another room just down the hall and I'm the asshole willing to auction her off.

I wanted to say no.

But she's so determined.

I know she's trying to find herself, and I feel all the more the villain for allowing her to step into this world. But I can't mix my personal feelings—which are most uncomfortable—into this.

I know her being on her hands and knees will get her all the hits from being positioned like that alone. I know she'll go for a high price. But all I can do is imagine what she tastes like and how she'll scream in pleasure.

Fuck. I need a release.

She arches her back and angles her face, the light bouncing off her ass.

Fuck.

I undo my belt and let my cock spring free. The relief I feel is momentary because I have so many other urges to be met right now.

I fist my cock, and my eyes all but roll into the back of my head as I watch her. I've never watched anyone during their photo shoot. *Fuck, I shouldn't be doing it with her.* But my cock—my poor fucking cock—needs this. I can't even stand being in the same room as her.

All my years of well-trained discipline and restraint have gone up in chaotic smoke.

The photographer instructs her to lift a belt and place it between her lips, and she does so, biting down. And at this angle, it's as if it's all for me.

Damn, I wish it were for me.

I glide my hand up and down my length, thinking back to the time in the closet with her, and how her lips felt along my cock. That bite. My cock jerks, and I glance down at my tattoo.

Is this an all-time low for me? Wanking over a screen because I want to abide by my own rules so desperately. But, fuck, does it feel good watching her. Every angle I could imagine ramming into her. I want to see how much of me her sweet lips could take in. To train her to take me to the back of her throat. I want to see the tears in her eyes as she gags on me. And then I'll return the favor.

"Fuck," I growl as I pull open the drawer and grab a handkerchief. Am I a fucking teenager now? But damn it feels good. She feels good. *Would* feel good. I want to have her squirm under my touch and listen to her breath hitch as I choke her.

I wonder if she tastes sweet, like honey.

She twists, her back now facing the camera, and wraps the belt around her wrists. The light reflects on her supple skin, and her hands rest beneath her supple ass.

I imagine shoving my thumb and a string of beads into that ass. I want to play with all of her. To train and force her to submit.

I throw my head back as my cock explodes, and I grunt with the thought of how she would taste on my lips. I take a deep breath as I wipe myself clean and throw the silk handkerchief in the trash.

Fuck, that felt good.

When I look back to the screen, I notice she's gone, which means she's getting dressed. I shake my head in disbelief.

Fuck, what is she doing to me?

A few moments later, I meet her at the entrance. She's wearing her jeans and jacket again, hugging herself as she reaches the front door.

It makes me feel even shittier for what I've just done.

"Let me drive you home," I offer.

Honey nods but doesn't say anything.

Maybe I should put a stop to this for her. She isn't the only one to get nervous and feel uncomfortable with the process. And I always want to make sure the others feel safe and empowered in their decision, but somehow it's different with Honey.

"Having second thoughts?" I ask as I open the car door. Plenty of people say they want to dabble in this but don't understand the meaning and the nerve required to go through with it. To use it as an empowering experience. And if she can't change her mindset, I won't let her go ahead with it.

I don't want her to have the same experience that many of my staff had in the past.

Or that I did.

She stops at the car door I'm holding open for her. "No, I just..."

"What?" I search her eyes, but she diverts them. "Honey, look at me." I tip her chin to meet my gaze. Someone so beautiful should never look at the ground.

She seems shy, and I want to figure out a way I can draw it out of her.

"It's going to hurt, right?"

My stomach drops. And I don't know why it seems like such an obvious question and answer. As easy as the birds and bees. Honey climbs into the car, embarrassed for asking, but I don't want her to ever be embarrassed with me.

I lean on the door and look down at her.

"Yes, it will," I tell her, then stand and close the door. I won't ever lie to her. She's already buckled in when I get in on the other side.

"Can I get drunk?" she asks.

"Now?" I question as I pull out of the parking lot.

"No, before I have sex," she says, exasperated.

I shake my head. "No, Honey, you need to be sober."

"That's unfair." She huffs.

"This is always your choice. You can pull out at any point. But I will tell you now, some have lost it in worse ways. You can take control of this."

I feel her gaze on me. "How did you lose yours? I know it's different for men, probably easier."

A dark laugh erupts from my core. If only she knew. She has no idea the question she is asking nor the ugliness that it brings to the surface. "Let's just say I was in unfavorable circumstances with no power."

She goes quiet, then her question creeps through the air. "Were you hurt?" she asks. And I can feel the wound wanting to reopen like her gentle voice is trying to coax it out.

I push it back down.

In my industry, it's mostly women who are considered victims. But if you're a male—

"I found my power," is all I say in response. I took it all back and built an empire out of it. I provided roles and security for those who also wanted to take theirs back.

Her soft hand lands on mine and rests on the center console.

I glance at Honey and the sadness that radiates from her pours into me. It makes me uncomfortable and yet soothes me all at once.

"I am not a good person, Honey," I admit into the silence of the car.

"Everyone's lying if they think they are," she replies and turns toward the window.

And I think it's more for my sake than her desire to avert her gaze this time. But her hand doesn't leave mine. And I'm painfully reminded this is why I didn't want to touch her.

Because I would hurt her.

Make her dirty.

But I'm the selfish prick who won't remove my hand, either.

CHAPTER 22

Dawson

The collectors in charge of the Ivanov Auctions stand across from me.

Anya sits there, the red lipstick starkly contrasting her rich porcelain skin. Her thick, glossy red hair is wrapped into a tight bun as she looks over a tray of unique jewelry with a magnifying glass. It's unusual for her brother, Aleksandr, not to be in the room, but I suppose they sometimes have to divide their business dealings.

Two of her guards stand behind her. "I didn't expect to see you so soon after we auctioned you off only a few months ago," she says thoughtfully.

I helped Crue with a personal task by selling myself at one of the Ivanov's events. And he owes me a favor for that. "What can I say? Business is going well."

She beams a smile. Anya, although beautiful, reminds me of a snake. Entrancing, but with a bite. And the Ivanov family is not one I'm willing to go against unless necessary, of course.

"Didn't the Torrisi woman end up dead only a month after you and Crue Monti last walked into this establishment?"

I knew it had been a risk involving Crue and that could even jeopardize my business, but I leveraged a return favor would hold a greater value in the future.

"It was very sad news to hear," I say with mock sadness as I remove my jacket and sit across from her.

She pouts and watches me. "Very sad indeed." Her Russian accent is anything but sympathetic. "But you could always return to my good books if you're willing to do something for me. Or many things *to* me." She eyes me.

I give her a smile. "Maybe you should have bid on me last time."

She laughs and snaps her fingers. One of her guards picks up the jewelry and leaves the room.

"Another virgin auction, then?" Anya asks.

Our agreement has always been they get a small cut, and I advise them when they have a particular client who is looking to dabble in the services I offer.

I nod. "The usual."

"Hm," she purrs. "You know my brother and I enjoy exchanging business with you. Our dealings have been transparent and mutually beneficial."

"I feel the same."

"Then I wonder if you're sorting your shit out," she seethes.

And there is the bite. The venom that sits just beneath the surface.

I offer a tight smile. "Regarding?"

"I've been advised that a man propositioned one of my security guards to try and find out information about our next auction. Someone who boldly announced that he works for you."

My blood drains, but I keep my composure. "And could he verify that claim?"

"No," she admits. "And my security is wary enough of commoners and police sniffing around to know how to avoid the question. I should hope that my people will not be approached in such a way again?"

"It's being handled."

"Hm," she says as if she can't hear me.

My knuckles go white. "It's being handled," I repeat. I can't very well ask Anya if her people can identify the man because it certainly won't look like I'm handling it. But I do know that someone is fishing around where they shouldn't be, and now it is affecting my business.

I keep my composure because the Ivanov siblings are best kept as allies. And we're already on fragile ground after the stunt Crue pulled by killing off one of their regular clients. One who bid for me to personally escort her.

Anya pouts as she walks over to me and stands between my legs. She presses her finger against my lips.

"But I could be lenient. Forgiving, even. I could put a good word in with my brother if you play nice."

Everyone knows the Ivanov siblings work in equal shares. She is the front, and the brother is the dirty work behind the scenes. But they are ruthless. It doesn't mean that I can't be any less cruel if needed.

I curl my fingers under her hand and kiss her knuckles. "I think you'll put a good word in for me either way. You will both receive your usual cut from the auction."

She seems pleased. A difficult thing to do with Anya Ivanov.

She offers another lingering gaze over me. "We look forward to doing business with you as usual, Dawson. But clean up your shit." And there's a hint of a threat behind her words.

Fuck. Too long.

We've taken too long to find this fucker.

No more.

CHAPTER 23
Honey

H e's waiting for me, dressed in a perfectly tailored suit. And I am wearing a white dress, per the instructions in the email I received earlier.

"Are you ready?" I nod as he holds open the door for me and offers me his hand.

"Honey?" I turn to find Rya walking toward the building, obviously coming home from work. Dawson looks her way but doesn't say anything. Her eyes scan him before they land on me and eye me up and down.

I can't tell her anything, so when she's closer, I stay still as a statue, trying to think of the best lie I can think of, but instead, something else falls out of my mouth. "Dawson is taking me on a date."

I feel Dawson stiffen behind me, and I'm not sure if she believes my lie because she eyes him with a narrowed gaze before she pins her gaze back on me.

"Are you sure that's a smart idea? Your dates with Kit have been going well."

"I know. And I like him. I'm just, you know... playing the field, as they say," I tell her and reach for the car door Dawson is holding open. Dawson steps away and walks around to the driver's side.

My sister eyes him the entire time. "Does Marco know about this?" she asks.

I bite my bottom lip. *Fuck.* "He's taking a nap right now."

Her brows furrow. "You spiked him?"

"Shh," I say, as if someone might hear.

"Honey, what the fuck?" she demands.

"I want some space for myself for once, okay?" And that's not a lie. She shoots a death glare at Dawson. Her mistrust of the situation isn't at all misplaced. "Rya, I'm an adult. I'm sick of being followed everywhere. I love Marco like he's family, but I should be able to go on a normal date."

She tucks a piece of my hair behind my ear. "But you're not a normal girl, Honey. And Dawson isn't normal either."

He scoffs at that, and I can't help but smile because I know she understands. "I know that. But please... I feel suffocated. I want to live freely. Like you have all these years."

She crosses her arms over her chest. "You know father won't be pleased when he finds out."

"So let him be disappointed in me for once."

She sighs. "I get it. But next time, let's think of another way to get distance from Marco. What you did breaks trust on so many levels."

"In my defense, he probably hasn't had a decent sleep since our father forced him into this role."

She nods once as if in agreement. "But it still doesn't make it okay. And you..." She points at Dawson. "So help me, Dawson, if you hurt my baby sister, I will find a way to put you behind bars... *for life.*"

He laughs it off, and that only seems to irritate Rya more. Although, I sense he takes her threat seriously. Where Crue might threaten, Dawson swipes it away. Both are equally infuriating.

But tonight serves a purpose.

"Have a good night," I tell her, clicking my seat belt into place. I take a shaky breath, and Dawson whistles as he drives off.

"You didn't tell me you were going to literally put your bodyguard to sleep," he scolds.

"Shut up." I swat his comment away as if I don't already feel bad enough about it. But the store clerk told me it was harmless. I'm twenty-seven years old, and I know Marco wouldn't let me go anywhere if he suspected. A date here and there, he might be fine with. But a date with Dawson? That's a big fat no, in his opinion. "There's no way my father can find out about tonight. For both of our sakes."

I feel selfish putting Dawson in this position, but I'm

grateful he took my request seriously. I've been mentally preparing myself all week.

I turn to see his hands glued to the steering wheel and his jaw locked tight.

"Are you mad because of my father?" I ask. I want to reach for his hand but think better of it. Tonight will kill whatever lies between us. I won't ever see him again. He'll get his cut of money. I'll be a free woman and wealthy woman too.

"No, I'm not mad about that." His grip eases, and whatever he was thinking about seems to have left his mind for now.

"Is it because I've put you in a bad position?"

He then looks at me, surprise in his gaze. "No, Honey. You've done nothing wrong."

It feels intimate, the way he says my name. I want to ask more about what's happening. There's obviously something going on with him, but I find myself at a loss. No, his problems are his, and I need to focus on mine tonight. I take his advice seriously, needing to mentally prepare myself for tonight.

We drive in silence for thirty minutes before arriving at a mansion. Someone is waiting and opens my door before Dawson can get there.

"Welcome, Miss Ricci." I nod to the man dressed in a suit.

Dawson comes around, grabs my hand, and pulls me toward the house and up the stairs.

I peek through the slightly ajar wooden door and see

at least a dozen men and one woman waiting, each with their own table and drink. I didn't even consider a woman could be a possibility.

I feel Dawson watching me, and my heart begins to race. Some of the bidders are attractive, some not at all. I recognize one as a well-known judge. I wonder what Rya would say if she knew that judge was into this sort of business. Not that I could ever tell her.

Dawson closes the door, so I can't peek any further. "Are you sure?" he asks.

I nod in silence and let him walk me to a room around the back with a single chair. He places me on it, studies me carefully, then leans close. "You want another man to fuck you?" he asks. His tone holds a hint of volatility, and I know he's purposefully trying to spook me. I'm starting to consider that he doesn't want this money at all because he's clearly trying to talk me out of it.

"I need to be fucked," I state, though it doesn't sound like me when the words leave my mouth. I try to take a deep breath, but he gets closer, his mouth almost touching mine.

All my thoughts dissipate at his proximity.

Right now, behind this curtain and in this room, it's only me and Dawson.

"You *will* be fucked," he says, and his gaze flicks to my lips. The tension is palpable. All that tension turns into jittery heat and expectation. I want to pull him to me, to press my lips to his and demand more from him. If he'd just fucked me, I wouldn't be here.

Neither of us breathes for what feels like years before he pulls away. I feel the loss and the immediate reminder of my decision.

Yes, I will be fucked...

... but not by Dawson.

And not by anyone I know.

He walks out the door, and soon enough, the television lights up, and I watch as Dawson comes on the screen and welcomes everyone. He's different—charismatic and charming, coaxing and promiscuous in all the things he promises on my behalf. I watch, transfixed, as he explains the process. Each person has a tablet with them to make their bids. A photograph of me, on my hands and knees, appears on the screen. And then, after Dawson's introduction, a woman I recognize from the group with him at the restaurant takes over. She's most likely his assistant or business partner or something.

She tells them I have an age limit, and those who don't qualify may leave or do as they please while the bidding starts. They can then come in on the next one.

The next one?

My heart races.

How many women are willing to do this tonight? I wonder what their reasons are.

The camera pans to the crowd, showing the bidders. I can't see them clearly, as they're sitting in the dark with only the dimly lit screens to light their silhouettes.

The bidding starts at one million, and I freeze as a bidding frenzy ensues. My hands are glued to the seat, and I feel them sweating. The bids come in lightning quick. One bidder constantly outbidding the others.

Oh my God, who is it?

What do they look like?

Are they kind?

Will they be slow and gentle with me?

How much will it hurt?

The bidding hits ten million dollars, and my jaw drops. I recall Dawson telling me the previous highest bid at one of these auctions was ten million. Surely, I won't surpass that? But the bids keep increasing. My heart is pounding, and I realize I have arms wrapped around my waist. *That figure can't be real.*

"Seems we have the highest bidding war to date," the woman says as the screen reads twenty million.

Who knew virginity could cost that much? I bet if most girls had the choice, they would rather make twenty million like this than lose it to an idiot. But Dawson's voice echoes in my mind. *Not everyone has that choice, and not everyone's first time is gentle.*

But once this is done, it's done. It's my choice and in my way.

The door opens and the same woman who was on stage walks in. She offers me a smile. "It's lovely to finally meet you, Honey," she says.

I give an awkward smile. I don't like that she knows who I am. But I suppose, as the auctioneer, she has to know those details. None of the bidders do. They just see a picture.

"I'm Lesley. I help with most of Dawson's affairs," she clarifies, and I realize my uncertainty must have shown. She holds out a piece of white silk. "You need to be blindfolded," she explains.

"Will I not be able to see who the person is?" I ask.

She shakes her head. "No, sorry. You had your requirements, and all were met. He requested you do not see him."

"Okay. I didn't know that was an option, but it makes sense," I say as she steps behind me and places the blindfold over my eyes and it also covers my nose. I try to calm my beating heart.

My choice. My power.

I repeat to myself like a mantra.

She grabs my hand, and I know it's her because her touch is soft. "I'm walking you to an elevator, and then we go up one floor to the main suite. If you have any issues, please yell and security will be at your door. You have the power here." She guides me, and I sense when we're in the elevator. When we exit, she takes me down a hallway, and I repeat my mantra to myself...

My choice. My power.

... and can feel it working.

A little.

I hear her open a door, and I'm led to what feels like a bed. She sits me down on the edge and sits next to me.

She places her hand in my lap with my own. "Do you feel safe?"

"Um... I guess so?"

"And you are sure you want to proceed?"

"Yes," I say, thinking about all that money. And freedom.

"Okay. Would you like something to help you relax?"

"I was told no drinking," I say.

"Yes, but there are other things we can give you."

I shake my head. "No, I'll be fine." At least, that's what I'm telling myself.

"I'm leaving now. Your winner is already in the room with us." I freeze at her words. I hear her footsteps as she leaves the room, and I begin to tremble.

What do I do?

I'm not familiar with any of this.

"Hello," I say as I hear some ruffling.

A hand touches my shoulder and gently lays me back. The hand leaves my shoulder but does not leave my body. It slides down ever so slowly, tickling me as it brushes over the swell of my breast and inside my white dress. I feel his other hand skim over my stomach and my panties, down my thigh, and to the hem of my short dress. He lifts it ever so slowly, and goose bumps break out all over my skin.

"I-I'm n-nervous," I stutter.

"Shh," he soothes.

Okay, I can do that. I guess, technically, he didn't pay to have me speak.

Maybe this is normal. *Why didn't Dawson tell me not to speak?*

My dress is lifted higher, exposing my panties. I feel him reach for them, and I lift my hips to accommodate as he slides them off of me.

I'm left bare, and I hear him swear, and a small smile touches my lips at his reaction. That is until his mouth is on me, and very soon, I'm spreading my legs even wider as his tongue starts dancing against my clit.

"Oh my God." I gasp, thrusting my hips up to meet his onslaught of heated demand. I didn't know it could feel this good. I thought it was only for their pleasure... but this is like nothing I've experienced. And I'm hungry for it. Desperate even. My worries fall away as I shamelessly ride his face.

Who gives a shit? It's not like I'll ever see him again.

He inserts a finger into my pussy, and I feel full. Then he slides it in and out while his mouth continues working my clit. He creates slow and sensual circles as he goes.

My hands find the sheets, and I grip them for dear life as if they're the only thing keeping me in this room. My back arches, and pressure crawls up my legs and builds in my core.

Oh fuck, am I...

Am I about to...

My legs begin to tremble, and before I can even stop myself, I have my first full-on orgasm.

It's hard and slow like it pulls on my every nerve ending. His mouth doesn't slow, and his finger doesn't speed up. His digit keeps the perfect rhythm as I ride the wave of pure bliss.

I have never felt anything so... *mind-blowing.*

When my breathing evens out, he stops, and I feel lost without his touch. I hear the tear of a wrapper and go to shut my legs, but he is already standing between them and stops me from closing them.

"Sorry," I whisper, instantly wishing to take it back. His hand slides up and down my leg, tickling it as he opens me wider. I feel him there, at my entrance, but he doesn't make any move to push inside.

His breathing is hard, and I wonder if he plans to go slow or fast.

Do I want him to get it over and done with?

Or do I want to savor the moment?

Let's be real. I don't.

After tonight, I plan to tell Kit I want to be with him and no one else. We've skirted around the conversation, and now I can give him this. But will it feel like this with him?

"Do it," I encourage.

His finger comes down on my sensitive clit and rubs slow circles. My legs open wider, and my hips start to move of their own accord. I am hungry and almost know what to do, and I play into it.

He inches closer, and I suck in my breath in suspense.

His tip is in me now while he continues rubbing my

clit, and I realize it's a purposeful and pleasurable distraction as he slowly pushes into me.

I stiffen when I feel it.

Damn, that hurts.

I only feel sharp pain now, but when he slaps my clit, it pulls me from the other pain and sends a shock through me. My hands grip the bedding again, and he keeps on pushing. I feel a tear leave my eye under the silk blindfold and hope he doesn't see it. But just as he fully seats himself inside me, his body comes closer, and his heavy breathing hits my ear.

"Cry for me," he says in a husky voice. Then he moves very slowly, so slowly that the burn is almost painful, but his hand on my clit feels so good.

It's like my body can't decipher which one it wants to feel.

Pain.

Or pleasure.

And I wish it were only pleasure.

His hips move faster, but not so fast that it hurts worse, just faster than when he first entered me. I can't say it's amazing because the burn is real, but part of it does feel good. And the part where he went down on me that was definitely amazing.

My hips begin to match his rhythm. It's not awkward but fluid, as if my body knows exactly what to do. His hands brush up my arms and bring them above my head, and the move feels oddly intimate. I can feel his breath on me and notice our pants are in unison as we ride each other in search of...

... bliss?

I feel another tear glide down my face, and I'm not sure if it's from the pain anymore or something else.

I hear him grunt, and when he does, he pulls out of me. My legs snap closed, and I feel his loss straight away, my heart pounding from the exchange. I hear his footsteps as he walks away and then the sound of running water. I don't move from the bed, unsure what to do next. Then I hear him come back, and something warm brushes between my legs, and I realize he's cleaning me.

Once he's done, I hear the door open and then close.

And I'm left lying on the bed.

Alone.

A few minutes later, a knock sounds.

I sit up and snap my legs closed. "Come in," I call out.

I hear the creak of the door.

"You can take the blindfold off," the woman says. I remove the silk as she steps closer, hands me a check, and smiles. "Pleasure doing business with you, Honey Ricci." She smiles and leaves. I look down and see the sheet beneath me has blood stains. And the cloth that was used to clean me is on the floor, also smeared with blood.

It's done.

I am no longer a virgin.

And I have no idea who I gave my virginity to.

CHAPTER 24

Honey

As I sit in my sister's kitchen, Marco sits across from me, and Rya mediates between us. I can't even meet his gaze. With everything that happened last night, this is a sudden, hard slap of reality. I was thinking clearly about my decision at the time, but even I admit that putting something in Marco's drink might have been extreme.

That and I have a weird lump in my throat.

I still haven't been able to process last night. I stayed awake for most of the night, my mind crossing wires on many possibilities of who the winning bidder could have been. *Was it the famous judge?* I mean, if it were him, he wasn't bad to look at, so I suppose that's okay. But what if it were someone I wouldn't look at twice on the street?

I take a harsh swallow as Marco sits there expectantly. The maid brewed us all a mug of coffee earlier. The only one who has taken a sip is Rya. It's her day off, and I'm sure this is not how she'd planned to spend it. But Crue isn't here, so at least I know I'm not stealing her away from him for too long. Lord forbid.

Rya clears her throat. "I think perhaps you should start with an apology, Honey."

Obviously.

My gaze darts up to Marco and quickly falls back to my hands, where they clench my dress. He's so pissed but hurt as well. It's the worst combination. Of course, I feel guilty, but it was the only thing I could think of to ensure he wouldn't track me down. Marco is a well-trained hound.

I clear my throat. I want to grab my coffee, but my hands are too shaky. I've stood up to many people in the past, but Marco is basically family, so it's different.

"Honey," Marco starts. "I need a very clear explanation."

I let out a shaky breath and want to burst into tears. Most likely a mix of still trying to process last night and now the consequences of my decisions.

I don't have any regrets.

I just feel really shitty.

I shoot a glance at Rya, who is casually blowing on her coffee to cool it down.

I roll back my shoulders. "I just..." The words fall short, and then I pin him with a stare. "Marco, I don't want you here anymore," I blurt. The hurt that overtakes his expression is immediate, so I quickly add, "And I don't mean it like that."

I sigh. "It's just... I want to be by myself, truly by myself, for a while. I don't want to be followed. I feel like I'm still being treated like a child. And it weighs on me that you had to leave your family back in Italy."

"I go where you go," he says dutifully.

"No, Marco, that's not fair," I exclaim.

He seems slightly taken aback by my outburst. And maybe it's because I've always been quiet. That's what I thought everyone wanted from me—to speak when spoken to, to be the perfect daughter and representation of the Ricci household, and to make my father and mother proud.

"Miss Ricci," he says. And I hate when he speaks to me so formally. He makes it sound, yet again, like a job, even though he has been as much of a father to me as my own because Marco has always been there. *Always*. And now, I want to breathe a little like Rya. I suppose it isn't a good point to make when two guards stand outside the kitchen door, but still.

"Honey," he starts again. "You know I can't leave your side. This is my duty. And the pressure lies as heavily on me as it does you to uphold the Ricci name. I swore from when you two were born that I would protect you with my life."

"But you have your own children, Marco. A wife," I say, almost pleading. I always worried that his wife, even his children, might hate me for taking so much of his time.

"And that was my decision to have both."

"And what about what *I* want?" I argue. "I came to New York to try and figure out who *I* am and what *I* want to do with my life. And it just feels like everything I do is still tracked. That I can't do anything right and I'm always being judged.

"I want to go on dates with boys. I want to go to a job where I'm not being collected like I'm still in school. I am smothered. And not by you. I know it's my father's hand by extension. But I wanted an evening to myself, and I hate that I hurt you and went to such measures to put something in your drink so I could do that. I never wanted to hurt you."

Rya is watching us. She probably assumes that I spent the night with Dawson. And that little white lie was so much better than the reality, even with her reservations concerning Dawson.

Marco exhales. "That act could've cost you your life, Miss Ricci."

I exhale in frustration. "No, Marco, I had a very lovely evening. I want to have what Rya has." I point to her. "I want to live my own life. No one here knows who I am."

"There will always be people who know who you are," he says.

I growl out a frustrated noise and stand up. "Yell at me or something, Marco. Be pissed off that I spiked your drink. But stop treating me like a child!"

I can see the muscle bounce in his jaw, and I throw my hands in the air.

"If your father found out about last night, I don't think you realize the consequences it would have on *me*," he says, banging his hand on his chest.

I open my mouth but shut it.

I do know.

I've seen Marco punished for the few escapades I had in my teens.

Goddammit! I feel defeated.

"I never meant to put you in that situation. And I'm sorry. I just don't know what to do. I feel like I'm suffocating," I say, pressing my hand to my head.

I've called my father multiple times since being in New York, and no matter how many times I "kick and scream" as he puts it, it was the agreed-upon condition. But guilt is a very real thing. Despite what happened last night, I want to be free.

Rya taps her long nails against her mug thoughtfully. "Perhaps I can speak with Father."

We both look at her.

"I've tried so many times," I say to her. "You know what he's like."

"Oh, I know what Father can be like. He had someone pretend to be my best friend for years just so he could keep tabs on me."

"But at least he let you come here without security." Tears prick my eyes because it's Rya. Strong, independent Rya. And I have always been the backup. Had to be made extra safe to secure the line and ensure contracts were at play. And now it's a habit. Something I don't know how to break free.

Rya seems remorseful, and Marco averts his gaze and sips his coffee. Not without sniffing it first.

I let out a small laugh. "Marco, I won't do it again."

"I never thought you'd do it in the first place," he grumbles before taking another sip.

"What if I suggest Crue's security take over?" Rya offers.

I'd just be moving from one set of chains to another. She gives me a look that says she wasn't done speaking. I sigh, and she continues, "But we have different conditions around it, and your phone is tracked. No walking you to and from work. No hovering on dates. And in bigger social gatherings they're to lie low, but someone will still be there."

"Your father won't trust someone else's security," Marco interjects.

Rya gives him an arrogant look, which reminds me so much of our father. She can truly bring men to their knees. What she says is law. And I'm, what? Nothing but a coddled backup.

"My husband's security is sound," Rya says, putting her mug on the table. "Not that I like it when they breathe down my neck. And anyway, Honey is trained in self-defense. She can look after herself. She's just never had the space to do so. Besides, our father arranged our marriage with the Montis, so he's not ignorant to their force. And, Marco, you can go back home and enjoy time with your family. Take a holiday for once. Woo your wife."

He snorts at that. And the energy in the room immediately shifts. And for the first time, I have hope. Another shackle is possibly being broken. A new space is being made for me to explore.

"Do you think it will work?" I ask.

Rya offers me a ruthless smile. "I've never gone into a debate where I've been told no. But you need to promise me that you will remain on your best behavior, within reason, of course. This is leveraging a lot on Crue's reputation as well."

I sit, almost desperate for the rope she's giving me. I place my hand on hers. "I'll try not to do anything that you would do."

And to that, she laughs.

CHAPTER 25
Dawson

Twenty-fucking-million my sweet honeypot went for.

It's the most we've ever seen at our virgin auctions. The next virgin for the night went for four million. My knuckles go white over the page of bidder names. I had to leave straight after as I couldn't face her. Our transaction was complete. There was nothing more to exchange. Whatever freedom she was after, I hope I was able to help her set free.

"Dawson." Lesley enters my office without so much as knocking.

"It better be good," I all but growl, not pleased at being interrupted.

Her expression is grim. Behind her stands Macy, one of our escorts, who is holding herself tightly. I look between the two in the heavy silence of the room.

"What happened?" I stand from my chair, waving

Macy in. She enters and closes the door behind her. I can tell in her body language—I know it well—that something was taken.

Lesley watches Macy as she ushers her to sit in the chair. I crouch in front of the woman who has worked for my company for two years. She came from a background of prostitution. I provided her with an alternative path. One where she is paid generously for her services and has security provided at all times.

"Macy, what happened?" I ask. A thick tension wraps around my throat. I already know what she's about to say, but I hope I'm wrong.

Tears well in her eyes and spill over her cheeks as I place my hand over hers. "I think I was raped," she whispers.

My heart drops, and immediately, I want to kill the fucker who did it to her. Every person who thinks it's okay to take what's not theirs. Who overpower and manipulate others.

She begins to sob, and I stand and lean against her chair to hold her closer and comb back her hair. Macy leans into me as I level a glare at Lesley, who has the same burning resolve in her gaze.

"Where was your security?" I hiss out.

"She wasn't on a job," Lesley says. My eyebrows furrow. Last I understood, Macy recently got engaged and wasn't seeking other partnerships outside her job. I can tell in Lesley's tone that I'm missing something here.

I crouch down again and meet Macy's tear-filled eyes

as I pull a handkerchief from my pocket.

"Macy, it's very important you tell me what happened, and I'll make that fucker pay."

"I don't know who he was," she says, sobbing. "I mean... I sort of do."

"Sort of?" I ask.

I give her a moment to control her shaky breath. Her resolve quickly begins to harden. A coping mechanism many of us have nurtured over the years.

"Macy, who did this?" I push.

She takes another deep breath and wipes at her still-streaming tears. "I had a drink with girlfriends a few blocks from where I was meant to meet with the client. I was an hour early, so I waited at the bar, and a guy sat beside me. He said he worked for you and that I had to advise my client I wasn't making it for the night."

I exchange another anguished look with Lesley.

"I would never send another escort on someone else's job."

"I know that," she says with a shaky breath. "But he was so convincing. He said he came straight from the office and, I don't know, the stuff he said sounded legitimate. And I did screen him because I know we must be careful, but I really thought you sent him," she says desperately.

"I know. I know," I reply calmly. It's the same fucker. It has to be. "Then what happened?"

"He ordered us a drink," she says. "And we just spoke about stuff. How our business was going. You know, general work small talk." Which means he knows the industry. "And then..." She hugs herself tightly. "I can't remember much more past that. I just woke up in a hotel room alone and..." Macy begins to sob.

I eye Lesley. "I want you to contact the restaurant she was at and find any information you can on this fucker."

"He's following your movements," Lesley warns.

The muscle in my jaw tics. This is personal, and I don't know why or who... yet. But when I find out, he will wish he never fucked with me or my empire.

"I should go," Macy says, shooting from the chair.

I hold her hand. "Whatever you want or need, you let us know."

She wipes away a tear. "I'm not going to sue or black-mail you or anything, Dawson."

My smile is grim. "I know, Macy, it's not even about that. What happened was not okay. I'll find who did this to you and kill him," I promise.

At my words, a scared edge comes over her but also an understanding.

Thank you, she mouths.

Because she knows I'll follow through on my promise.

Getting my hands dirty to protect what I built and those who put their trust in me is not only a necessity but an honor.

I pull out my phone and call Crue.

I don't want to call in that favor, but this hits too close to home, and this fucker is going to be buried for it.

CHAPTER 26

Honey

Since I lost my virginity, I haven't seen Kit.

It's been almost a week, and I'm unsure how to feel. The fact I have no one to talk about it is the worst part. I mean, I guess I could call Dawson. He is the only person who really knows what happened and the one person I can speak to about it. I've fought with myself for a week about reaching out to him. We said we were done, and I haven't seen him since the auction, but not talking about it is eating me alive.

Me: *Can we meet after work?*

It doesn't take long for him to reply.

Dawson: *I'll be there in ten.*

I look at Alana and then at the clock. I don't finish for at least another hour.

Me: *I still have another hour, so after that?*

I pocket my phone.

However, in true Dawson form, he arrives precisely within ten minutes. I'm restocking shelves when he fills the entrance. "Fuck," I curse under my breath.

Alana is bringing out another box when she sees him walking in, and she cocks a lopsided smile. "You've been making your rounds a lot more lately. I'm starting to think I'm either going to be fired or I'm due for a pay raise," she says in a way of greeting. I imagine few could joke with Dawson like that, but since her husband does his accounting, I figure that may have something to do with it. "Or maybe there's another reason?" she boldly adds as her gaze flicks to me.

I give her an unimpressed look, and she tries not to laugh. Now, she's outright teasing me.

"I need to take Honey. Will you be okay without her?" he says.

"We can make do," she replies.

"I can finish my shift," I argue. Even though I requested to meet up with Dawson, I didn't mean during my shift.

Alana raises her hand. "It's fine, Honey. You've been picking up extra shifts while Talia has been sick. Just don't do anything I wouldn't do." She wiggles her eyebrows. I'm almost gobsmacked by her audacity in front of Dawson, who seems unfazed by the insinuation.

As I walk past her to the back to collect my things, I whisper, "I thought you were warning me away from Dawson only weeks ago."

Her smile is wide as she replies, "But I'm also a total gossip and a married woman living vicariously through everyone else."

"Shameless." I laugh. "But it's not like that."

"If you say so," she sings out as I collect my things from the locker. "Quick, you better sneak off before your not-boyfriend comes and picks you up."

I bite my lip, trying to hide the smile.

Officially, Marco returned to Italy. We dropped him off at the airport yesterday, and despite how much I wanted to see him go, I was also sad to see him leave. He was everything familiar to me. He had always been there for me. There was a lot of back and forth with my father, but he'd finally agreed to Rya's new deal. The terms included that when I return to Italy, Marco would be by my side again. And if so much as a slip-up happened while I was still in New York, he would return.

Despite it all, I genuinely think Marco was grateful. Not that he would ever admit it, because, you know, duty and all. But he could finally spend time with his wife and children. I feel guilty for taking so much of him up until this point.

Dawson is inspecting items near the door. When I appear beside him, he opens the door for me. He looks like he hasn't slept in days. His usual smooth demeanor is slightly off. And to most, he probably looks the same as usual, but I can sense the exhaustion that lies beneath.

When he walks toward the car, I stop him.

"Just a drink down the road? I need to talk to someone before I go crazy. And you're kind of the only person I have."

He looks back to his car and then pockets his keys. "Lead the way," he says, waving his arm. Today, he is dressed in a blue suit with a long, dark blue coat. I pull my coat tighter around me as we walk down the street. We stop at the nearest bar and find a seat at the back.

He's still acting normal. Whatever normal looks like between us. But I sense I'm the only one carrying the weight of what happened that night. Then again, he does this often. I suppose I should be grateful that he can make the time for me.

"So, what's up?" he asks, motioning the waitress over. She stops at the end of the table and takes our order. I request a glass of Moscato, and Dawson orders whiskey on ice. "And are you sure you're allowed to spend time with me, especially without your bodyguard? I know Rya has reservations about us meeting," he says.

I nervously bite my lip. "Well, Rya isn't in charge of me. And Marco left for Italy. Turns out, I get a sliver of freedom."

Dawson's lips kick up in a smile. "Except for the gentleman at the table behind you who is closely watching us, right?"

I go to turn but stop myself. I don't need to see what he looks like, and I agreed to my phone being tracked. And although it's still annoying to know I'm being monitored, I agreed to Rya's and Crue's terms. At least he's attempting to be discreet. "Small victories." I shrug. I don't know how long I'll be in New York, but I can at least cling to the illusion of being free.

"Anyway, I know this is awkward, but I think we are past that stage. I mean, I bit your dick, turned you down, then asked you to find someone to take my virginity."

Dawson's quiet at first as if he's surprised by how blatant I'm being, but a smile slowly blooms on his lips.

"Yes, awkward isn't really our thing now, is it," he agrees. The waitress delivers our drinks, and I pick up my glass of wine and down it all. She stares at me, and silently, Dawson raises two fingers to order another two glasses.

"Or should I just order a bottle, Honey?"

I shake my head and wait for her to leave, and then words spill from me, "I enjoyed what happened that night. Is that bad? I mean, it hurt, but I enjoyed it." His gaze darkens at my words. "Please don't act weird. I need someone to talk to, and you're it."

The waitress comes back with a bottle of Moscato.

I almost want to laugh at the ridiculousness of it, but I'm not going to say no. I don't drink too often and only socially. So why not?

"Thank you," I tell him as he pours me another glass.

"I haven't done anything yet," he says.

"You haven't walked out."

"Do you want me to walk out?"

"No. I told you... I want to be friends with you. Can we forget about everything before right now?" I ask.

"Forget?" He raises an eyebrow.

"Yes. Let's start fresh. Be friends."

"Most of my female friends, I fuck. Unless they work for me."

"I work for you... and I'm no longer a virgin," I remind him, smiling.

"Touché." He sits back, and I take a sip of my wine. "But I also don't get my friends' lips tattooed near my cock."

I choke, and his smile brightens up the entire fucking restaurant. He laughs as I gasp for breath and take another sip to push down the first one.

"Well, that's also kind of crazy," I add as I wipe at my mouth, mortified.

"I never said I was sane."

I arch an eyebrow. "No, you give off this aura that you're always in control." I use my hands to articulate this imagined aura.

"Is that what you like about me, Honey? When I'm in control?" The insinuation of that question lingers in the air.

I try to avoid his gaze because, damn, sometimes he's just too intense. I get it's part of his job to be fawned over. But that's not us—we're just friends. "Stop trying to charm me."

He chuckles. "Who said I was trying?"

I give him a mock glare that he finds equally humorous.

"Anyway…" I make a point to change the subject as I linger on the remaining thought of how strange it is that he tattooed my lips near his cock. "I googled how to soothe *down there*, and I feel good. But I don't know who won me, and that is eating me alive a little because he requested a blindfold and, I don't know… I was wondering if it's enjoyable for a man when the woman is a virgin." He chokes on his drink and covers his mouth at my question. "Was that too much?" I ask.

He waves a hand at me. "I get reprimanded for being charming, yet your directness, Miss Ricci, is alarming."

"Shut up." I laugh. "I'm serious."

He stares at me for a moment longer, that expression darkening and heating again.

"Do you mean is it enjoyable for a cock to slide into a tight, untried pussy?"

I shrug, a little taken aback by his expression but never uncomfortable with it. Only regretting how my body responds to it. "Well, yeah."

"Yes, sex is enjoyable full-stop, Honey. It's fucking amazing. And let me assure you, if a man was willing to pay twenty million for it, you can be assured he most certainly enjoyed his time."

I don't know why, but that eases some of my tension and worry about what we did. Crazy to think I don't even know who it was, but I want to somehow feel validated that I was worth all that money.

It offers me confidence.

"The next time I have sex, will I enjoy it more?"

"So, you did enjoy it?" he asks, and I casually shrug again.

"I mean... yes and no. It stung, but it also felt good. So I wasn't sure what it would feel like next time. And if I did it right in the first place." I should be embarrassed as a twenty-seven-year-old asking these questions, but despite whatever Dawson and I are to each other, he's never made me feel silly for asking a question.

"Do you want me to show you?" he asks, leaning in.

"What do you mean?"

"I mean, let's go back to your place, and I'll show you how good it feels."

A short laugh escapes me. "So now that I'm not a virgin, you're willing to fuck me?"

"Yes," he answers without hesitation.

I want to laugh again, but I can't. The sheer desire and lack of hesitation have me heating in places that have hungered for Dawson since the day I met him.

This back and forth between us. Constant desire and denial. It's fucked-up.

But maybe dabbling in a little danger wouldn't be all that bad. I mean, I called him here, didn't I? Do I really only want to talk?

"Okay," I say quietly but try to nonchalantly shrug it off.

If this man can promise all the dark and feel-good things, then shouldn't I have a little taste at least?

Isn't that why I came to New York?

To try new things.

To taste some delicacies.

To embrace this time in my life where I can have my freedom.

CHAPTER 27

Honey

Dawson stands, reaches for me, and tosses far too much money on the table before he leads me out the door and to his car. A nervous flutter erupts in my stomach as we walk in silence with pure focus on where we need to be, and then suddenly, the short drive we are about to take to my apartment feels like a lifetime away.

But as he opens the door and gently ushers me into his car, his hand never leaving mine, his gaze burning with pure desire and need, my gut tightens with the same instinctual pull. *I'm safe with Dawson.*

After he slides into the driver's seat and starts the engine, his hand is on my thigh and squeezes, pulsing with need as he maneuvers down the street. The tension is palpable, and memories of all the moments and heated exchanges we've shared flood my mind.

And now, what can be.

As soon as he pulls up to my building, we both get out of the car and he walks around to me. My feet freeze on the spot as I look at him. "I work for you," I remind him. More so as a warning because if we actually do this, there is no going back.

"I know."

"I might bite you again," I add, trying to lighten the mood.

"I hope you do." He smirks, which in turn causes me to smile back at him.

I hear my name, and when I turn around, Kit is standing there. He stares at me, his hands in his pockets.

"Kit." I say his name, and he looks from me to Dawson and back again. "This is a surprise." I haven't seen him since I lost my virginity. In fact, we've only exchanged a few messages since then as I've tried to sort out all my thoughts and emotions.

"Yeah, well, I know you've been dealing with some stuff this week, so I wanted to check on you. Is this your brother?" he asks, motioning to Dawson.

"Her boss, actually," Dawson answers, and there's a dark undertone in his words.

Kit doesn't realize it, but he takes a step back and looks between us again.

"Okay. Well, can we talk?" he asks, and I turn to Dawson.

I'm stunned.

How is this for shit timing?

But I waver on my decision. Is this like divine intervention? Something telling me maybe Dawson is a bad decision? Kit is the embodiment of a nice guy, something new and normal. And isn't that what I wanted only a week ago? I swallow. At every moment with Dawson, there's always been something to stop us. *Surely, that's a sign.* My mind jumbles with confusion, and I realize then that Kit has been watching me silently this whole time.

"Dawson, I'm sorry. I have to cancel our plans. Can we talk later?" I ask.

A cruel expression crosses over his features. And for a moment, I think he's going to say something. My heart races just thinking about it. I don't want to hurt Kit. I don't want a showdown in front of my apartment building.

Eventually, Dawson nods, but I can tell he is not pleased with me.

I feel shitty. I wanted to take Dawson to my apartment, but I don't want to turn Kit away.

Fuck. What was I thinking?

"Goodnight, Honey," Dawson says before he gets in his car and drives off.

Right now, I can't help but think maybe I didn't make the right decision. But how could I blow off Kit so obviously like that?

"He seems like more than a boss," Kit comments.

Fucking tell me about it.

"He's just my boss. We had to go over some things," I tell him awkwardly, shoving my hands into my pockets. Because, quite honestly, I don't want to invite Kit up to my apartment just yet. I thought I did all of this so I could get closer to him, and now I feel guilty and awkward.

"So, what brings you here? Do you want to go for a coffee or something?" I ask, pointing in the direction of the café across the road.

He shakes his head. "Look, you're great and everything, and this has been amazing, but to be honest, I need to…" I stand there staring at him. *Is he breaking up with me?* "Well, I know who you are," he adds awkwardly.

"You know who I am?" I ask, confused.

He leans in and whispers, a little unsure, "I saw you, well, the photos. You should have told me you were a virgin." My body freezes at his words, and I feel the color drain from my face.

How could he know that?

How does he know about the virgin auctions?

"Honey," he says and leans away. "Say something. I would have helped you if it was money you needed."

"I…" What? *Kit is a normal type of guy, isn't he?* Sure, he works for a well-known accounting firm, but this society is on a whole different level.

"I have money, and I would have paid you." He licks his lips.

"Excuse me?"

He smiles coyly. "You know, virgins are quite rare."

"Rare?" I ask, and I feel my blood boil despite the cold slap of confusion.

Kit was meant to be a Mr. Nice guy.

Kit was meant to be normal.

"Yes. We could have made it special."

The guilt and uncertainty wash away. Was Kit propositioning me now because I'd been a virgin?

"Okay, I think it's time you leave," I say angrily, stepping away from him.

"I can pay you... if it's sex you want. You'll still be nice and tight. I could even teach you a few things."

Goddammit! I look at him with disgust. "I'm not some prostitute, Kit." I all but hiss out the words, completely offended.

He offers a half confused, half cocky smile. "Well, you are. I mean, you've done it once. And I don't know, it's a hot fantasy."

Did he really just say that?

How could I have been so wrong about him?

I mean, three dates in, and we chatted regularly. I thought I had a good impression of what Kit was like as a man. And all this time, the asshole's a disgusting pig.

Are all of the men in New York like this?

Or just men in general?

"You need to go before I call security."

"Are you serious?" he asks, baffled. "I thought things were going well between us. I don't understand why you're mad."

I don't even have the words to deal with him and how offended and pissed off I am. This is a part I wanted to keep to myself. I didn't want anyone else to know. And to be propositioned like this when I thought I had a spark with him leaves me astonished. "You need to leave," I reiterate as I walk away.

"Call me if you change your mind. I'd still fuck you, Honey," he shouts.

My skin crawls. "Yeah, that's a no," I call back, shaking my head and heading to the elevator to get as far away from him as possible. And all I want to do is cry. Because, for some reason, now I feel dirty. And disappointed. And disheartened.

I actually thought Kit was one of the good ones.

But I now realize that might not even be a thing.

Or maybe it's not a thing for me.

CHAPTER 28

Honey

It's been two days since I last saw Dawson and had the confrontation with Kit. And besides my regular dinner with Rya and Crue, I've holed myself up in my apartment baking all types of treats. I've gone back and forth with Kit's words. And how offended I was by the prospect of being considered a prostitute. It made me feel... less. Dirty? New waves and notions I didn't understand developed but then I realized I didn't care what he thought. And who cares if I accepted money for what I did? It doesn't make me less of a woman. In fact, I feel invigorated by it. And *as if* that asshole could fucking afford me anyway.

I'm walking back from the shelter on the outskirts of town. I baked so much that I didn't know what to do with it, so instead of throwing it out, I hope it brought some less fortunate people joy.

I know Crue's bodyguard is following me, and I'm

okay with it. I still have a small container in my bag as I walk past the homeless man who is regularly at the park. He's there today, so I drop off various assortments of sweets. And it always brings me joy to see someone cherish my cooking. The only person who has appreciated it in the past was my nonna. I touch my necklace, thinking of her. I wonder *What she would think of all of this?* She was just as strict as my father but always had a soft spot for us girls. When our father was strict with us, she'd be lenient or slip us a treat. I wonder how lenient she'd be about this.

I'm strolling through the park when a voice gains my attention. "Oh, I know you. You're the woman from the lingerie shop." I turn to find the woman who was with Dawson the first day he entered the store—the cat lady.

I look around, almost half expecting Dawson to be with her. But she's by herself, just like me. Well, sort of, I have the guard following me.

"I am." I half laugh at how excited she seems to have bumped into me. She's definitely a little strange but seems nice. "I'm Honey. Sorry, I didn't catch your name last time." I offer her my hand.

She adjusts her handbag over her shoulder and grabs my hand with a bright smile. "Daphne." She shakes my hand vigorously, and I'm almost slapped with her bountiful amount of energy, but it's charming.

I pocket my hands. "Did you get that role you were after, with the cats?"

She huffs out a laugh. "Strangely enough, no. Apparently, they already had a girl in mind before the auditions started, but that's fine. Maybe next time. Anyway, I got a hot-ass lingerie set out of it, so I can't complain."

"I'm sorry to hear that," I say and smile. She waves me off as if it's nothing. So, Dawson also let her have things from the store for free. I think back to the jacket he gave me. Perhaps it's something he does regularly.

A mischievous grin lights her face. "Hey, are you free? I know we don't know each other well, but you have good taste." She waves up and down at my clothes. "And I'm looking for a dress for a date tonight. If you're free, I'm happy to offer a coffee in exchange for your opinion."

"I—"

"Oh, do you have plans? I'm so sorry." Daphne's hands fold over her chest. "I blurt a lot, and Dawson tells me I can be too friendly." She laughs nervously.

I can understand it now, her charm and allure. And I haven't had much girl time, except with those I work with or my sister. And let's be real, I will probably go home and bake more treats if I don't occupy my mind.

"Sure, I was just going to spend the day watching movies anyway. I can help." She claps happily and hooks her arm through mine. I'm startled at first, but I just go with it. Unlike my sister, I'm not averse to physical touch, but I'm not usually so easygoing with strangers.

"Anyone who's friends with Dawson is usually good people, and I can already tell that you're super nice," she says as she leads me in the direction of shops.

I consider asking if we should call a cab, but instead embrace the change of the day.

WE END up in the shopping district in a store with brands I've never heard of. We've spoken mostly about trivial things up until this point, and, as promised, she purchased us a coffee from a cart, which isn't half bad considering how horrible I find the coffee here. I do miss home for some things—especially coffee.

Daphne starts picking items off racks.

"So, who's the lucky man tonight?" I ask, and it's been a very real burning question from the start.

Is she seeing Dawson?

They have a contract, right?

It has to be Dawson.

A mischievous smile touches her lips as she appraises a dress and then puts it back. "It's not Dawson if that's what you're asking."

"I didn't say that," I let slip, almost too quickly. Daphne gives me a pointed look, and I avert my gaze.

"Well, yeah... I mean, you two have a contract and stuff, don't you?" I ask casually.

"He told you about that, huh? How interesting."

"Interesting?"

She seems to touch every single item, simply for the texture, but she's only handed a few items to the clerk.

"You know, you aren't Dawson's usual type. But I can tell he looks at you differently."

"Not his type?" I question, and she seems almost amused. But there are so many layers to Dawson that I don't understand. And she seems to know him better—a lot better.

"Yes, he likes *experienced* women. Women who usually look like me." She chuckles. "Not that you aren't beautiful, because you are stunning." I wish I had her confidence to so easily call myself beautiful and to say it so matter-of-factly. "But you also look soft, tender, sweet. Not his usual type."

I'm a little offended. Not because it's not the truth but because it hits the mark. It's everything I'm trying to free myself from and become a better version of myself.

"And you don't?" I ask. She's bubbly, happy-go-lucky, and nice.

She scoffs. "No, I'm friendly and can be nice. But I'm harder around the edges. Just means I've been broken a few too many times." She shrugs. "Plus, you're a blonde, and he likes brunettes." She chuckles. "Well, I guess that's past tense now since he has a thing for you."

I almost laugh, but keep it in. "Dawson has a thing for me?" Because I'm pretty sure he's found a way to escape every time we've almost *maybe* had something. But the last time was definitely on me.

She walks into the change rooms and speaks over the door as I sit and wait.

"People have been talking all about you around his office, you know?"

"Why?"

I can hear that she's struggling to do the zipper up as she speaks. "Because he never visits employees. He may pop in briefly to check on a store, but he's visited your store more than once. That is unusual for him. But, anyway, changing the subject, what do you think of this?" Daphne steps out and twirls around in a circle while I focus on the task at hand and not Dawson.

"It's for a date, right?" I ask, and she nods. "Do you plan to fuck him on the first night?" I ask, hoping I don't sound too judgmental. She laughs, and I feel at ease being myself around her.

"Shit, you're right." I smile at her as she looks down at the outfit. The shirt she has on is basically a bra, and the skirt is so short that if she bends over even a fraction, I'll be able to see her panties. "I'm not used to worrying about those things. With Dawson, I wore whatever because it all ended up on the floor." She shrugs. A small twist of something knots my stomach. *Jealousy?* Which is so not okay, considering he's not mine.

She goes back to change, and I take time to build the courage to ask, "Do you still sleep with him?"

She pops her head out. "Would it upset you if I said yes?"

"No. I am just curious."

She smiles. "If you say so. But you're in luck. Since

you've been in the picture, I don't think he's slept with anyone. Which is so unlike him."

"What do you mean?"

She returns, this time dressed in a slightly longer skirt that hides her panties and a lace shirt. It's short but looks phenomenal on her. Quite honestly, anything she wears would.

Daphne assesses herself in the mirror, running her hands over the material again. "We had a schedule. Sometimes it would be sporadic, but I usually knew when he'd want me."

"And did you enjoy it?"

She chokes out a laugh. "Dawson is the best fuck I have ever had. Plus, he's a decent man."

"He is, huh?" I say.

Daphne steps back into the change room after I give her the thumbs up. It isn't long until she walks back out, and her phone starts ringing.

"Daphne, you have a call," I tell her.

"Could you answer it? I won't be long." Okay, that's weird and kind of awkward, but I lift her phone to my ear. "Hello."

"This isn't Daphne." His voice is like butter, smooth and silky.

"Um, no, she'll just be a second," I tell the man.

"Honey?"

"Dawson?"

"Yes," he answers. "Why are you with Daphne?"

"She wanted help finding clothes."

"You two are shopping together? It doesn't bother you that I've fucked her?" he asks.

"Should it?"

He doesn't seem to have an answer to that. Being in the line of business he is, I doubt jealousy is a thing. So does he think it would bother me because I'm not in that business?

"How was your date? I hope he at least made you come... *hard*. That's what I intended to do."

That's one way to change the subject.

"Would it bother you if I said yes?" I ask, repeating Daphne's earlier question.

"Yes. I may very well find him and... kill him."

"That's a joke, right?" He stays quiet on the other end, not answering me. "But, no, he broke it off with me, actually. I have to talk to you about that."

"Good. You can do better anyway. And why? What did he do to you?" I can hear the feral edge to his tone. I look back to the change room.

Maybe Daphne wasn't lying.

Maybe I mean something to Dawson.

Or maybe it's sheer sexual curiosity.

"Because he knew what I did the week before."

"What did you do?" he teases.

"How I lost my virginity. He knew," I tell Dawson. The line goes quiet, and I hear the tapping of a keyboard before he speaks again, "Don't associate yourself with him again," he declares, then hangs up.

I stand there, shocked that he just hung up on me.

And what was that supposed to mean, Dawson telling me not to associate with Kit?

"I'm going to get both." Daphne comes out with a smile. "I mean, if he's great on the first date, I plan to get some action on the second at least." She winks, then looks at the phone still clutched in my hand. She takes it, says a few hellos, and then looks at me, confused.

You and me both, girl.

You and me both.

"Who was that?"

"Dawson," I tell her.

She laughs as she walks to the register. "Speak, and the devil shall appear."

If only she knew what the conversation was about.

"Is Dawson a dangerous man?" I ask.

This grabs her attention. "I mean..." She thinks about it briefly before continuing, "Not to those he cares about, which is very few. But yes, he is. He's even involved with the mafia and stuff." She whispers the last part. I want to roll my eyes. If only she knew that 'said mafia' is also my sister's husband and my father, mafia men surround me.

She pays for her clothes, and we leave. Fuck, I hope Dawson doesn't kill Kit because that's the only conclusion someone like Crue or my father would come to, being the dangerous men they are.

"Are you still free? Do you want to come back to my place to help me with my hair? Your hair is perfect, I want mine the same." She touches my curls, which I added the night before.

"I actually have to get back home," I reply quickly. I have to try to get ahold of Dawson. But I know there is never any way to tell a powerful man that killing isn't okay.

She holds out her hand. "Give me your phone." I hand her my phone, and she types in something, then her phone starts ringing. "Okay, I'll let you know how my date goes. Thanks again for your help." She leans in and kisses me on the lips.

On. The. Lips!

I'm startled at first.

What is she doing?

But she simply smiles before she turns and saunters off.

Did she just kiss me?

CHAPTER 29
Dawson

I hold my gun to Kit's head.

He pisses himself.

"Who told you about the auctions?" I demand.

Not only do I want him dead for touching Honey, but this breach could jeopardize everything I've built. Someone like this asshole could never afford our services, let alone have the social standing to hear about the auctions. Which means there's a leak.

His eyes are closed as he stammers. One of Crue's men stands behind me. I don't require security, but he's here if I need cleanup. I don't kill lightly—it doesn't come as easily to me as it does to the likes of Crue. But I've done in the past what has been necessary.

Kit trembles through sobs. "I-I'm sorry. I d-didn't mean it. I d-didn't know it w-wasn't okay. I want no trouble with the m-mafia." I don't correct him. "I didn't know. I-I was told about it by a m-man who approached me at a b-bar. He said h-he had my back because it l-looked serious between me and Honey. I d-didn't know she works for the mafia."

Humor doesn't even reach my eyes at the assumption that Honey "works" for the mafia. Then again, he saw us together the other day and she said I was her boss. Again, I don't correct him. It might be better for her safety if he thinks that.

"And what did this man look like?" I question. I already know the answer before he says it.

"I-I-I don't know. He was wearing shades and a hat. Never said his name. He just told me. I won't tell anyone," he promises. "And I'll never speak to Honey again. Please, man, just let me live."

Shit. It's the same fucker who's been tracking my movements for the last month.

Fuck. He knows about Honey and my association with her.

That's bad.

Very bad.

Because if anything were to happen to her...

I pull the gun away from Kit's head, too aware that I'll probably pull the trigger in hopes it'll simmer this rage boiling inside me.

My phone buzzes, and I know I've received a text message, but I start speaking before dealing with it, "Know that I hear and see everything. If I so much as catch a fucking hint about this, I *will* find you. You and your family back in Oklahoma, and even your high school girlfriend."

His eyes go wide. Of course, I have everything I need to know about him. This chump is a pawn. Minor to the actual problem I have at hand.

If Crue were here, he would shoot him.

Leave no loose ends.

But I also know what it feels like to be a pawn in someone else's game. To be caught in the crossfire. And I don't believe people should die for that.

I straighten my suit and take out my phone, surprised to see a text from Honey.

A cold shudder runs through me at her demand.

CHAPTER 30

Honey

> Me: I think you should come over.

I wait for him to reply, and when he doesn't, I decide it's time to shower. Once I'm done, I hear knocking on the door. I expect to see my sister on the other side, but Dawson stands there. His expression is dark and ominous, but the moment his gaze roams my body, it changes. That tension he had a moment ago twists into something else. He smirks when he sees me wrapped in only a towel.

"Ready and washed for me just to get you dirty? That's so kind of you." He steps inside and shuts the door behind him.

I step back because the way he's looking at me right now makes me second-guess inviting Dawson over. I feel comfortable with him, and I'm hoping he can give me a good experience for my second time having sex and show me that it doesn't have to hurt. Don't get me wrong, it was good the first time until it stung. And, boy, did it sting.

But the second time isn't supposed to sting as bad, is it? I hope not.

"Will it hurt?" I ask.

He leans against the counter, his knuckles going white as if he's fighting with himself. He knew what I insinuated by him coming over, right? Again, I'm suddenly unsure if he wants this too.

"Look, if you don't want to, that's fine. I can't with this back-and-forth thing," I admit.

"I'm not good for you, Honey," he says. But his gaze devours me, and I have the impression that his tight grip on my kitchen counter is the only thing holding him back.

I'm so sick of people telling me that, so I cross my arms in defiance. "I just wanted to tell you, I don't want you to kill Kit."

His face scrunches, and it's so different from the usual mask I see him wear. The charm, the desire, the put-together man. The danger coils so tightly beneath, and I can't help but wonder if anyone else ever sees it.

"Don't mention him ever again. It's dealt with."

"But—"

His stare turns feral, and I close my mouth. I don't want to know his methods, but I hope he's done this for me. I'm sure the only reason was to protect his business, but I can't help but hope a small part was for me too. Surely, he didn't come over just for that, though.

I take two hesitant steps toward him. It's like watching a cornered beast. "Will it hurt?" I repeat.

I can see the tension slowly ripple from him. This other face of his that only I see, releasing to bring me back the Dawson I know.

"Just a little, but in the best way," he says as he licks his lips. Unhurriedly and thoughtfully, as if still trying to hold back from himself, he lifts his hand and reaches for my towel. Dawson pulls the end that's tucked in and lets the material fall to the floor. His gaze roams over me, his jaw tight as he takes in my naked body. He makes me feel good, very good.

"Daphne is nice," I blurt out the words, there is no stopping me. And I know I'm pushing it. But I want to feel like the only one. I am dancing a dangerous line because I might not be, and Dawson is many things, but a liar he is not.

"Hm," he hums with a wicked smile, then takes a menacing step toward me. I think he's so mesmerized that he might not have heard me.

"Did you sleep with Daphne a lot?"

"Why are you asking about how I fuck other women?" he questions. He pushes my hair back off my shoulder before he leans in and runs his fingers over my shoulder blade. Goose bumps run over my skin as his mouth lowers, and he kisses me in the same spot. It's so hard to focus on anything but his touch.

"Do you still fuck her?" I ask. I already know the answer but want to hear him say it. And weirdly, pushing him is... turning me on.

"No, I want to fuck you. How does a contract between us sound?"

Before I can question him, he wraps his arms around my body and lifts me, his hands on my bare ass as he stalks toward the bedroom. Then he stops, changes direction, returns to the kitchen, and places me on the counter. It's cold on my ass, and I flinch.

"I don't know about a contract... the last one was a lot for me," I admit. It's oddly arousing, teasing almost, as I watch him as intently as he watches me. But then I feel his loss as he turns around and starts opening my cupboards. I'm not sure what he's looking for, but by the swell in his pants, I don't think he's leaving me any time soon.

"The auction contract?" he asks absentmindedly. "This one doesn't require vows unless you want to be on your hands and knees again." He's still searching for... I don't know what.

"Do you make the other women take the same vows?"

He shuts the cupboard when he finds what he's looking for, then turns back to me, and I see a bottle of honey in his hand. His smile is devastatingly gorgeous, a dimple popping in one of his cheeks. "No, I just enjoyed having you on your hands and knees," he says.

Confused, I look at the honey as he steps between my legs. My heart is pounding. "Um, what are you doing?"

He lifts the bottle and squeezes some of the honey onto my breast. "Figured I would have dessert first." He smirks before he lowers his mouth to the mess he made on my skin. I freeze as he starts to lick it off, tasting me as it begins to slowly glide toward my nipple. His mouth continues the assault on my other breast. *Fuck me, that wicked tongue.* My head lolls back as he goes lower, his tongue forcing my focus to my pounding clit.

I go to move, but his hands pin mine on top of my thighs. He offers a devilish smile, and I want to feather my fingers through his hair and push him down to fulfill my demanding need.

Without instruction, he steps back and places his lips just above my clit. He pushes my legs farther apart shamelessly, and then his mouth is *there*, devouring me, and I moan at the contact. *Fuck, that wicked tongue is dangerous.* One hand leaves my thigh and slides between my legs until he slips a finger inside me.

"Ohhh..." I moan, but he doesn't stop. I don't want him to ever stop. I sift my free hand through his hair as his mouth works wonders and his finger pumps inside of me. He inserts another finger, and I feel so full and good at the same time. He releases my other hand, and I find myself sliding both hands back now, accepting the pleasure he offers. I have to right myself, conscious of the recently baked cookies that might end up as collateral damage.

Fuck. The heat in my core spreads down my legs as he sucks hard on my clit. Dawson pulls and tugs at every nerve and promiscuous need. This is so much more than I thought it would be with him. This is...

My breath becomes shaky, and I frown in confusion. *Oh my God.*

"There you are," he says while I come undone, as if at his command. My body trembles when I ride the waves of pure bliss. *Holy shit. Oh my God.* "That's a good girl. Come for me," he whispers, his breath warm against my skin.

"Oh my God!" I scream, my hands stuck in the one spot, my body locking tight as I feel the release light me up from the inside. Dawson moves back, and I take a moment to catch my breath. I hear rustling, and when I look up, I find him undressing.

Yes, yes. That's what I want.

If he can give me this...

I *want* all of him.

I *need* all of him.

Sudden clarity hits me.

"Wait!" I scream and jump off the counter. He seems perplexed as I run into my room and go for the top drawer of my nightstand.

I bring out an unopened box of condoms, and he grabs them, a chuckle erupting from him. "That's very sweet, Honey, but regular won't work."

I frown. "I once saw a video of a guy stretching a condom over his leg. They're stretchy and—"

"Honey." My name on his lips brings me back to the room, and my chest swells with lo—

No. It can't be love. Admiration, maybe.

It's something, though, because I feel safe and not embarrassed around Dawson.

He pulls out his own condom and holds it in the air pointedly as he lifts me up and places me back on the counter. His fingers trail down the remains of the honey on my stomach and flick off at my clit. "Now, where were we."

In what seems like seconds, all of his clothes are piled on the floor, and he efficiently applies his condom. He reaches for me, but I stop him.

I take a moment to admire not only all the defined muscles I expected under his shirt but also the unexpected tattoo across his chest. A crown marks the top, and roses are twined into a word I can't properly read. The tattoo is old, almost clumsily done, and yet beautiful. It's unlike anything I expected of the clean-cut Dawson that he presents daily.

He catches his breath as he watches me, and then my gaze drops to the tattoo of my lips next to his very hard cock.

My mouth hangs open. *Fuck me, he is huge.* I almost forgot.

"I'll send you a photo later, honeypot." He smirks and I'm suddenly back in the moment when he reaches for me. Dawson lifts me so my legs wrap around his waist, and then he walks us to the window that looks over the streets beneath and slams my back into it.

At first, I'm speechless. That is until I feel him at my entrance. He pauses when only the tip of his cock enters me, his gaze solely on me. I'm trying to look down between us, but I can't see anything because our bodies are locked tight.

"Honey."

"Hm..." My eyes find him.

"Watch me." I nod submissively as he lowers me, and his eyes somehow darken as he ever so slowly fills me. It doesn't hurt as much as the first time, but there is still a small stinging sensation when he enters me. Once he's fully inside, he pauses again, licks his lips, and leans forward. His mouth claims mine, and I feel the stickiness of the honey still on my chest spread between us. He doesn't seem to care, though, and I tighten my hold around his neck as I feel the urge to move up and down. I do it without waiting for him, and as soon as I do, our kiss stops, and our lips rest against each other. Breath for breath. Our focus is on the sensation of me gliding up and down his cock.

"Fuck," he utters against my lips, which fuels me with more power and confidence to keep on moving while he squeezes my ass. It feels good. So fucking good that I never want it to end.

Soon enough, he adjusts himself, complementing my rhythm as he slides in and out of me. My fingers feather over his strong arms, the muscles bunching from holding me.

And fuck me, it's hot.

I love this.

Him.

Us.

I never want it to end.

I feel powerful.

Like I have full control of this man right now.

My nails dig into his shoulders as we move faster. His mouth is eager to find mine again, and this time, he bites my bottom lip as we continue to fuck.

My clit is being rubbed with each movement, and I can honestly say I understand why people become addicted to sex.

It's exhilarating.

The buildup comes again. Dawson doesn't slow, and it comes even faster and harder. And soon my mouth forgets to move, but his doesn't as he continues to kiss me. Who knew the second time I had sex, I could come twice? Tears well in my eyes, and one spills over my cheek.

"That's it, cry for me," he says, continuing to pump a little harder. I scream his name as I come, and a crude laugh escapes him before he comes as well. He leans in and bites my neck when we stop moving. As I come down from the bliss, I realize what he just said.

And how he said it.

"Cry for me?" I repeat, the words echoing memories.

"You just put two and two together, didn't you, Honey?" he asks, pulling away.

I close my legs.

He seems perplexed as to how to handle me when I stare at him with wide eyes and my mouth slightly open in shock. His jaw tightens, his resolve hardens his gaze, and I know I've lost him again.

He steps back, the distance a contradiction to what we just shared, and quickly throws his clothes on.

My hand goes to my chest, too confused to ask the question on my lips that I already know the answer to.

"I'll let myself out," Dawson says, not making eye contact.

I still don't speak, not sure what else to say.

I just had sex with the same man I lost my virginity to.

Of that, I am sure.

And I'm utterly lost for words because Dawson said he would never have sex with a virgin.

That he would never have sex with *me*.

But he paid millions of dollars to do so.

CHAPTER 31
Dawson

The look of recognition on her face said it all.

She's worked out exactly what I did.

I never intended for her to find out, but when I saw her that day waiting, I knew I couldn't let another man win her. Though I had denied it for so fucking long, she was mine from the moment I first saw her.

Even if she was a virgin.

To be honest, that was the main hurdle between us. I would've made Honey sign a contract and been fucking her from day one if she weren't.

Goddamn! I have no control when I am around her, and that's dangerous. Especially considering I'd gone over there to cut all ties. To tell her to stay as far away from me as possible. With a psychopath on the loose who's aware of our association, I can't put her at jeopardy. But I am.

I could only think of one thing when I saw her standing there in that towel.

I've built my entire life around discipline and control, and around her I fall to pieces that only she can glue back together. She's in every part of me.

I got a tattoo of her lips on my dick and passed it off as an irrational moment. I stop by her work, convincing myself it's because I own the store. If she worked anywhere else, I probably would have acquired the business. And her body. *Fuck!* How she makes me feel alive. Her rants and random questions. She's my honeypot. And I have no right to her. But I'll be damned if I'm going to let anyone else have her now that I've tasted her.

I hope I can get her to sign a contract. Because now I've had her twice, I know she's my new favorite thing, and I will want her repeatedly. But the shock on her face, it was like I betrayed her by not telling her it was me who won her at the auction and took her virginity.

I don't have time to dwell on this problem, though. I'm still no closer to finding the identity of the man who seems hellbent on bringing down my empire. He's done enough damage as it is, and if I don't find him soon...

A startling reality comes to mind. Because Honey might be the only thing I'm unwilling to lose, which makes her a weakness.

"Is it written in another language?" Daphne asks. My gaze shoots up from the paperwork I've held for the last five minutes.

I look at it again—actually look at it this time—and ignore Daphne's mischievous grin.

"I wonder what else could be taking up your mind," she chirps as I look over a deal she's been offered to model for a fashion line.

"I always have a lot going on," I reply, reviewing the finer details. She has always approached me for this, and I don't mind reviewing her contracts. "This looks sound."

"I like her," Daphne says.

"What?"

"Honey. I like her. I'm meeting up with her today."

I shake my head, irritated by how observant she is. "She has work."

Daphne looks at her nails and innocently says, "Does she?"

I know when Honey works because I have her schedule right before me.

"Because last I heard, she quit." She plucks the contract out of my hand. "Maybe she had a tyrant of a boss."

"*Daphne*," I all but growl.

But she's already walking out the door and waving goodbye. "Thank you for your help."

I call the store, and Alana answers.

"Where is Honey?" I demand.

She goes quiet momentarily, then softly says, "She quit this morning, sir."

I hang up the phone.

CHAPTER 32
Honey

Daphne sits across from me, trying to defend Dawson, but it goes in one ear and out the other. I've been circling my finger over the glass of Moscato for the last ten minutes. I know she thinks highly of him, but that doesn't mean I have to too. A part of me is glad to know it was him who won me in the auction, but the other part feels betrayed he could do that to me without actually telling me. For a man who boasts how he doesn't fuck virgins, he sure knew how to fuck me.

Daphne tells me about her date and how she slept with him on the first night and hasn't heard anything since. She also tells me that she wore the revealing outfit. I laugh at her, and she simply shrugs and tells me it's been a while for her, what with having a contract with Dawson for so long. And though there was no exclusivity clause, she didn't try to date while under contract with Dawson.

"He really is a good guy. I just want to add that."

I know he's a good guy. I've seen it. I've met a lot of dodgy men in my time due to my father's business dealings, and he's never given me any of those vibes whatsoever.

"And you don't need to tell me, but I know about the twenty million," she adds.

I don't bother to ask how she knows. Daphne seems like the type to know everything that happens in Dawson's line of work. But I think she's also smart not to talk about it. Unless, of course, in a situation like this.

I nod. I vowed I wouldn't speak of it, and I'll abide by that vow.

"I'm actually incredibly surprised it was him. He told me he has this whole thing with never wanting to touch virgins."

"He's said that to you?" I ask.

"Well, it's very well-known. It doesn't suit his *usual* tastes, but he's never expressed why. But also, virginity makes so much money for him. I mean, look at how much money you made from him. That's evidence in itself."

I can't help but think there's something else to Dawson's aversion to virgins. Surely, there's a deep-set reason behind it.

"How can I ever trust him again? Did he tell you I found out about it by accident?"

She finishes taking a bite of her pasta then wipes her mouth. "No, I haven't spoken to him about it at all. How did you find out?"

I like Daphne, she has this easy-going nature about her, and she's someone you want to be friends with, even though we've been with the same guy. Surprisingly, it doesn't bother me because she has been nothing but upfront about it, and I can tell there's no romantic relationship there. And that is even more frustrating.

Is it because I want a romantic relationship with Dawson? No, it's only sex. Right?

"I invited him to my apartment a few days ago, and, you know, we proceeded to have sex. And as I was coming, he whispered something into my ear that the person to who I lost my virginity also whispered to me. So I knew right then and there it was him."

She briefly studies me, then says, "It's baffling because it's unlike Dawson to slip up. What did he say?"

I hesitate because it feels oddly intimate. "He said, 'Cry for me,' " I tell her, and her eyes widen.

"He never said that to me." She shakes her head. "Actually, come to think of it, when it came to our contract, we didn't talk much at all. It was just transactional fucking, which he is great at. So, tell me, how many times did you come?" She grins.

I can't help but laugh at how easily she lightens the situation. "Twice." She lifts her hand for a high five, and I slap it.

"Hell yeah. It sucks he's such a dick, but at least his

dick isn't bad." She laughs at her own joke. "Trust me. Some men have terrible dicks. They think they're great, but in reality, they suck." Shaking my head, she goes on, "For example, you know the guy I told you about? Well, he didn't do any foreplay. He just stuck it right in and thought that was getting the job done. I listened to him grunt and moan for sixty seconds before he was done and pulled out of me. I at least thought he was going to touch my clit and get me off, but he did nothing of the sort."

"Oh God, that sounds awful."

She holds up her hand. "Then he proceeded to stand up, go to the bathroom to relieve himself, then came back, completely naked, hands on his hips, and asked me if I had somewhere else to be." Daphne shakes her head in disgust. "That man gave me the shittiest lay of my life and then basically told me to leave." Her face is red with anger. "You know what, fuck this. I'm going to tell him how much his cock sucks." She pulls out her phone and starts typing.

"What are you saying?" I ask, leaning over to see what she is writing.

I want you to know that the sixty seconds you spent in my vagina was the worst of my life. Please take lessons before you inflict that on another woman.

She hits send, turns to me, and smiles. "Done."

"I can't believe you just did that." I laugh, half shocked but more so impressed.

"Believe it," she says.

CHAPTER 33
Honey

O ver the next week, I don't hear from Dawson. My sister asks me why I'm not working, and I simply tell her I found an online job. Because I'm rolling in money now, and she's going to see me spending it and asking me how I'm getting it. As thoughtful as my father's allowance is, it's limited compared to my lifestyle before moving here. Most likely intentionally to ensure I eventually go back.

"Are you ready?" Rya asks. It's Crue's birthday, and, as expected, a party is being thrown. Although I suspect Crue will only make an appearance at his own party before he whisks away his wife for a private celebration.

I slide on my light-pink dress and matching heels, then grab my black bag.

"Ready."

"Dawson will be there," she tells me as we walk out. I feel her gaze and unasked questions.

"Figured as much."

I haven't told her about what happened between us because I have a feeling if she knew, she'd find him and rip his balls off. And I'm not really sure I want that to happen, considering he needs them, especially when he knows how to use the part attached to them so well.

I've been using my vibrator every single night, getting off to the memories of Dawson. I try to think of someone else—anyone else—but it's always him that pops into the back of my head.

And his words echo in my ears as I come. *"Cry for me."*

It's become like a mantra I love to hate.

I can't help it that my eyes water every time I come.

"How is it going with him?" Rya questions.

"It's not going anywhere if that's what you mean," I tell her, smiling as we get in the car where Crue is already waiting. He nods to me and pulls my sister closer to him. I sit across from them, trying to look anywhere other than his wandering hands.

"Good, I hope it stays that way," she says. For someone who gets along with him great, she certainly has an issue with me becoming too friendly, which I can understand.

Bad guy and everything.

Rya makes small talk with me for the rest of the car ride until we arrive at one of the restaurants Crue owns. I'm starting to think he owns half of New York. There's already a room full of people—a handful I recognize from their wedding and others I don't know. They're the same sort of company my father keeps. Powerful men and women who border on the line of mistrust but have to be nice enough to keep their alliances tight. I now realize how tiring it all is. It's all for show and power plays.

The one person I knew would be here is leaning against the bar, holding a glass in his hand as he stares at me. Dawson's gaze eats me up while he takes a mouthful of his drink. Beside him is the woman who auctioned me off, Lesley.

Is he fucking her too? Gah. I hate myself for even having the thought.

A few people greet us as we enter, and I feel his stare burning into the back of me. I slowly make my way to the bar on the other side of the room. And as I place my order, I know without looking that he's standing next to me. He smells of spice and vanilla.

"Are you avoiding me?" Dawson asks. My drink gets placed in front of me, and I try not to look his way. "Oh, so you are." I go to walk away, but he steps in front of me. "We don't have to talk when I take you home and fuck you into oblivion." My harsh gaze cuts to him. "Aww, there she is," he purrs.

"Cut the bullshit," I say, and he actually smiles. "You left me high and dry at my apartment. I won't play this game with you. It's giving me whiplash."

He acts wounded. "You quit your job to avoid me."

I shrug. "Felt like a career change. I've recently come into a lot of money. So it appears I don't need yours any more," I say as I lift the glass to my lips.

His smile quirks. "I know you've thought about that day since I left your apartment, and I know you want to do it again."

I hate that he's right, but I don't admit it. "Why? So you can do your disappearing act again? You're getting good at that," I spit venomously. Spiteful in how my body wants to reach out and touch him. I knew it would be hard to see him again but fuck me, this is toxic. I can't breathe around him because I want to fuck him.

"I'm not good for you. But also, it's fucking evident I can't contain myself around you either."

Interesting. But it doesn't mean he won't leave me high and dry again.

"What would you like to do to fix this?" he asks.

I don't even want to ask what "this" is.

"Go away," I reply, stepping around him. I walk straight over to where my sister is and feel him follow. I honestly didn't think he would, considering she may very well kill him.

"Rya, Crue," he greets, sliding in beside me.

Rya looks at me before she smiles politely at Dawson.

"Good to see you, Dawson. I hear you've been keeping busy," Rya says.

"Yes, your sister keeps me busy."

Shit! I almost choke on my drink. It's the complete opposite of what I told her earlier.

"Is that so? And you see her often?" she presses.

"I've seen her multiple times. When was the last time? At your apartment?" Dawson asks me.

"Yes, I think it was. And I heard you were very interested in the fact that you wanted to intrude on my lunch with one of your girlfriends. Do you call them that, the women you fuck?" I ask him.

Everything seems to go quiet.

"I'm not sure. What would we call you? Is girlfriend the term you're hoping for?"

"Dawson, I think we need to talk," Crue interrupts and places a hand on Dawson's shoulder. I look away from Dawson and blow out a breath. Crue drags Dawson away, and Rya pulls me in to whisper to me, "I thought you said nothing was happening. Are you sleeping with him?"

Fuck.

"Yes," I admit.

"How many times?"

"Does it matter?" I sigh. "Twice."

She blows out a heavy breath and shakes her head. "Are you sure about him? I don't want to tell you what to do, but Dawson isn't a one-woman man. As far as I'm aware, he has multiple women under contract.

"I'm fine, Rya. I'm a grown woman who can make my own decisions. Even took the training wheels off the security guard thing, remember? Fully-fledged adult."

I can tell she doesn't appreciate my tone, but she then says, "Okay. Well, do you want me to save him before Crue kills him?"

"Nah, he'll be fine," I reply, lifting my glass and finishing the wine.

CHAPTER 34

Dawson

C rue is a scary man, there's no denying that. I've known him for many years, and there have been a few times where I thought he might want to kill me, and today is one of those days. I would usually say it's through no fault of my own, but this time it's completely my fault. I've been fucking his sister-in-law, and I don't intend to stop. I can't help myself.

"You make my wife mad, which in turn makes me furious because she won't let me touch her because she thinks I did nothing to help," he says calmly. "I like you, Dawson, but if she told me to kill you, I would."

"I'm not sure I would allow you to do that," I reply. I do not doubt if Crue wanted to kill me, he would most likely succeed. But over the past few years, my empire has grown to a level that rivals his, and his goes back centuries. It's why we've grown closer over the years—he has supported me, and I him.

"Fair call. Don't piss my wife off," he says, shaking his head.

I stand there watching Rya, waiting for her to come over.

She doesn't.

"A Ricci girl, eh?" he notes, leaning back in his chair. And it pisses me off how much satisfaction he has at being right.

"Fuck off, Crue."

He stares at his glass of whisky, somber now. "It's not the right choice by her. And I trust in my security, but now, with your involvement, I will have to put more guys on her."

I side-eye him, knowing he's right. *Fuck me, I know it.* I've fought this off so fucking much.

"I know." I don't have to tell him how hard I tried to stay away.

"If this guy hellbent on ruining your empire is already aware of your involvement with Honey, she's not safe with you."

"She's safe with me," I state adamantly.

"You're not always with her," he reminds me. And the reason I'm not is because it takes away her freedom.

"Any closer to finding out who he is?" I ask.

I had to call in my favor. To ask Crue to get his informants on this guy as well. Whoever he is, he's good at covering his tracks.

"Not yet, but soon. Whoever he is, he's good at slipping between the cracks."

I nod, expecting as much. "Then business goes on as usual until I take him down."

Rya walks over, and I notice Honey walking to the kitchen.

Rya looks seriously pissed as she approaches, and I offer Crue an apologetic smile. "Happy Birthday."

I leave before Rya arrives, not because I'm avoiding her but because there's another Ricci girl I want to be talking to right about now. Truthfully, talking isn't what I have in mind.

I walk into the kitchen, the staff not daring to say anything, and sidle up behind Honey, who is discussing one of the plates and its ingredients in depth. The chef seems to shrink under my looming presence behind her. I know she's aware I'm there, and so I wait.

She huffs out a breath and turns on me. "I thought in your line of business, stalking would be a big no-no."

I choke on a laugh. And she crosses her arms, even more furious.

She's fucking adorable. Delectably so.

"You didn't have to quit work because of me," I tell her.

"I did. You lied to me. You had plenty of time to tell me it was you." Hurt crosses her expression.

I grab her elbow and pull her into a storage room. There are a few shelves with packaged ingredients. I close the door behind her because I don't want anyone over-hearing this conversation.

"I wasn't planning on it being me, at least not until that night when the bids kept increasing. I knew I couldn't let anyone else have you."

"You didn't have that choice."

"I did, actually. It was my event."

"Oh, so because it was your event, you could allow yourself to fuck me as a virgin? Put me on display just to fuck me in the very way you said you'd never touch me?"

I want to rip my hair out. I clench my fists. *How do I get through to this little honeypot?*

"I can't stop fucking thinking about you. I have tried so fucking hard to stay away from you. Time and time again. And you just keep appearing like fucking tempta-tion itself," I roar.

She chokes on a wild laugh. And I wonder if anyone else gets to see this side of her. This wild, ferocious little thing. "You're struggling? You walk away every time anything happens between us. Do you know how that feels? For someone who sells pleasure, you certainly leave a bad aftertaste. I can't keep being fucked over by you, Dawson."

I break, frustrated, gritting the words out so I don't shout at her, "It's only you I want to fuck over, in every which way possible... doggy, cowgirl, cowboy. You name it, I want it from you."

Her cheeks go red, and tears sparkle in her eyes. *Fuck.* I wipe my hand over my jaw. I don't know what else to say. How do I get through to her? Hell, I don't even know what I'm asking for. I throw my hand up on one of the top shelves and think. "I've never had issues expressing myself. But, fuck, you make it hard," I grumble.

"Why, because I am not in a contract?"

I eye her. She doesn't know what she's talking about or why they're important.

"You can have anyone, Dawson. Look at you," she says. "I want you, but I can't keep doing this. You have contracts to have sex with whomever you want. So if that's what you want, find one of them to do it with."

"I don't have any contracts left."

She takes in a sharp breath.

"I haven't slept with anyone else since I first laid eyes on you in Italy. I don't understand it, but here I am. I've always taken what I wanted in this world. But I won't take from you. Not unless you're willing to give it."

I don't even know what I'm promising her at this point.

I wait for her reply, and she steps forward.

"This does not mean I forgive you." She drops to her knees. I'm momentarily confused, but I don't question it as I grip the top shelf tighter. Her hands hastily undo my belt.

"Honey—"

She palms my cock, and my head tips back. My knuckles go white with my hold on the shelf, and my semi-hard cock springs free, so responsive to her touch.

I look back down, and she's the perfect vision in pink. So beautiful on her knees before me. I'm at her mercy as she wraps her lipstick-stained lips around my cock. Her wet tongue glides under my cock, and she sucks hard. Honey grips my hips as she bobs back and forth, sucking and pulling me deep into her throat.

"Fuck," I hiss. I want to fist her hair but don't, willing to take what she will give in her own way. And then she bites down, an immediate jolt hitting my dick as pre-cum leaks into the back of her throat.

She pulls back with a smile and wipes her mouth before placing a kiss on the tip of my cock, and then she stands up. As she goes to walk past me, I grab her elbow.

"What are you doing?" I ask.

She offers me a sickly-sweet smile. "You're not the only one who can walk out any time they want, Dawson."

Mischief and humor is glinting in her gaze as she slips through my grasp and walks out, closing the door behind her.

Fuck my life!

CHAPTER 35

Dawson

"I didn't think we'd leave Crue Monti's party so early," Lesley says as I drive us back to the office. "Didn't have anything to do with a certain little bumble bee, did it?"

I eye her, unimpressed with her attempt at teasing. I swear, it's bad enough that I have Daphne on my ass, I don't need Lesley jumping on board too. "We have a few things to go over before tomorrow night."

She agrees as she looks through the details on her phone for tomorrow's event. "Everyone invited has accepted and is due to come."

As was expected.

It's an annual event that anyone in the know won't want to miss, where many of the escorts under my banner sell themselves for the following year.

"Are you sure we should still go ahead with this? It's

risky," she says. "And, I don't know, you seem distracted lately."

My knuckles turn white over the steering wheel. Because I know who she is insinuating is the distraction, and she's not wrong.

"We continue business as usual. Neither Crue nor I have found a definite answer on who's keeping tabs on my business, and they will want to be a part of this event. In whatever form, he'll slip up."

She keeps flicking through her phone. "Dangling bait can backfire, and this is the elite of your services, staff and clients."

"And what other idea do you have?" I ask.

She shrugs. "I think it's the best idea as well. It's just risky. But we have to find this fucker. He's put too much doubt on your reputation already. And he needs to pay for what he did to Macy."

The car is silent.

"How is she?" I ask. I'd visited her once since and deposited a large sum of money into her account. Money can't make up for what happened, but there isn't much more I can do in the meantime, the guilt riding me hard that she'd been caught up in this.

"She's strong," Lesley replies. And after a beat of silence, she asks, "And who will you have attending the event by your side?"

"I haven't decided yet."

"Hm..." She puts down her phone and turns to me. "Do you have a contract with Honey?"

"No."

"Hm..." I can hear the disapproval in that hum. "You're playing with fire, Dawson. She's a Ricci. Her father will put you on a spike for bringing his flower into your world."

"He can try."

"I just hope you're not risking your empire for one woman."

"I don't pay for your advice on who I fuck, Lesley. Maybe you should remember that *you* work for *me*."

She blows out a whistle and shakes her head but says nothing more.

Honey's father and family are no fucking saints. But this is my world. Pleasure, sex, pushing boundaries. There is money and power in it. But it comes with its own expectations, something that I'm not entirely sure Honey will fit into.

And maybe there is only one way to find out—to throw her in the heart of it all. Because if she wasn't scared off by the virgin auctions, then this might be what turns her away from me.

It will be her last chance to escape.

He has a thing for showing up unannounced. Like right now, as he stands at my door, I stare at him.

"Honey." He says my name, and it feels like feathers all over my skin.

It's selfish, really, for him to have that much power. It's only a day after Crue's birthday, and he seems to have bounced back quickly after I left him in the storage room with a raging hard-on. In truth, I felt fucking good leaving him in that state, but I didn't want to deal with the consequences. Because the way he'd looked at me, I could tell he wanted to tear off all my clothes, and if I hadn't walked away, I would've let him.

"I have a work event. Are you free to attend with me?" He's dressed in a tailored white suit. Perfectly immaculate as always. Such a contrast to the tattooed man beneath. Well, the man he's shown me, at least.

"You couldn't ask someone else?" I ask nonchalantly as I lean against the doorframe. Admittedly, I'm enjoying this bit of control and power I hold over him. This man who takes whatever he pleases but will not take from me unless I give it.

"No, it's a mixer of sorts. One of my parties, and I want you by my side."

"What does that even mean?"

"It means my escorts and high-profile clients come to mingle. It's speed dating for the rich. Basically a tasting menu."

"And what, you want me to go to taste test other men?"

His laugh is sinister.

That's a big fucking no.

"No, you won't be doing that. I prefer to have a woman by my side. It's not just male clients, female clients are looking for male escorts as well. Many of them like to come up and ask how much for my services. Which, I might add, are not included."

"So if I paid you, say... twenty million, I could have you for the night?" I tease.

"You can't, not for money. But I'll indulge *you* for free," Dawson replies, teasing me back.

"I'm still mad at you, so why should I?"

"You haven't closed the door in my face yet," he points out.

I arch an eyebrow with my arms still crossed over my chest.

"And you left me to relieve myself in the back of the restaurant, so I think you can do this much for me."

I chuckle. "Did the poor lettuce leaf get abused?"

"There was a pack of napkins, it so happens," he says with a tentative smile.

I throw my head back and laugh. *Fuck, maybe I do feel a little guilty now.*

I bite my lip, unable to stop the smile and throw my hands up in defeat. "What do I wear?" I ask, stepping back to show him I'm dressed in a nightgown, not expecting to go out tonight at all.

"Do you have a gown?"

I raise a brow at him. "It's that fancy?"

He nods. "I'm afraid so."

"Okay. I'll be ready in twenty." I try to shut the door in his face, but he stops me.

"Are you not going to invite me in?"

I smile sweetly and say, "No, I am not," then push the door shut. I stand and wait, thinking he'll open it, and when he doesn't, I head to my closet. I know the exact dress I can wear. I bought it when I first arrived and haven't had an occasion to wear it. I have hundreds of gowns back home, but there's something I love about this one. Perhaps it's the honey color. I pull it out and admire it once more before slipping it on and going to the bathroom to fix my hair and apply some light foundation and lipstick. I'm determined to give him the bare minimum.

Events like this, I'd always be fussed over for hours. I

had to have the perfect hair. The perfect makeup. The perfect presentation. Now, I feel comfortable throwing that to the wayside. Dawson will accept me how I am or not at all.

When I'm done, I check myself in the mirror. My lips are nude, and my silk dress perfectly drapes over my breasts and hips. I look over my shoulder, appreciating the low cut-out back. I can imagine Daphne exclaiming, "Fucking hot!" and clapping in approval. It brings a smile to my face.

I walk out and pull open the door to find him still waiting. "I'm ready. This better be worth it because I can't decide how angry I should be at you yet."

"Angry sex is the best sex, but we can play later," he drawls.

"So you think," I shoot back, stepping into the elevator with him. We stand in silence, the tension a living, breathing thing between us. I'm certain as he exhales, I inhale. We walk out of the lobby and to a waiting car with a driver holding the door open and ready for us. Dawson offers his hand as I step in, cautious of my honey-colored heels. The contrast in color is perfect against my tan skin. He enters on the other side of the car, sitting beside me.

He adjusts himself as the driver takes off. I watch him carefully, fighting all urges to mount him. It's cruel that he should be so fucking beautiful.

"You don't want to play later?" Dawson asks, turning to face me.

"Not at all. You needed help, so here I am. I expect you to return this favor one day. I am a Ricci, after all."

He cocks a smile as he puts his hand on my knee. The heat radiates through my body, and my clit begins to pulse for him. Expectantly, demandingly, and almost blindly.

"Oh, so is that what we're calling this? A favor?"

I pull my gaze away from his hand, thinking of all the things those fingers can do. "Is it not?"

"I return favors in other ways."

"I'm sure Crue is a very happy man, then. A beautiful friendship the two of you have."

He laughs at that, and I can't help but smile and look away.

"You look awfully beautiful tonight, but do you want to know when you look better?"

I don't indulge in asking him when, but he doesn't care and answers his own question anyway. I'm trying to avoid his gaze because my body is a treacherous thing. Surely, I can last two minutes in a car with him before ripping my clothes off.

"When you're coming. Fuck, it's the hottest thing I have ever seen. When your eyes roll back into your head, your hands clutch together, and your body gets this perfect arch. I want to photograph it and put it up on my wall." His expression is dripping with lust.

I try to let my hitched breath escape evenly. *Fuck, I want his hand to glide farther up my leg.* I swallow, hard.

"Maybe one day I'll let you. I mean, if the price is right," I tell him.

"Will twenty million cover it?" he asks.

"I think by the time I'm done with you, you may very well be broke," I joke.

"I'd happily go broke for you."

I eye him, hating how I react to his words—almost hopeful they're the truth. I know they are, but it's because I want something more with Dawson. And I'm not sure if the man who is used to contracts and control can give that to me. To say he'd go broke for me is interesting. We are both people who come from money. Dirty money, earned money, old money. *Of all the things that it can buy, love is not one of them.*

I turn away. That thought and word coming up again. *Love.*

Is someone like Dawson even capable of it? Do I even truly comprehend what it is?

We sit in comfortable silence, his thumb tormenting me as it rolls back and forth over my knee. Every glide up, I wish it would go higher and higher.

The car slows down, and the scenery begins to change as we enter a wealthy area of suburbia.

"Where are we?" I ask.

"It's one of my many houses," he says as the car stops, and he lets himself out. Shortly after, he opens my door and offers his hand to help me out.

I look up to the beautiful two-story mansion. It's classic in its own right, chic and polished, much like its owner. Two grand staircases lead up to the oversized balcony on the second floor. The wooden entrance doors are open, with wait staff on either side. The inside is lit up by large chandeliers, and music drifts outside.

"So you don't live here?" I ask, admiring the beauty of this place. "Are you like the Gatsby of New York?"

He laughs because the house screams lavish events, high society, and leisure.

But not... *home.*

"I'm sure you're used to amazing places," he comments as we walk toward the front doors.

"I am, but this is *very* nice." However, it does make me wonder what home looks like to Dawson because this is all business. A showpiece for his clients. I want to know what his house looks like because where a person lives often says a lot about them. Well, that's what my nonna had always told me.

Dawson's hand stays on my lower back as we enter the mansion. People start to greet him, throwing curious glances in my direction but asking for no introduction. I'm used to events such as these and honestly prefer when people don't speak to me. Unless, of course, I'm hosting personally. Not once does his hand leave my lower back.

I find a small bit of satisfaction in the fact that when he shakes other people's hands, he doesn't really give anyone much more attention than they deserve, and his attentiveness continues to circle back to me.

We walk through the mansion and arrive in a room where most of the people are mingling. It's as expected—

large chandeliers, grand art pieces, marble flooring, and screams decadence. But I still don't see Dawson living here.

A lady walks over, holding a tray of champagne. He grabs one and hands it to me before taking one for himself.

An energy buzzes through the air upon the announcement of Dawson's arrival. If people weren't mingling before, they sure as hell are now. I find it fascinating to watch. I quickly realize that those wearing a red bowtie or red choker are the escorts. And they're all beautiful. It's like they all stepped out of a magazine, but it's more than that. They ooze ease and charisma. This is the elite, and I feel like I'm stepping into another part of Dawson's world. Had he started as an escort? He still has so many secrets.

"Should I have a red choker on?" I ask him. I can tell he's been studying me more than the group around us.

He leans in, his lips brushing against my ear as he whispers, "The only choker you'll ever wear is one I provide you."

As he pulls back, I can sense the shift in him. His hand applies more pressure to my back as an older lady walks over.

"Dawson, this year's picking..." She shakes her head and looks at me. "Oh, tonight you have a pretty date. I approve. Now, find me someone," she says, smiling at me. But I feel judged by her. Being scrutinized was something I dealt with at these types of events back home. I was either judged for being my father's daughter, a possible match for their son, or as competition. But this party is based on vanity and companionship alone.

"Mrs. Henderson, I supply you with the best, but you never like any of them," he replies.

She lays a hand on his shoulder. "It's because I'm waiting on you, dear."

I want to laugh at her forwardness.

"I'm sorry, but I'm already taken," he says, which surprises me.

"I'm sure she wouldn't mind sharing you. Would you, dear?" she asks me.

"Oh, you can have him." I smile, and her eyes widen, but Dawson pulls me closer, squeezing my hip. I can hear his unsaid "behave."

"She's joking. The sense of humor on this one. I don't share. Sorry, Mrs. Henderson. Please enjoy your night," Dawson says, pulling me away. I give her a little wave, and she smiles in return as we walk off.

"You would share me?" he asks as we reach an empty table.

"You aren't mine."

"But I want to be yours. Or at least make you come again." He smirks.

I hold up the glass of champagne. "If I get another one of these, I very well may let you." He hands me his glass, which he hasn't touched. "I was joking."

"You shouldn't joke and play with my feelings like that," he mock scolds as a man approaches us. He comes up behind Dawson and glances at me briefly before he focuses on Dawson.

"Edgar," Dawson greets.

"Dawson."

"Everything okay?" Dawson asks.

"Yes, just a quick update. Do you want to discuss this in front of your customer?" Edgar asks, nodding to me.

"I'm not..." I shake my head, and he eyes me.

"I saw you auctioned off. I know you're a customer."

Shock invades me, and I gasp.

"Edgar, I don't pay you to talk, so shut up and handle the situation." I watch as his employee walks away and feel extremely judged. I assumed that no one here would know who I was. But then again, every exclusive society group only has so many fish in the pond.

Dawson turns to me and carefully takes the glass from my hand. "Don't get upset. Edgar has a mouth, but he is good at his job."

"I didn't come here to be judged, Dawson. Maybe I should leave so nobody is confused by our 'friendship.' " I go to leave, but he grips my hand.

"No one can leave. Once all the members are here, the doors are locked."

"What? Why?" I ask, looking to the doors and seeing guards there.

"It's for protection. Cameras can't be snuck in, and people who aren't invited can't enter."

"And even you can't leave?"

"No, not even me. It's a rule for a reason, Honey."

I look around, feeling trapped as the people around us socialize. "You didn't tell me any of this before I came in," I hiss. "I won't stand here and be judged as your plaything the whole night."

"You are *not* my plaything," he says seriously, and his hand reaches for one of the curls that frame my face. It's oddly intimate. "Though, I do have a room here that no one else is allowed in or has the key to."

In the middle of all these high-society, beautiful people, it feels like it comes back to Dawson and me. Like everyone else is irrelevant. And I certainly didn't come here for this. I came here for him.

"Take me to it."

He doesn't hesitate before he grabs my hand and moves.

CHAPTER 37
Dawson

"Dawson." One of the regulars, who has gone home with every escort I've ever had on my arm at events such as these, taps my shoulder as I try to escape with Honey. Honey pulls free from my grasp, but I reach out to grab her again. I couldn't care less what these people think of her. They don't know her, and I don't intend for them to know her. Bringing her here was never about them. It was all about her and whether she could accept this part of my world.

She shouldn't make herself small to make room for them.

She might have done that at her father's events, but she would never do that at mine.

This beautiful woman is above all of them.

"Oh, Dawson, one day you will join us. Please say you will," Mrs. Laddle gushes. She has always propositioned me like this with the fantasy of me joining one of the escorts in her unique sexual tastes.

Quick to assess the situation, Honey accepts my touch. "Dawson," Honey says commandingly from behind me, clasping my hand in hers.

"Don't you know the rules? It's rude to interrupt someone," Mrs. Laddle snaps at Honey.

"I'm sorry," Honey says, stepping up beside me. "But what did you just say to me?"

There's no need for me to interrupt because I can see the fire in her eyes.

She's mad, and it's hot.

"You heard me. Do you think just because you managed to get your claws into this one, you have more rights and are above us?" Mrs. Laddle snaps.

I find the situation almost laughable. If these people knew who Honey really was and the family she came from...

Honey's gaze narrows, and it's the same glare her father and sister offer when they're looking down on someone. "If I were you, I would shut up right about now," she warns.

"Luckily, I am not you. And I don't take orders from *little girls*"—the older woman puts her nose in the air and then says for all to hear—"you nasty whore."

Honey's hand releases mine, and before I can even stop her, her fist connects with Mrs. Laddle's face, and the crunch of bone is audible.

I've seen violence far worse than this. But from

Honey, I was not expecting it. And she was so goddamn fast and precise. She steps back, brushing over her dress, ensuring nothing is out of place as if she weren't a part of the ordeal herself.

The older woman is on the floor, holding her bleeding nose, as a few of my staff assist her.

"You need a lesson in manners, bitch," Honey says and spins away, her hair flicking as she does, then moves in the direction we were heading.

I hear Lesley lecturing me tomorrow about Honey's behavior, but I will never apologize for anything Honey does. If anything, I learned that my sweet honeypot isn't as helpless as I once thought.

"You're just going to let her do that?" Mrs. Laddle shrieks.

"I'm sure you're aware that we don't condone behavior or language that criticizes our services. The term 'whore' is not something we take kindly to." I snap my fingers and point to Mrs. Laddle, and security comes to hurry her away. "But the party will continue, amongst friends only," I add.

Whispers bubble around me, but my staff and escorts are quick to lighten the mood with smiles and small touches of favor. The ordeal, a lesson, is quickly dismissed.

In a few strides I'm by Honey's side again.

"I really hate the company you keep," she says. I grab her hand again as I lead her up the stairs, but by the way she's walking, you'd think she owns the mansion.

"I'll fire anyone you don't like." Her eyes narrow on me as I reach for my key and pull it out. Unlocking the door, she walks in, her hands on her hips as she starts pacing.

"I hate all of this too." She waves a hand toward the area we just left.

I can feel the muscle in my jaw jump. And I can't help but take it somewhat personally. These groups are what I've built my empire on.

"Would you ask me to stop attending events like this?" I ask.

She looks at me then say, "What? No."

"Because I could." I mean it. I can step aside. Only make appearances at certain events instead of all of them.

"Stop trying to soften me," she screams, frustrated. My cock twitches, and I don't know why I find her hot temper so fascinating and enticing.

"Is it working?" I ask, going to the bed and sitting on it. When she doesn't answer, I question, "Who taught you to hit like that?"

"You think Rya was the only one who knew how to fight?" She huffs. "We were both taught various forms of fighting from young ages. Though all my other fights ended up with me and the girl on the ground hitting each other."

"Who won?" I ask.

She flicks her hair behind her ear. "Me, of course."

CHAPTER 38

Honey

I'm not sure I like the way he's staring at me. It's different from how he usually looks at me, and I can sense something has changed in him. I'm not going to lie and say that he hasn't always looked at me with want, but right now, I know that's what it is, and maybe more.

I remain where I am, and Dawson stays where he is seated on the bed. He tells me so many things with only his eyes, and I don't entirely understand how I know. I never have. But it always feels inevitable. He removes his jacket and places it next to him on the bed before he taps the spot on the other side of him, indicating for me to sit.

"I didn't come in here to have sex," I tell him.

"No, you didn't. But we will," he says, then taps the bed again.

Fuck, I hate his arrogance. And I hate how much discipline I lack because he's right, we probably will.

I throw my hands in the air. "Why did you bring me to this event, Dawson?"

He blows out a breath and watches me carefully. Those intelligent eyes give nothing away.

"I can never understand what you're thinking," I admit. And I've grown up around men like him my entire life.

But with Dawson, I want to understand.

I need to know.

I need to know I'm not being used.

That I'm not the only one who's vulnerable in whatever this thing is between us.

"I wanted to see how you would react in this situation."

I scoff, angry. "This was to test me? Because I just decked one of your clients."

"Well, that was an added bonus. But no, not so much to test you." He seems to struggle with his words.

"Oh, for fuck's sake, Dawson. Speak," I demand. "Just give me something, at least."

He seems hesitant as he brings his hands together. "I have, for as long as I can remember, used my body to display affection. This world I'm in is so much a part of me in every way, Honey, and you are not from here."

I wrap my arms around my stomach, finally hearing a crack of vulnerability from him. This powerful man is finally giving me something to grasp on to.

"I have tried to fight my attraction to you. Yet here

we are. I wanted to bring you here because, honestly, I thought you'd run."

"You want me to run?" I ask in surprise.

"It's selfish, but also, I can't let you go," he admits. "*Won't* let you go," he corrects, and a dark, brooding expression comes over him. "All of this is a part of my ugliness. And I've never at any point in my life had the urge to compensate or apologize for that. Until I met you. I'm not a good man, but I want to be the best version of me for you."

I scrunch my eyebrows in confusion. This moment of insecurity is the last thing I expected from Dawson. But it suddenly makes sense with the push and pull. The back-and-forth. The moments when I think he's not entirely okay. And it's the most honest any man has ever been with me. Not even my own father would reveal his weakness to me.

Slowly, I take a seat next to him. So this is his form of what? Approval? Maybe even acceptance? A man who doesn't need or ask for any of that requests that of me? And not just any man. Dawson. Cleanly polished Dawson. He is a ruthless man. But I realize now, for me, perhaps, he is something *more*.

I feel myself heating up.

I want this.

And he knows that.

I can't lie and say I don't enjoy everything he does to me because I do. All of it. And I wonder if you're supposed to feel this way toward every single person you sleep with. I don't have much experience in this area, but I have always felt incredibly attracted to Dawson. There is absolutely no denying that whatsoever.

"I don't think we should have sex," I tell him, and I can sense his appreciation for the subject change.

"I think we should. I know how to make you feel good," he counters.

"There are a ton of people downstairs." I wave a hand behind me, glancing at the door. When I turn back to face him, he's standing before me. He picks me up, then resettles me on my back, higher on the bed.

"Who cares? Let them hear."

"Oh, you mean let them hear you telling me to *cry for you*?" I say with an eye roll as he hovers above me. He lifts a hand to the side of my face, next to my eye.

"I love it when you do. It's only a few tears that escape. I know then that you are in a state of bliss. It's hot..." He pauses. "I'm going to undress you now."

"You first," I say.

Dawson nods and steps back, his gaze intent on me the entire time. I watch as he removes each article of clothing until he is completely naked.

"Your turn," he says.

I climb off the bed and turn around to give him my back. I push my hair to the side and look over my shoulder at him. He doesn't waste any time before he steps up closer and ever so slowly unzips my dress, his fingers lightly brushing my skin on the way down. He slides it over my hips until it drops to the floor. When I turn around, his eyes are firmly on me. I'm wearing an expensive lingerie set from his store—the honey-colored one I loved so much. I didn't wear it with him in mind. I just like expensive things and how they feel on my skin.

"Beautiful," he breathes out as his fingers touch my breast and drag across it, making my skin prickle with need.

I stand, letting him look and touch, and all the while, my insides are screaming at me.

"I just want sex. Don't go down on me. I want to know if it's enough," I tell him.

"But I like to taste you."

"You can taste me after." I smile, then grab his hand and pull it down between my legs. He immediately slides a finger between my pussy lips.

"Crotchless panties." He raises a brow, and I smile seductively. "You're already wet for me," he growls, then steps forward until the back of my legs hits the bed, and I fall backward. I scoot farther up the mattress, and he climbs over me. He leans down and bites my nipple through the lace before he pulls off and does the same to the other one. All the while, his hand is between my legs, stroking me up and down my clit, then in and out.

I thrust my hips and reach down to grab his cock.

"My needy girl," he croons as I spread my legs wider and pull him even closer. He moves his fingers away, and his cock slides between my folds teasingly. I start to get restless and want him to move more, to inch into me and bury himself deep. I have this overwhelming need for him to be inside me. I lift my hips and feel his tip at my entrance. "Are you sure you're ready for me?" he asks. I move, and he grunts but stays still, just the tip breaching me.

"Dawson," I growl.

"Oh, there she is," he says and smirks. He leans down and bites my lip as he ever so slowly slides into me. My body tenses, and I stretch, taking him in. As soon as he's fully seated, I open my eyes to find him watching me.

"Keep your eyes open," he demands.

A knock sounds on the door, but we both ignore it.

I don't bother replying to him as he starts to move. He leans back down and kisses me.

I've been told that a lot of women can't come like this, that they need clitoral stimulation. But the way he is moving inside of me, our bodies so close, I can feel the friction on my clit.

And damn, it feels good.

I wonder if any other man would fuck me this good.

Or if I got really lucky with Dawson and no other will ever meet the standard he's set.

I know this is a fling.

But I try to embrace the now.

How can it work between us?

My father sure as hell won't approve.

He didn't like Dawson when they met at the wedding, so what would make him like him now?

And if my father found out that he paid a lot of money to fuck me, well, I'm sure he would find a way to put a bullet straight into Dawson's head and not even blink while doing it.

A hard bite on my breast startles me, and I cry out, suddenly back in the room. Bite marks circle my tit as Dawson looks at me almost impatiently.

"Am I not demanding enough?" he asks, sounding insulted.

I laugh. "You actually fucking bit me."

The tension ripples out of him as he kisses it better. "Now you know how it feels."

My hands clutch the bedding as he continues to move in and out of me, and I have to remember not to squeeze my eyes shut. But just as I'm about to come, he pulls out. I open my eyes, not realizing I closed them, only to feel his mouth at my clit, tasting me, before he slides two fingers straight inside me.

"That's it... cry for me," he says, but I'm already arching my back in pleasure. And his mouth is moving at the perfect pace again. I feel the loss of his fingers before I do his mouth, and as I come down from the ecstasy, he's thrusting his cock back into me. I grip his hair, hungry for more, only to feel the pressure building yet again.

He fucks me harder and faster this time. I'm screaming his name as loud as I possibly can. And then he's coming too.

And when I look at him, I notice he's drinking in every moment. He pulls out of me and lies next to me, his cock still semi-hard and a smile on his face.

"I could do this every day," Dawson says.

"If it feels that good, so could I," I tell him honestly. "Does sex always feel like that?"

"No. You will have bad fucks, but never with me."

"So other men…"

He doesn't answer right away, and when I turn to look at him, I find him staring up at the ceiling.

"Don't mention other men when I just fucked you senseless."

"Don't talk to me that way if you ever wish to fuck me again. Understand?" I bite back and sit up.

He pulls me back down and kisses my neck. "I'm sorry."

"Hm…" I hum in response.

"Forgive me."

And I do because he then proceeds to show me exactly how sorry he is.

CHAPTER 39

Dawson

I grin at the photo sent by Honey only an hour ago. It's of her squeezing honey over her tits. I shift my hard cock to a more comfortable position. *Fuck, she has no idea how beautiful she is.* And that temper I saw last night... my cock pulses. That perfectly polished mask of hers slipped, and I delighted in the underlying ferociousness.

I wanted to see what Honey thought of the event last night, but I received so much more than simply her approval or appraisal. It was hard to go our separate ways when I had work matters to attend to.

Lesley knocks and lets herself in. When she sees me, she stutters to a halt and glances around the room, then looks behind her.

"Were you just smiling at your phone?"

I set the phone on my desk, the screen down. "I received good news."

"How nice," she drawls. "How did the event go last night?"

"It went as well as expected. I've had service requests coming through all morning."

She nods and tosses some photographs on my desk. "I heard Mrs. Laddle ended up with a broken nose and was blacklisted."

I can't help the smile. I can tell Lesley wants to be mad at me, but she also breaks out in a smile. "I have to give it to the little bumble bee... I didn't think she had it in her. But at least we don't have to deal with that old hag anymore."

I pick up the pictures as Lesley sits across from me and flick through them. Various security footage images of those on the grounds last night. All were invited guests. Which means our mystery fucker was smart enough not to come on the premises.

"The street security?" I ask.

"Henry is working on it now. He says it shouldn't be too long. Do you think the guy fell for it?"

"I do."

CHAPTER 40

Honey

Dawson has invited me to his house. I was surprised when the text came through. I didn't expect it nor reciprocate the picture of his cock. I'm staring at the screen, my head tilting as I gnaw on my bottom lip. I have girlfriends who have told me they hate receiving dick pics, but they've obviously never been sent the right one.

I'm leaving shortly, but I'm tempted to pull out my vibrator first. I look at my top drawer thoughtfully. I mean, I still have an hour until I need to leave, right? So why not?

But just as I've decided to go for it, my sister walks out of my wardrobe triumphantly. I quickly close my screen.

"Aha! I knew you stole it," she says, holding up one of her shirts.

"You can't just assume it's yours because it's black, Rya." Black is basically the only color she wears.

She gives me a stern expression, and I look away with my tongue in my cheek. It actually is hers.

"Are you sure this is the right thing to do?" she asks as I apply my lipstick. She has the afternoon off from work and came down to speak to me and, of course, drill me about Dawson before she leaves for her belated honeymoon with Crue.

"What?" I reply, playing dumb.

"I know you're going to see him."

I smile in the mirror. "How do you know that?"

"Honey, you care what your parents think. It's always been how you are. Our father arrives here tomorrow. How do you think you'll explain to him that you're seeing someone he dislikes?"

"I don't. I won't tell him," I say, shrugging.

"If he sees you two together, he'll work it out. He's a smart man."

"I know. He just needs to get to know Dawson better."

"You are Daddy's little princess, Honey, and you always have been. I rebelled, and you stayed glued to him. He won't take this easily, and Crue and I will be away, so no backup from us."

"I won't need backup."

She coughs "bullshit" under her breath.

I roll my eyes. "If you say so."

She walks into the bathroom and hugs me from

behind. It's nice because she's not one to often offer physical affection. "Just be safe, okay? I get it's all exciting, and sex is fun, but just because you're having great sex with him doesn't mean you won't with someone else." I feel my cheeks redden at her words.

The only person I have really spoken with regarding sex is Dawson. I feel comfortable talking with him about all those things, and I know that's probably a weird thing to do, but who better to discuss it with than someone who sells it for a living? And he listens to me without judgment despite the fact I'm sleeping with him.

"I'm going back upstairs. Call me if you need anything," she says.

"Oooh, I'll be up shortly to grab my baking tray before you go. I only have one."

Rya rolls her eyes. "Shouldn't you own like a million of those?"

"No, I only have the ones I stole from your kitchen. And besides, I'm a woman on a budget."

She shakes her head and leaves as I touch up my mascara.

I'm unsure if I should go to his house late or early because I'm eager to see where he lives. He's been to my place multiple times, and I haven't once seen where he lives, and I'm curious.

I put my mascara away. It doesn't take away the nerves of my father and mother coming to New York. I've only just started feeling like I'm establishing a new life, and I know they'll try to convince me to return to

Italy. And if Dawson comes around when my father is here, I'm outright terrified my father might shoot him.

The possibility of that is extremely high because he already dislikes Dawson and doesn't even know what he does for a living. If he did, well, let's just say I don't think he would be too pleased. Then again, my father probably has intel on him and knows exactly who he is.

I love my father, and he was good to us girls and my mother, but that doesn't take away the type of person he is. It wasn't long after Rya left for New York that, at thirteen, I stumbled upon my father behind our shed with a gun in his hand, standing over a dead body. I realized how much Marco had protected me from seeing that side of him and the business up until that point. I knew about it, but seeing it is different.

That was my first glimpse of how dark my father is.

He is a killer.

I also had it in my head that if I ever did get a boyfriend or lose my virginity, I'd walk into the back shed and find another man in there, but this time, it would be someone I was seeing.

My front door opens. "Honey." I hear Rya call my name as I slide on my heels. When I walk out, I find her standing there with my parents. "Look, Father decided to surprise us early. Aren't you lucky," she says and pulls me by my hand to her side.

My father looks me up and down and asks, "Are you going out?"

"We just went out. She was going to get

undressed, but you showed up. We met in the elevator. How's that for timing," Rya babbles. She hugs our father, and I can tell she's giving me a moment to adjust to the situation because I am shocked. My mother gives me a hug, and although Rya and I have different mothers, mine has always accepted Rya as her own.

"Honey, you look beautiful," my mother says. "Glowing, really. Is this because of a lucky man?"

My smile is tight. Count on my mother to jump straight into it.

"Yeah, how about that, Honey?" Rya asks with a smile.

I smile again and give my father a tight hug. I can tell he doesn't miss anything as he looks around the apartment. "Come in, are you hungry? I could make you something."

"We are, but we wanted to go out with you both if we can," my father says. And I can tell the small space of my apartment isn't to his liking.

"Sure thing. Let me go up and tell Crue. We have a few hours before we leave," Rya says, kissing my father on the cheek and then abandoning me.

"This is a nice place," my father comments, and I know it's a lie, but he's trying. I just nod, unsure of what to say. I need to message Dawson because there's no way I can go over there now.

"I'll be back. I'll just touch up my makeup if we're going back out," I tell them.

Walking back to my room, I grab my phone and bring up his name.

Me: *Can't make it. Change of plans. Rain check?*

He replies almost instantly.

Dawson: *I prepared my favorite dessert.*

And then he sends a picture of a bottle of honey. I cover my mouth as the laugh escapes. I don't bother replying to that.

I don't plan to ditch my family when they have just arrived. However, a part of me is trying to figure out how I still can.

CHAPTER 41
Honey

They have been grilling me all evening, and I get it. They want to know what I've been up to. The last time I spoke to them, I had a job, and now they want to know why I quit, and I'm doing, in their words, "Some pointless online job."

I told them I decided it was not the path for me, and I'm still figuring things out.

And that also has me worried.

Shouldn't I know what I want to do at my age?

Shouldn't my life be all figured out by now?

I feel like it should be.

My sister knew all along what she wanted to do and how she wanted to live her life.

And yet, here I am, still trying to figure things out. I mean, I know everyone is different, and we all have our own struggles, but it's the part of me that really annoys me the most. I feel like I'm failing at life. But I also feel that by living here, I am starting to become who I'm meant to be, by starting to love myself and find out who I want to be. And none of that will align with my parents' expectations.

"Honey, have your fun here and come back home. We never forced you to work, and you really don't need to," my mother says empathetically as she takes a small forkful of her salad.

I sigh. I know she's trying to help, but she isn't. My sister watches me carefully, and Crue looks... bored? Probably pissed that he's had to push back their private jet a few hours for this dinner just to listen to me be scolded.

My father waves at the waiter for more red wine. He and Crue both ordered the steak—bloody, of course. I haven't touched my meal.

"You've been here for three months," my father adds. "We were expecting you to come back home by now."

"I'm rather enjoying my stay," I tell them.

"But don't you miss home?" my mother asks. "Unless there's a special someone you're staying here for?"

My father's glare is piercing. I let out a sigh. My parents have always been like this. My mother encouraging a dating life because she enjoyed her youth before meeting our father, and my father adamant I'm not to see anyone because I'd be married off. Now I'm certain he wants me to die a sweet, innocent angel. Alone and a virgin, preferably.

"Honey's been making progress," Rya says on my behalf. I appreciate the support, but it also makes me feel insignificant that I need her to stand up for me. "She's made friends and is enjoying the differences in cultures. And she's learning new things with this online job."

Part of me just wants to tell them I have twenty million sitting in the bank right now, so they back the fuck off. Naturally, I can't tell them how I earned it.

"Asking your sister to send Marco home is what had us worried," my father adds. "He's miserable."

I roll my eyes knowng that's far from the truth. "I love you both dearly, but I'm twenty-seven. I don't need protection. And I don't need to be scrutinized for my life choices when I only moved out of your home three months ago."

They're quiet for a moment before my father dives back into it. "And how many more months do you think you'll be here?"

I exhale. Once again, I'm ignored. As I've always been when I've voiced my own wants.

"Papa, enough," Rya scolds. "She's not a child, so stop treating her like one."

I sag into my chair. That alone makes me sound even more like a child. "I need to excuse myself for a moment," I say, pushing back my chair.

"Honey," Rya shouts, but I beeline for the bathroom. I'm glad to find I'm the only one in here. I grab both sides of the basin and take a shaky breath. I feel like kicking in every piece of furniture in this room.

I look to my left and see a high window. A small smile creeps on my lips as I think about the time Dawson and I snuck out. I wonder if I could use the same method now. But who would be my booster in the grand escape this time?

The door opens and I quickly turn away from the window as my mother steps in. She looks sympathetic as she holds my shoulders. I exhale, trying to release my anger. I don't want to direct it at her.

"We don't mean to be harsh. We just miss you," she says. I know it comes from a place of love, but it's suffocating. And I'd once used that word on my mother and she sobbed.

My father loves us all, but even she isn't the exception to his expectations. Things had to remain in place to uphold the Ricci name.

"I just need you both to give me some space. I came here to find out who I am. I'm glad you're both visiting, but not if you're going to lecture me the whole time."

She nods in understanding. "I'll speak to your father."

"Thank you," I say gratefully.

She offers me a beautiful smile and taps on my shoulder. "He only wants the best for you. You're our baby."

I sigh again. "I know." But, shit, there has to be a line when it comes to coddling your child. But I suppose in the world in which we were born and raised, caution was instilled. Had I been a son, I probably would've been taught how to use a gun. But instead, because I was a girl,

I was raised to smile and be polite and was taught to defend myself but never leave without my bodyguard so I'd never have to use them. In his opinion, only a man can protect a woman.

And I don't know how to change that kind of thinking in my father.

But it's now beyond crippling, and everything I'd run away from has followed me here.

CHAPTER 42
Dawson

M y insides boil with anger the next day as I watch her walk in with another man. I've never been jealous, but I am right now. Is this the reason she blew me off last night? Did she have a date with somebody else?

I watch them stroll down the sidewalk for a good five minutes, stopping to look at various shops before I decide to get out of the car.

Coming up behind them, I hear her laugh at something he says, and I hate that someone else made her laugh.

Am I fucking falling for her?

I shouldn't be.

She'll want more life experience than just settling for me. I've been her first and only fuck, and I know how curious she is with everything. She asks me questions that most people in their early twenties would usually ask their best friends. Hell, even as teenagers.

A part of me loves that she trusts my opinion, but the other part wonders why no one has shared things with her before. Has she lived such a sheltered life? I completely understand that she comes from a background where what your father says is law.

But then I look at Rya and wonder why Honey isn't the same.

Not that I want her to be anything like Rya. At least when it comes to how forward Rya is compared to how reserved Honey is. Well, how reserved she is with everyone but me.

She laughs again, and I tap her on the shoulder this time. She turns, and the man's arm is still linked with hers. And when he turns with her, I see it's not just any man.

It's her father.

Fuck.

My sour face instantly changes as I see her surprised expression turn worrisome.

"Dawson," she chokes out, then composes herself and continues, "You remember my father." She waves to him, and I offer him my hand.

"Yes. A pleasure to see you again, sir." He glances at my outstretched hand and doesn't bother to take it before he looks back at his daughter.

"We should go, your mother will be worried."

Yep, still hates my guts.

Honey pulls away from his hold. "You go. I want to chat with Dawson for a moment. I won't be long." She leans in and kisses him on the cheek. The whole time, he gives me a death glare. The feeling equally returned as I offer him a half-cocked smile.

He turns reluctantly and walks away.

She finds us a little alley between two stores where he can't see us anymore. When I know we're alone, I pull her to me, slamming my lips to hers, our bodies so dangerously close that there's no air between us. She kisses me back at first, our tongues sliding together. Her arms wrap around my shoulders as mine circle her waist. I glue her to me, but then she seems to remember exactly where we are and breaks the kiss.

"My father could see us." She pulls back.

"Is that an issue?" I ask.

She pushes my possessive hands away from her waist. "Yes."

"Why?"

She cocks an eyebrow, and I already know the answer. I just want to hear her say it out loud. "Father doesn't like you, but don't take it personally. I don't think he will like anyone with me. Unless he chose the man himself." I stand there quietly. "Hold on. How long have you been here?"

"Not long. I saw you and wanted to bring you back to my place." I reach for her again, and she doesn't pull away this time. "Tell me you'll come."

I sound like a fucking lost puppy. There are so many

papers and contracts I could be signing at the moment as I wait for Henry to give me useful information.

But this woman is my distraction.

My procrastination.

A break-time snack.

Call it whatever the fuck you want, but I need her.

She shakes her head. "What are we?" she asks.

"Two adults having great sex," I reply.

She huffs out a breath. "A fuck buddy doesn't stalk me down the street as I take a stroll with my father."

"In all fairness, I didn't know it was your father at first."

She laughs. "I mean, the sex is great. And I know you do contracts with most people. So what are we? Because we don't have a contract."

"Do you want a contract?"

"No! I would actually be offended if you gave me one," she says, and I feel her tense beneath my fingers.

"I'm not asking you to sign one."

"Good. I wouldn't sign one anyway," she states, staring right into my eyes.

I don't know what else she wants from me. I've never had a non-contractual relationship. And sure, I know what normal people do in terms of dating, but she and I are far from normal—our circumstances are completely different.

"Come back to mine. Please."

She bites her bottom lip. "I could use Daphne as an excuse."

I kiss her with a smile. "A reason I can finally enjoy you two being friends."

She slaps me on the chest. "Hey! She's actually really nice." Honey peers around the corner, searching for her father. "I have to go and get some things and will give it an hour or so before I break it to my parents."

"Do you want me to come and grab your things?" I ask.

"I think that will only make it worse," she says. "I can come to yours later or—"

"I'll wait."

She nods, and before she can pull away again, I tug her back to me and kiss her. Her hands clutch my sides, and I kiss her for all the days I missed out on kissing her. She smiles against my lips before she backs up.

"I won't be long. Am I staying the night? Just so I know if I have to pack anything."

"Yes," I say without hesitation. Waking up next to Honey sounds like a fucking dream. One I am eager for.

She nods before she walks off, and I watch as she leaves.

I'll happily wait a lifetime for her.

But an hour or so is better.

CHAPTER 43

Honey

My father is looking at me with his stern "father look" as I like to call it. It's not the normal mad look he gives to people he hates, or even those he likes. No. For Rya and me, he has this other look. It's him trying to be mad at us, with a hint of disappointment mixed with love.

It usually fails and we end up getting what we want.

"You're going to see that man, aren't you?" he asks, and I walk over and kiss his head.

"Papa, he's a nice man. And no, I'm not. I'm meeting with a friend named Daphne."

"He is *not* nice," he declares. "Do you know what he does?"

My mother laughs behind us and he scrunches up his nose at her reaction.

"Love, do you forget what you do?"

"But this is our daughter."

"It's not like she's marrying him."

"Yet," my father tacks on.

"I'm telling you, I have plans with a friend. Calm down."

Unfortunately, my father is the suspicious type and has a nose like a hound when it comes to lies. And I feel somewhat guilty for lying to him, but it's easier this way. For everyone.

"Do you love him?" Father questions.

I laugh. "Papa! I'm visiting a friend. But if you must know, I think you and Dawson are more alike than you think."

He scoffs at that.

"It's true. Like you, he says it how it is, no bullshit. And I've never been mistreated by him," I insist. *Dawson only mistreats me in ways I prefer*, but I keep that thought to myself.

I would never be stupid enough to tell my father about the auction for my virginity. I'm pretty sure if he ever found out, he would storm out of here after locking me in my own apartment and hunt Dawson down and kill him.

And I still need that man.

My father is unconvinced. "Good. Don't let your heart interfere. Just because you're here and dating now, does not mean all men are good."

"Remember how I said the overprotectiveness is too

much? This is what I'm talking about," I say, pointing at him.

He crosses his arms over his chest, and I look past him to my mother, who mouths, *Be safe,* before I walk out.

CHAPTER 44
Honey

Dawson is where he said he would be, waiting for me.

"Sorry it took so long," I tell him. He offers me one of his smiles before he takes my bag and walks toward his car.

"Your father let you go?" he asks, surprised.

"Yep. Not without a warning, though," I say, smiling as he opens the car door for me. Putting my bag in the back, he walks to the driver's side.

I feel like a teenager sneaking around and lying to my parents about who I'm seeing, but it's kind of nice in a weird way. Because I never really did this before. It's foolish. But also fun.

"You hungry?" he asks, and I nod. "Anything in particular you want before we head to my place?"

"Do you have food at your house?" I ask.

"Yes. I'm not a complete savage," he jokes. If only he knew that my sister never had food at her apartment before Crue. I'm just grateful she has a personal chef now to make sure she's actually eating meals.

"Okay, well, just keep driving, and I can cook us something."

"You like to cook?"

"Yep, very much so."

"Lucky me." After a beat, he asks, "So, how long will your parents be in town?"

"I'm not sure. We haven't really discussed it."

He doesn't seem too happy with my answer, just grunting in response.

We drive for about thirty minutes before he pulls off one of the main roads and then turns down another street. The area has plenty of greenery and space between the houses. Some have ranches, and others are situated along the water.

It's very different already to the mansion he took me to the night of the event. Dawson pulls into a driveway with a large black fence wrapped around the property. He leans over and puts in a code at the gate, and when it opens, he continues down the driveway, the outside lights flickering on as we approach.

I make out a house that looks like it came straight out of the Hamptons. I think it's a cream color, but I can't be sure because it's nighttime. I admire the front of the home, with its two large wooden doors, as the garage automatically opens. The inside of the garage lights up, showing another three sports cars. Doesn't the saying go "Boys and their toys"?

"No Gatsby comment?" he teases.

I smile as we step out of the car, and he grabs my bag. "That has yet to be decided."

But it feels different here. It's grand and magnificent, yes. But it already feels more homey. Probably because he lives in it, and it appears to be smaller than the other mansion, and I don't know why, but I like that. The other one felt... vacant.

He pulls one of the doors open, and I'm instantly met with gleaming white marble tiles. He flicks on the lights and leads me down a short hallway until we enter an incredibly large kitchen.

"Do you have cooks?" I ask, eyeing the beautiful, spacious kitchen. It almost reminds me of the one back at home in Italy. Stepping past him, I run my hand over the marble counter—white with gray streaks running through it.

"Yes, they come on the weekends to pre-cook my meals for the week," he replies.

"Wow."

I turn to the two-door fridge and pull it open. I find an array of ingredients and start reaching for things I can use.

"What do you plan to cook?" he asks, and I hear the amusement in his voice.

I look over my shoulder at him. "Are you allergic to anything, or is there anything you won't eat?"

"Just mushrooms," he says. "But you won't find any in there."

"Okay, good."

I pull out pots and pans while he goes to another refrigerator disguised as a pantry and pulls out a bottle of wine.

He pours two glasses, and I start cooking.

"Pasta? What type?" he asks.

"What you like to classify as carbonara," I reply. I usually make the pasta from scratch, but Dawson doesn't have all the ingredients, so I use the packaged pasta in the cupboard. My nonna would hate it, but it can still taste amazing if you nail the sauce.

Being in the kitchen puts me at ease because I want to check out every crevice of his home, but I don't want to be obvious about it.

"Who taught you to cook?" he asks.

"My mother can't cook. Actually, I don't think she even knows how to turn the stove on." I laugh. "My mother's mother was a great cook. And after Rya left, I spent more time with her, and she taught me most things. Then, in the summer, I would sign up for cooking classes. It was amazing. I really enjoy baking as well."

"So why are you working in lingerie?"

I stop stirring the sauce and look up at him. "What do you mean? I quit."

"Hm..." he hums as he slips his hands around my waist. "I heard your boss was a tyrant."

"Oh, he was," I deadpan. "I think he was compensating for other things he lacked."

He squeezes my sides, and I laugh. He rests his chin on my shoulder, and it's nice. It's easy and comfortable, and I wish we could stay like this forever.

"I'm serious, though. What are you doing with your life?" he asks.

I blow out a breath. Wow! It's like the conversation with my parents all over again. Except I don't feel like I'll be judged by Dawson, and he will hear me out earnestly.

"I really don't know," I say thoughtfully. "I'm not like Rya. And with everything after the arranged marriage falling through, I want a moment to decide what I want. And I suppose three months isn't enough to figure that out yet."

He considers me, his grip around my waist tight, which is comforting. "And will you go back to Italy?"

I stir the sauce, contemplating that for a moment. "I really don't know."

Silence passes between us, then he presses a kiss to my cheek before moving beside me to slice the bacon into small cubes.

"Not just a pretty face," he says, and I smile.

This feels... domestic, and I'm almost surprised by his shift but grateful to know that we can do something other than have sex even though it's mind-blowing.

This is... nice.

And I wonder if we would remain like this if I decided to stay in New York. Or would our fling end at some point, and we'd part ways? And that thought leaves a bitter sadness that I don't want to confront.

"I know what you're going to do. I'll buy you a restaurant."

My heart skips a beat, and I turn to him. Did he really just say that he plans to buy me a restaurant? I'm not sure how to take that. Does he not remember that I have twenty million of his dollars already? The one he never took a cut of? How much money does this man have? Starting a restaurant in this country is not cheap, especially in a city like New York.

And then there's all the butterflies it adds to my stomach.

Surely, he doesn't offer every girl these things? But I'd be a fool to think I'm special. I push those feelings aside, not entirely sure what to do with them.

"W-what?" I finally stutter out.

He smiles like it's the best idea he's ever had. After adding bacon to the sauce, he grabs his wine and sips it.

"It's your passion, right? So why not? Hell, I'm sure Crue will love the idea, so he can money launder through it."

I give him an incredulous look.

"Okay, maybe not the last part. But if this is what you love, then why not do it?"

He has a point, but I've never thought about having a restaurant. How does one even go about that? I do like the idea, and in my head, I'm already picturing all the types of food I could serve. But maybe a café would be easier? Something small to start, where I can bake every day? And serve some decent coffee.

"You can picture it now, can't you?" He grins, and I smile back.

"I can. Maybe a bakery and coffee shop could be fun as well."

"Good."

"But I wouldn't even know how to start a business."

He nudges me. "Lucky for you, you know someone who is especially phenomenal at starting businesses."

My heart feels light, and my body buzzes with excitement. I don't know why I never thought of it before. It could be fun. "I won't take your money for it, though," I inform him. "Did you forget I already have most of your money?"

"You have a small fraction of my money, Honey."

"More than enough to start a business." I poke my tongue out. He laughs, and I have the impression he's far from claiming defeat.

I dish up the plates and slide his over to him. Giving him a fork, Dawson doesn't wait before he starts eating. He closes his eyes, moans softly, then looks up at me. "Marry me."

I laugh and wave him off before serving up my plate

and joining him. When I sit next to him, he's already eaten half.

"The restaurant is a must. But if you can bake as good as this, then bakery it is."

"Yeah?" And I don't know why I'm asking him. "Maybe."

I smile, finally taking a bite for myself.

CHAPTER 45
Honey

Dawson climbs onto the bed with me, and I push his shoulders back and then hook a leg over his hips to straddle him. He looks up at me, and I kiss his mouth gently, taking my time to taste him. We're both naked, and it feels like it's been forever since we were last together, even though it was only days ago.

I feel his hardness between my legs but don't yet take him. I grind up and down his length, giving myself all the stimulation I need, and his hands are squeezing my ass. There's a laziness to our touches. A different type of exploration. I look at his chest again, the tattoo catching my attention. "When did you get these tattoos?" I ask.

"Honey," he growls.

"Oh, shut up. I know you think my questions are cute."

He grabs my hair and pulls back my neck so he can kiss down my throat. I laugh.

"I think many things are cute about you. But I don't share the same focus of asking about my past while my cock is only inches from impaling you."

I chuckle as he releases my hair, and I grab his cock, angling it toward my entrance. But then I stop. His hands lock on my hips as he growls.

"Promise you'll tell me after?"

He cocks a grin. "Are you blackmailing me?"

I position myself over his tip before pulling back up. He grunts. I brush my lips against his before whispering, "Think of it as a transaction."

"And you told me you weren't business savvy," he says with a grin. "I promise. Now, fuck me, Honey."

I chuckle when he grips my ass hard before he slaps it. I feel the sting from his handprint, but it only eggs me on. Our kisses pause, but our lips don't leave each other.

I move a little higher until I feel him at my entrance, and then I slide down, pushing him all the way inside me.

Dawson groans into my mouth before he bites my lip, and I moan at the fullness. I start moving before I can think better of it. One part of me wants to move fast to feel it everywhere, while another part wants to stay still while he's deep inside me to feel the connection with him.

His hands make the decision that I was struggling with, and he pulls my ass up and down, rocking me on his body.

And it feels good.

Really good.

Feeling him slide in me while I have full control, but he is guiding the movements, is way too good.

Will every time we have sex feel like this?

Because not once have I had a bad experience with him. Even when I lost my virginity, it was amazing at first, but I was sore toward the end, which is to be expected.

I can't help but continue moving, sitting up, and squeezing my breasts.

"Fuck, you're beautiful," he says, and when I look down, I find him watching me. I place one of my hands on his mouth, and he takes my finger between his lips and sucks it.

I ride him hard into oblivion, finding the same drive to make him come, so he blows inside of me. I'm satisfied when he does. Knowing I can pleasure him like this. That we can share this moment. It makes me feel powerful and sexy.

We fall into a heated, sweaty mess. Our breaths nothing but harsh air moving in and out of our lungs. I face him, our heads on the same pillow, and laugh.

He pushes back my hair. "What are you laughing at?"

"I honestly don't think I will get enough of this."

Dawson's hand stills as it traces my jawline. I sense the shift in him before he continues the movement. And it's nice, almost like being petted.

"Right. You owe me a story about this." I point at the

tattoo that I doubt anyone suspects resides under his clothes.

"You want to ask about that and not the one of your lips near my cock?"

I shrug. "I was there for that."

He huffs out a humorous breath. "It's not a nice story, Honey," he says, pushing back my hair thoughtfully.

I grab his hand. "Stop trying to show me only the nice sides. I want to know about the warts and all."

His lip kicks up in an amused smile. "I don't have any warts."

"You're deflecting."

He sighs. "I considered getting it lasered off once. I was young when I had it inked. Angry with the world and the hand I got dealt. I thought a tattoo would make me... I don't know... scarier... less desirable, maybe."

I frown. "Why would you want to be scarier or less desirable?"

He averts his gaze, and it's the first time he's ever looked away from me. I cup his cheek, and the tender touch brings him back to me. He seems hesitant to continue, but I say nothing, slowly and patiently drawing it out of him.

"When I was fifteen, I was forced into the industry. My mother and I both."

My brows furrow. "When you say the industry..."

"We were prostitutes. I was fifteen when I was first forced to take on a client. We had no money, and my mother got caught up with the wrong people. And for payment, they not only took her but said I had a pretty face and physique, so it was decided I would help her pay off her gambling debt."

Ice runs through my veins.

"So I dutifully performed for three years and got this stupid tattoo, thinking it would deter customers."

"Dawson, that's awful." I feel tears prick at my eyes.

"It's not as bad as some have it. Some don't even make it out alive. There was another guy my age. We hung out a lot, trying to get through it. My mother and I were able to buy out of our debt by the time I turned eighteen, but he wasn't able to. And I hated that. I hated that everything was taken from us.

"It's never just sex. It's a give and take. But there's so much money in it. After her debt was cleared, my mother moved on. I've always hated her for putting us in that position. I provide for her to live a luxurious lifestyle now. But I still hate her."

I stroke my thumb over his clenched jaw. Could anyone blame him? I now feel guilty for all of those times I thought ill of him. "So why did you s-stay?" My voice breaks, and his gaze snaps to mine. He offers a wavering smile as he absentmindedly wipes my tears.

"At eighteen, I had no other skillset, so I went into escorting and realized I was good at it. And I thought if I could create a safe place for the transaction to happen, then perhaps it wouldn't be so bad. And maybe I could earn back all of that money if not more than what was traded for my services involuntarily for those three years."

It dawns on me then, his hesitation around my virginity. I suspected there was a deeper reason, but this is horrible. "The virgin thing?" I need to know. Need to confirm.

He sighs. "I agree it makes a fuck ton of money with the right clients. Mine was bought for one hundred dollars, and it was a fifty-year-old woman."

I bring my hand up to my mouth in shock.

He tucks my hair back behind my ear. "I don't want you feeling sorry for me, Honey. It's made me the person I am today. It's the reason why I protect my staff and have built a lucrative business. Contracts and all. But no, I never wanted to touch a virgin because of that. It was... unappealing to me."

I furrow my brows and can feel the tears spilling down my cheeks. "So why did you take mine?" I feel bad.

Had it been painful for him?

Did he regret it?

Did it make him uncomfortable?

"I couldn't let any other man touch you, and that's the goddamn truth. Turns out I'm a selfish bastard. But I wanted your experience to be—"

"It was," I'm quick to say, interrupting him. And there's an understanding that passes between us. "I'm glad I lost it to you, Dawson. I'm honestly so glad I met you. Thank you. You've given me a beautiful gift."

His thumb rolls over my cheek. "Likewise. Even when you give me hell."

A chuckle rises from my throat as I wipe away my tears, and I feel the tension leave his body and leave the room.

"I've never told anyone that," he admits. And my heart fills with warmth, sadness, and the want and need to protect a teenage Dawson. "Did you know Dawson isn't even my birth name?"

I prop my head on my hand and look at him. "Really?"

He shakes his head. "Another reason to hate my mother. A lot of days doing drugs, and she gave me a god-awful name because she couldn't think straight when I was born."

He says it with a hint of laughter, and I can't help but play into it.

"Now I'm curious."

"You're always curious, Honey." He laughs as he turns my back to him and scoops me into a hug from behind. I rest my head on his arm, stroking his other hand that hangs over my waist.

"What's your birth name?"

"If you tell anyone, I might have to kill you."

I laugh. "Please. You like my pasta too much."

He laughs and then sighs, defeated. "Bear."

I bite my lip and grimace. He's right. That is a shitty name.

"Your silence says it all, Honey."

I laugh. "Well, I guess you are like a rugged bear now."

"Shut up." He chuckles as he squeezes me from behind.

I nestle into him, my mind reeling with everything he's just told me. All the mystery and the masks. I realize now they have been Dawson's way of survival. He's never really had a home except for the one he built for himself.

"Thank you for telling me your story."

Silence.

Dawson rummages around the bed and then throws a blanket over the both of us. He kisses my cheek. "Goodnight, Honey."

CHAPTER 46
Dawson

Her hair is fanned across my bed as she sleeps, a light snore passing through her lips. I let her sleep after we showered and played again.

Why didn't I think to bring her here before now?

That would be because no one comes to my place. More precisely, no one is ever invited.

Honey says something in her sleep, and I pull her closer to me. She's still naked. Neither of us bothered to put on any clothes after what we did all night.

What's the point? I can't keep my hands off her.

And it's not just the sex, it's her. I could listen to her speak for hours on end, asking me the most random questions.

And I would answer every single one.

Because it makes her happy.

I brush my thumb down her cheek. Precious. Beautiful. Stern but fair.

She is the only person I've ever told about my past. The ugliness that I've tried to hide all these years. Why I needed to hone such a polished mask so no one would be the wiser? I built this empire on that, and yet I realize now that besides all the money, power, and recognition, it now feels like it has a purpose if I can share that with her. A surprising thought and harsh realization. I'm too selfish to let her go now.

Who knew that months ago, in a supply closet, I would fall into a pot of Honey?

Fallen, hook, line and sinker.

I'm not sure I want to come up to be resuscitated, either.

Her eyes slowly open and she offers me the softest smile.

"Morning. Your bed is comfy," she says and turns so her back is to my chest. Her ass pushes against my cock, which is already hard. "I can feel you're happy this morning." She giggles.

"Waking up with you does that," I tell her, my hand slipping under the sheet and finding her side before I drag it down and to her hip. I pull her back so her ass cradles my cock, and she wiggles.

"I haven't done doggy before. Care to indulge a girl?"

See, perfect. Always happy to ask for what she wants. It's one of the many things I love about her. And there are a lot of things.

"You aren't sore?" I ask, reaching around to slide my

hand between her thighs. She opens her legs slightly, and she's already wet.

"A good type of sore, but always ready to play," she teases. I remove my hand, flick the sheet away, and climb off the bed. Dragging her over to me, I turn her around so she's now on her hands and knees.

"Feet on the floor, hands flat on the bed," I order.

She slides off and does what I say. I step back and admire the view. And what a spectacular view it is. Walking to my closet, I find one of my many toys. I haven't used this one yet and bought it with her in mind. She loves clit stimulation, and this one is the perfect toy for that. It sucks the clit if you hold it there.

I wrap her hair around my hand and push her farther down, her ass tilting higher into the air. My other hand snakes around her waist to her clit. I turn the device on, and instantly she jumps, but I have hold of her hair, keeping her locked in place.

"Oh my God, what is that?"

I ignore her question and tell her to spread her legs wider. She does as I say and goes to move her hands, and I pull on her hair. "Keep your hands on the bed." She listens and moans as the vibration picks up. I pull it away and position my cock at her entrance. Honey pushes back, wanting it, and I slide in slowly. Just before I push all the way in, I bring the toy back to its spot, and she groans loudly. Using my grip on her hair as leverage, I slide in and out of her perfect fucking pussy, and straightaway I feel her starting to come. Her pussy milks my cock, and I fucking love it. *She* loves it.

I'll have to remember to ask her after we experiment with all the toys which ones she loves the most.

"Oh God, fuck! Dawson." Her head falls to the bed as I let her hair go. I grip her hips as I fuck her, and my thumb slides over her ass and straight into her asshole. She gasps and looks back over her shoulder, biting her lip.

"In due time, this ass will be mine too," I tell her because I can see how much she loves that too.

"You can have it all," she says breathlessly.

I fist her hair again and pull it back, a smile immediately lighting her face. "Be careful what you offer."

She fucks herself on me, the slapping noise echoing through the room as I grunt. *Fuck, I will never have enough of her.* Her hands fist the sheets as she moans my name, and I know she's close to the edge.

I flick the toy to the next level, and her entire body convulses. *Fuck.* In two more thrusts, I grunt and blow into her, her pulsing pussy milking every drop as she loses the strength in her arms. I let go of her hair as she tumbles to the bed, her hips still angled high and gliding back and forth slowly.

"Wow, I really like that position," she says through a heavy breath.

I glide my hand up her back, over her neck, and around to her throat. She purrs at the touch as I kiss her shoulder.

"Your wish is my command," I say as I pull out of her.

She giggles as I yank her ankle, then throw her over my shoulder and stride toward the shower. I turn the faucet and wait for it to heat as I look at the mirror. She's watching me with a heated stare. I beam a smile and slap her ass hard. She squeals and bites her lip as I lower her to her feet. I push back her hair as she traces the lines of my chest tattoo.

Perfect. So fucking perfect.

"What do you say to us giving this a go?" I ask.

Her silver-flecked gaze reaches mine, and her head drops to the side, confused. I love it when she looks at me like that—innocence and curiosity.

"What do you mean?"

"You asked me yesterday what we are. There's no way I'm fucking letting you go now."

She bites her lip. "Are you going to make me sign a contract?"

I let out a heated laugh as I dip my head to kiss her. The kiss is tender and sweet.

"No contract. But I worry," I admit. "Because if you say yes, Honey, I'm a selfish man, and I won't let anyone else touch you. I don't want you feeling like I'm your only experience."

She mulls this over for a moment. I know it makes her happy as she bites on her bottom lip. "Why don't we become swingers if you begin to make the sex boring?"

I grab her ass and twist hard in punishment.

She chuckles and rises onto her tiptoes to kiss me. But as she pulls back, I know there's uncertainty. Hesitation. *Fuck. Maybe she doesn't want this.* But like hell, I can let her go.

"If we do... you'll have to have dinner with my parents."

I drop my head back and blow out a breath.

"Dawson, I'm serious. What my parents think matters to me."

I growl, frustrated, as I follow her into the shower. "Your father hates my guts."

Water washes over her hair and body. I watch as it trails down her silky soft skin, my cock already twitching at the visual.

"Then do what you do best," she says sweetly as she wrings out her hair. "Be charming."

M y only saving fucking grace is that Crue is out of town and not at this table to give me shit.

Honey's father stares across the table, absolutely disgusted. His wife reaches over and grabs his hand trying to defuse the situation.

We're still waiting for our meals to come to the table. I'd hired out the restaurant just for us because, honestly, one of us will probably end up dead. Three of her father's guards circle the room, and the waiter steps over timidly with the bottles of wine.

Honey is looking between us both. She's wearing a beautiful light-green, free-flowing dress, and, fuck, she couldn't look any more innocent if she tried. I look like the big bad wolf stealing away a delicate flower.

"So, Dawson, tell us a little about yourself. We didn't get to talk much at the wedding," Honey's mother says as she takes a nervous sip of her wine. Mr. Ricci is steadfast with his hardened stare.

I flash her a smile, and in my peripheral vision, I see the vein in her father's temple pulse. "What would you like to know, Mrs. Ricci?" I ask. And, no, we didn't have much time at the wedding because I'd cornered their daughter in a damn storage closet.

"Well, you seem like a very capable man. Wealthy and presentable. What drives you to that level of success?" she asks. And I know she's doing her utmost to aid the situation. Despite Honey's father hating my existence, her mother is delighted by the idea.

"Have you ever killed a man?" her father suddenly interrupts.

"Papa!" Honey growls out. "Be civilized."

He mumbles in Italian, and she reprimands him again. Her hand has been clamped with mine the whole time.

There is no way this man will approve of *any man* being with Honey—I am certain of that much. Crue got a fucking hall pass because their parents had signed a marriage contract. But Honey's the last in the nest. And although she compares herself to Rya often, she is loved beyond measure and it has crippled her growth.

"I prefer to use other methods than killing to deal with threats," I reply and bring the whisky on ice to my lips.

"At home, we need men who are strong, who are

good providers, and can keep their wives and families safe."

"Papa! We're not getting married," Honey interjects.

Mr. Ricci raises his eyebrows. "Oh, so you wish to have some 'fun' with my daughter until the next woman comes along, huh?"

"I care for your daughter very deeply."

He laughs at that, and it's all menace and mockery. "What does a street urchin know of love when he couldn't even get it from his own mother?" he says.

"Papa! How dare you," Honey says, outraged, and stands, but I raise my hand. As expected, he dug deep, and I wouldn't expect anything less.

"We live on tradition. Loyalty. Strength. I see none of these in you, boy."

"I wonder if the struggle here is not who I am but that you're unwilling to let Honey spread her wings."

"I keep my family safe," he spits back.

"You diminish her wants and goals to fit your own agenda," I argue.

His temple pulses wildly as his wife sags ever so slightly in her chair. The defeat is evident in her expression. This was always going to go to shit anyway.

"Honey doesn't know what she wants, and she needs guidance," he states.

I offer a ruthless smile. "Honey is capable of so many things. We were only discussing last night her potential to open a restaurant."

Her mother and father look at her, and she pales.

Fuck. I didn't think she would shrink into herself so quickly. My heart aches when I think back to how excited she was by the prospect of her own restaurant.

"You want to open up a restaurant?" her mother queries.

"Here! In America?" her father shouts.

Honey's gaze meets her glass, and I realize I've fucked up. But I want to shake her, bring that fire I know is there to the forefront.

She rolls her shoulders back. "We were discussing it last night, yes. As an idea. You both want me to have purpose and accomplishment, right?"

"Not here... *in America*." Mr. Ricci sighs. He speaks Italian under his breath, and his wife shushes him.

"And where will you get money for this, Honey?" her mother asks.

She's silent again.

"I'll buy it for her," I tell them.

Mr. Ricci stands, his chair screeching against the floor. I stand to match him and tower over her father by at least a foot. His guards tentatively move closer.

"My daughter is a novelty to someone like you. Something to pass the time until you're done with her. You are not worthy of her."

Honey is standing with me now. Her fingers interlaced with mine. In a front of unity, though, I know she's terrified. The tension is palpable.

I offer him a malicious smile. "Maybe not. But I sure as hell know I will do everything possible to make her happy. Which you seem to be failing at." I look at the knife on the table pointedly. "And to answer your previous question, I've only ever killed when it's served a purpose."

It would only require a signal for him to order one of his men to shoot me where I stand. I know he wants to, and I know that part of me is fucking daring him to do it.

"This was a m-mistake," Honey says, and her broken voice draws me back to her.

"Oh, Honey," her mother says as she reaches over the table.

Tears well in Honey's eyes as she tugs on my arm for us to leave. "We're leaving. But, Papa, Dawson does make me v-very h-happy." Her voice cracks. "And if Rya is allowed to have that, then so should I. I'm sorry I don't live up to your expectations, but I can't live in her shadow anymore, either."

His expression twists momentarily into one of pain. For all his ruthlessness, his girls sure as hell know how to hit the mark as sharp as a bullet.

"Dawson, take me home," she pleads.

All my fight and bravado escape me.

I failed her today. *Fuck.*

I nod to Mrs. Ricci in parting as I let Honey lead us out.

Immediately, Mrs. Ricci begins to yell as the waiters stand at the door, confused, with plates of food in hand.

Goddammit! We didn't even make it to the entrée.

G roveling is not something my father does.
But an entire day of missed calls and not
replying to their messages have led them into
my small apartment. My father sits across from me,
finding sudden interest in the wallpaper. He's a proud
man. One who uses action as opposed to words.

My mother enters the room with coffee and places
the cups in front of us on the coffee table. I wish Rya
were here in times like this because she's always good at
this. *Mediating.* Not that my father and I ever had a need
for that before.

The dinner was horrible.

Worse than horrible.

Hideous.

Appalling.

Loathsome.

And I'd only sent a few texts to Dawson as I tried to

think about what I actually want instead of what everyone else wants for me. And, surprisingly, he's respected that space when I thought he would be kicking down my door. Dawson spent the night here after the dinner. We didn't have sex and barely spoke. Instead, he held me, and I was grateful for his compassion.

I was shocked when he mentioned the idea of the restaurant in front of them, but as I thought about it more, I'm coming around to the idea. Well, a bakery and coffee café, at least.

"I don't like him," my father says, referring to Dawson.

"Leonardo," my mother bites back, and he looks away.

"You don't have to like him, Father, as long as I do."

His gaze lands on me.

I roll my shoulders back again, uncomfortable with his stare. "So what if Dawson and I end up as a fling? It doesn't matter if it's him or anyone else. No man will ever be to your liking."

"He's flashy and arrogant. A pretty boy," my father begins.

"And you're a ruthless killer, but Mother was able to love you."

They seem taken aback by this statement, and I throw my hands in the air. "I'm not a child. And you need to stop treating me as such. Let me make my own decisions and mistakes. Let me stumble and fall. At least

I'll know it was because I made that choice and not because you told me to."

They're both quiet, and I realize for the first time I'm being seen.

I'm actually being heard.

"I don't want to have to choose between my family and whatever it is I want to seek out. Whether it's a relationship or even if I want to build a café. Maybe it'll go well. Maybe it'll flop. But at least I tried using my own merit."

My mother takes a sip of her coffee, a small smile edging her lips, encouraging me to continue, "When Rya said she wasn't going to marry Crue, you allowed it. So why can't I have the same sense of freedom and choice?"

And despite what happened between them, they still got married.

But that isn't the point.

"What about your life back home? Your friends? The extravagant events you enjoy?"

A bubble of laughter creeps up, and my father looks at me as if he doesn't even recognize me. "I've never enjoyed those events. And my friends with their superficial tendencies? The friends that you strategically placed for me as a child? I have made only one friend here. And Daphne is worth more than all those "so-called friends" back home." I use air quotes to get my point across.

I knew my life had been set up for me, but I didn't realize to what extent until I came to New York.

"So either you support me. Or you leave."

My father's brows knit together, and I feel my stomach drop. He isn't a man to be pushed. And the consequence of him dragging me back against my will is an incredibly real and palpable possibility.

"Chasing the American dream," my father grumbles under his breath.

I stand from my chair and crouch in front of him. "No, Papa, I'm just finding out who I am. And if this place allows me to do that right now, then this is where I need to be. I'm not saying I'll be here forever. But for now, I want to stay."

My father tries to avoid my gaze, which is extremely uncharacteristic. But I edge my head back into his line of sight, and he sighs. "I've been given stubborn girls. It's a blessing and a curse."

My mother chuckles as she sets down her coffee, and I know I've won.

Just a little for now.

But a weight feels like it's left me.

Another shackle undone.

"I still don't like him," he grumbles.

I pat his hand. "Yes, Papa, because he's pretty," I say with a smile as I stand to grab the cookies I baked yesterday to accompany our coffee.

M y knee is bouncing, and I don't even realize it until Lesley takes a pointed look over her phone. I stop immediately. We're sitting in a restaurant where I've just met with a potential collaborator. I intend to create a new line of luxury sex toys. With all the shit that is happening, including having no clear identification on the bastard who's messing with my business, my mind can only keep going back to Honey. The dinner with her parents had been a total clusterfuck, and if I'm being entirely honest, I've never been in a position where I couldn't sway or charm someone. But Mr. Ricci is on a different fucking level, and Lord forbid someone come between him and his girls.

"That went well then," Lesley says as she eyes a few prototypes lined up on the table. I grab the polished gold anal beads thoughtfully. *I wonder how many Honey could take.*

"Very," I reply absentmindedly.

I'm growing impatient that we haven't yet identified the stranger who had hovered around the estate taking photographs the night of the event. The car he used was later found abandoned.

I'm not getting any closer.

I'm frustrated.

And annoyed.

"Do you have a name in mind for the new line? I'll start putting everything in place and bring the final contracts to you once I'm done."

"Mr. Taylor," Henry intrudes. He shoots a glance at the toys on the table, and his throat bobs. No wonder my girls tease him so much. "I found something on... well, you know... that person."

He sounds coy, but no one else is in the room. Lesley slides over to the edge of the booth, so she's looking over my shoulder. I wave him over and he hands me his phone.

"I've continued tracking him since he staked out your place and abandoned the car. I was able to track through security cameras that, eventually, he took the night ferry. So I thought it might be a good idea to flick through the cameras from the last month to see if it's a regular occurrence. That maybe he's not from these parts," he says.

I swipe through the various images with different dates of him boarding the ferry.

"I still can't get a clear image of his face. He's good at

avoiding the cameras. And he always wears more coverage around his face after he's approached our members with beanies, hats, stuff like that. But since he's not from here, I was able to track the general area he lives in through street security. It's harder though, because the security cameras really begin to dwindle in that area. But I've narrowed it down."

My finger stops on a picture of the man leaving the ferry. My eyebrows scrunch as I zoom in as best as the graphics allow before pixelation. Henry stops talking as he looks at what I'm so intently studying.

My throat constricts as I stare at the purple wristband tattoo. I flick back through other images, and it's always concealed by the suits and dress shirts he wears. But in this one picture, it's visible, and it dawns on me who this fucker is. Old wounds resurface as I scan through the narrowed-down suburbs. It turns out that no matter how much I thought I'd run away from my past, they'd find a way to get to me. I go back to the photograph with the purple wristband.

"I know who it is," I say, and my hand drops into my lap with the phone. "His name is Timothy Lett."

"Are you sure?" Henry asks as he grabs back his phone, excited by this breakthrough.

"I want you to track him and find his address. Will the name help?" I ask.

"Yes." He nods excitedly. "It might take me another day or so to track him because he is good at keeping to the shadows. But I'll get you to him."

"Make it no more than a day," I grit between my teeth.

Henry nervously nods before excusing himself.

"Who is he to you?" Lesley asks over my shoulder.

I glance over my shoulder at her. "The past," is all I say.

Because I don't trust even Lesley with my past.

It was buried, and an empire was built on top of it.

Or so I thought.

D aphne is squealing in delight. "Yes, yes, and yes! Oh my gosh! If you open a café and bakery, it'll be so cute." She grabs my hand. "Can I be a barista?"

I give her a skeptical look. "Do you know how to make coffee?"

She waves her hand around in a 'never you mind' fashion, and I raise an eyebrow. "Okay, fine. I'll just take the money from the customers. I'm good at that." She winks.

We walk, arms linked, wearing heavy jackets as the cold sets in for the season.

I laugh. "This is progress, though, with you and Dawson, right?" We're walking through the city to a tattoo parlor she booked three months ago. Today is the day, and she's dragging me along because she's scared of needles. Again, I don't even know why she's getting a tattoo considering her fear, but who am I to judge the journey of Daphne.

"Maybe, but my father still can't stand Dawson," I reply.

She laughs again, still delighted by the faceoff I told her about. "I must confess, I love the idea of Dawson not being able to charm the pants off your dad. It must have come as such a shock to him."

We enter the tattoo parlor, and a small bell jingles over the door. The woman at the reception desk smiles and tells us to sit and the wait time is ten minutes. The walls are covered with marvelous creations—admittedly, it's the first time I've stepped into a place like this.

"It's not an ideal situation, but baby steps, I suppose," I confess as I continue to look at the art on the walls. The pieces vary in size. There are some full-sleeve tattoos ranging from dragons to geishas, but I prefer the smaller, daintier designs.

"Maybe not, but I'm starting to think your dad is a hardass. It's pretty damn hot, to be honest."

"Eww." My skin crawls at anyone calling my father hot. She rolls her eyes and giggles. If only she knew the harsh reality of how deadly my father is. I'd left out certain parts of my story to cover that fact.

Eventually my gaze lands on a particular design, and I'm immediately drawn to it. It's small, possibly even trashy, but I love it. A rush of adrenaline runs through me as Daphne eyes me and the small tattoo.

"You know... you could get a tat with me. I'm sure

we could convince them to squeeze you in if it's a small one."

"A tattoo? Me?" I laugh. She nods her head with an encouraging smile.

"You only live once, right? And besides, that's why they have lasering... if you have regrets, you just get it removed."

"I heard that hurts more than getting the tattoo."

She pales at that. "Well, just make sure you're certain about the one you get."

It's madness to randomly get a tattoo, isn't it?

But then again, I can do whatever I want.

It's my choice.

CHAPTER 51
Honey

I've just finished cooking in Dawson's kitchen when I hear him pull into the garage. He gave me a spare key after staying here with him the first night, and I wanted to surprise him a little. Then again, his security cameras feed his phone, which probably took the surprise away.

Dawson walks in with a bottle of red to complement the pizzas I've just made. I have to rectify the situation where he thinks the pizza joint he took me to has the best pizza because it is, in fact, my nonna's recipe that is the best.

His gaze sweeps me up and down as I remove my apron, and he walks over to me. He lifts me into his arms, his tongue hot and demanding as it invades my mouth. I feel the stiffness in his muscles under my fingertips, the only small tell he has when something has happened.

"I could get used to this," he says as he wipes something from my cheek, and I realize it's a bit of flour. "You look good in my kitchen."

"You look good in my bed," I reply, and his gaze darkens. Dawson steps away, and I'm left slightly jarred. I lean against the counter and cross my arms over my chest as I watch him unscrew the cork from the wine bottle like a man on a mission.

"Everything okay?" I ask.

He pauses momentarily before continuing, and the pop echoes through the room. "Just work stuff."

"You need to be more specific with me because when my father says 'work stuff' it may very well entail that he was a part of a drive-by."

"I doubt your father does that himself these days," he says, clearly distracted.

"Dawson," I say impatiently. He sighs and licks his lips. Something has really got him bothered. "You can tell me anything?"

"It's being dealt with. I want to selfishly enjoy tonight with you. Please."

It's the please that undoes me. I want to push further, but his mind is on a wild rampage. And if I can distract him from that, give him a moment of peace, then I'll happily fulfill that role.

He pours us a glass of wine and takes a whiff of the pizza. "It smells delicious."

I can't help but smile, always pleased when someone appreciates my food. But especially Dawson.

"I did something today," I say with a mischievous

smile. His own smile is slow and playful, even though he doesn't know what I've done. "But it's a secret."

"I love keeping your dirty little secrets," he jokes.

"I got a tattoo."

His eyebrows flick up. "Fuck me, Honey! If your father didn't think I was a bad enough influence before, he will now."

"That's why it's *our little secret*." I press my finger to his lips, and he nips the tip of it.

"Okay, show me."

"You have to be gentle because it's still sore." I lift my free-flowing yellow dress. His gaze darkens when he realizes I'm not wearing any panties. "I haven't been able to wear anything because of where it is."

He leans over and sucks in a small breath as he admires the artwork. He brushes a thumb close to its edges. "You got a little bear," he says quietly.

I drop my dress suddenly, too embarrassed. "Well, I figured since you got my lips tattooed on your cock, then maybe I could do this. But also, you know... if this doesn't work out between us, I can laser it off. It's no biggie and—"

He cuts me off as his hand grabs my jaw, and he pushes his lips to mine, claiming me. I melt into him immediately. His kiss is tender, then demanding and possessive. His grip is firm on my jaw as he devours me, and I let him.

He picks me up, his hands on my bare ass, and he places me on the counter.

"No!" I snap. "We are not letting this pizza go cold. Dinner first."

Dawson dips his head to my shoulder with a grumble, and I laugh when he nips at my exposed shoulder. He perks back up, his gaze meeting mine. The desire is still a real and burning thing, but there's something else there that I don't yet entirely understand.

"What do you think your father would say if we told him we were getting married?"

I freeze at his insinuation. I haven't really thought about marriage since my arranged disaster with Crue. And it seems like a sudden conversation with Dawson since we only just decided to be what? Boyfriend and girlfriend? Exclusive?

"You just want me to sign a contract," I reply with an eye roll.

"Nope. No prenup, no contracts. Just you and me."

I'm shocked because Dawson loves contracts, and I can't tell if he's serious or still playing. Dawson also knows how serious a commitment like marriage is to me —to my family and our name.

After the Crue and Rya incident, I wasn't sure if I wanted to get married. But as I thought about it more, I realized it was still something I sought. Something I want. I don't ever plan on divorce. I'm not saying that divorce is a sin. Some people need to be divorced from their partners for any number of reasons, and that's why I plan to take my time and be careful with who I pick as my permanent partner. I want to make sure my instincts are correct and that I'm marrying the right person.

"Are you serious?" I ask, pulling back from him.

"I've been thinking about this a lot. Thinking about you," he tacks on. "I have never once felt anything for any other woman the way I feel for you. When I told you I wasn't willing to give you away, I meant it. The only way you're escaping me is if you shoot me. So, in due time, prepare for it because it will come. I will ask you to marry me, Honey Ricci, because I literally cannot see myself with any other person in this world but you."

"But..." I shake my head.

"I know you aren't sure. But by the time I ask you, you will be," Dawson confidently says.

My heart is racing, and I feel hopeful joy and confusion at how quickly it's come up. Is everyone's relationship like this?

"How are you so sure?" I ask, my hand pressing lightly on his chest.

"Because it's you," he says simply as if that explains everything. "And *you* are *mine*."

I smile at his words, but I'm unsure of them. However, having someone claim me as theirs does feel nice. And the fact he isn't afraid of my father? I like that too.

It might be just a moment because of whatever pressure or stress he's having at work, but if I can be the person here waiting for him, reassuring him, and stealing kisses for myself all day long, then doesn't that make me the selfish one?

"Wow! Maybe I put special mushrooms on this pizza," I joke to lighten the intensity of the moment.

He laughs and rests his head on my shoulder, and I feel the tension ease out of him as I comb my fingers through his hair.

"I brought something for you for dessert as well," he says into my chest as he presses kisses along it.

"And what's that?" I ask, hugging him. Embracing this powerful man and claiming him as mine, even if it's only for now. But hopefully, it'll be forever.

"Shall we try some anal beads tonight, dear?" he asks and looks up from beneath thick eyelashes. His smile alone promises all the sweet and new things. Exciting things. My clit pounds, and I start to feel too hot in this dress. The idea of trying something new excites me. I know Dawson is introducing me to his world bit by bit.

But I want it all now.

Fuck the pizza.

CHAPTER 52

Honey

Dawson had to leave early this morning. An emergency came up at work, and he didn't go into further detail as he quietly tucked me back into bed, kissed me on the forehead, and left.

I'm sitting in a bar now, in a yellow pantsuit, scrolling through my tablet as I show Daphne the few design ideas I've come up with. *Thank you, Pinterest board*. "I want it to have chic Italian décor," I tell her.

Daphne and the bartender have been eye fucking for the last hour we've been here. And after two drinks, she's anyone's. Though he is cute—not that I think Daphne has a particular type—and part of me is envious of her free spirit. I wonder if I could be like her and sleep with multiple men. I mean, I want to say "yes, I can," and could have that much fun "tasting the menu" as Daphne called it once. But I know I'm not that type of person.

"Can we also add how much I love how girl-boss you

are right now?" she says as she takes a sip of her Long Island iced tea. "And those Louis Vuittons? Damn, girl, you're going all out. Do you have a business meeting after this?"

I laugh. "No. But we are having dinner with my parents in about two hours. And I felt like showing them a new side of me. Rya always looks so smart and stylish, and I love her wardrobe, but I always thought that style was only for someone like her. So I've stepped out a little."

"You didn't steal this from her wardrobe, did you?"

I laugh. *What are little sisters for if not raiding their sister's wardrobes?* "No, I did some shopping this morning."

She gasps. "Without me? Blasphemy. Oooh, what about that one!" She points out a shop front as I scroll through properties on my tablet. I stop immediately to check it out.

"This one?" I ask, looking at the super run-down joint.

"That location is great," she exclaims. "I remember going there as a kid. It used to be a candy store, but then the wife got sick and passed away, and shortly after, the husband closed up shop. He wasn't willing to sell despite how prime the location is. He would have been offered so much for it. Maybe the old man finally croaked." I give her an unimpressed look, and she raises her hands with an awkward laugh. "What? I know it's a sad story. But it's a really good location."

"I mean, I guess I'm not against ripping out some-thing old and refurbishing it into something new," I muse.

"Yeah, and I can help. Like, not with the labor side of things, but, you know, with advertising and bringing in customers for a grand opening. Your girl here has over one hundred thousand followers. We can really blow some shit up. Plus, you have a hottie boyfriend who's dealt with renovating heaps of places. You can't possibly fail!"

I laugh and take an appreciative sip of my wine. Who would have thought six months ago I'd be here, with what feels like my first genuine friend, scrolling through real estate in New York, and with a hot as fuck boyfriend.

Daphne giggles at the bartender as they continue to talk. Apparently, they used to go to the same high school. And who isn't a sucker for the idea of a second chance? Although, supposedly, he used to be the nerdy type and has clearly had a serious glow-up.

"I'm finishing up now, but maybe if you're not busy later, I can take you for dinner?" he asks her hopefully.

I bite back a smile as I take a sip of my drink. He's obviously been listening in on my conversation and knows I'm meeting with my parents later. It's their last night here, and Crue and Rya are returning to join us. It will be round two for Dawson and my father to try not to kill each other.

"You can have her now if you'd like." I interrupt

them as they exchange numbers and potential meet-up times.

Daphne looks at me over her shoulder. "Are you sure?"

I smile at her and see the thank you in her gaze. "Dawson is supposed to meet me here in the next hour or so, and I'm busy starting an empire," I joke, but I love how those words sound. If it goes well, I could franchise, maybe? Or am I getting ahead of myself?

"Yeah, that'd be cool," he says eagerly. "Let me just punch out."

"Oh my God, do I look cute?" she asks, and I roll my eyes.

"You're always beautiful. But no sex on the first date," I tell her.

She throws her head back and laughs. "Why stop a good thing now? You might be locked down, but I am not."

I laugh and wave her off. She downs her Long Island iced tea and meets him at the entrance.

I pick up my phone, surprised that Dawson hasn't responded to my earlier photograph. I'd sent him a pic as I explored the anal beads again this morning by myself. Usually, I receive an immediate response.

I try my hardest to push away the sinking feeling in my stomach.

I'm just being paranoid.

CHAPTER 53
Dawson

I step out of my car, adjusting my suit.

Onlookers are watching me.

Half of them most likely fucked-up on God only knows what substance. I hate it here. I fucking hate every single thing about it. This place is where people come to die. Whether they take their own life or someone else takes it for them. And I can't even pity them. Not when the scum that live in these parts were so happy to throw a fifteen-year-old into prostitution for a few dollars.

I tell Henry to wait in the car. He insists on following me, but I quickly deny him. He's not the violent type. Though, with his skill set, I'm sure he's had to fish through graphic images and videos, it's very different from watching cold-blooded murder take place firsthand in front of your eyes.

My gun sits comfortably within my suit. And in a

place like this, it will go unnoticed. Easily forgotten and removed, just as I had been. I step through the overgrown grass to a door that hangs off its hinges.

Last night, Honey offered me a moment of reprieve. But I couldn't rest, even with her in my arms. I meant what I said last night. I *will* marry her one day. I'm not a good man. Or at my true core, even an attractive one. But I will never let her be at risk.

Confronting Timothy like this has brought back memories of what we'd endured together, and although I don't know his motives, I don't care.

The two stairs creak as I walk up them. I've already called Crue to arrange a clean-up once this is done.

The partially open door lets a horrendous smell waft through. I choke on it, lifting my arm to my nose. I peek inside to see a small box on the floor with a half-eaten bowl of cereal on top of it, but I don't hear anything.

I carefully open the door wider on its one hinge, and the horrendous odor bombards me. *What the fuck is that?*

I peer into the cereal bowl, which appears to be only a few hours old. I walk around the small home. It's chaos. Litter. Rodents. The furniture torn and broken. I raise my gun as I step into the back bedroom. The edge of a mattress on the floor is visible, and I push open the door.

My stomach curdles when I realize what the stench is. A woman's half-decayed and eaten body is sprawled on the bed. My gaze lands on the picure frame beside the bed.

Recognition hits me.

It's Timothy with a woman I recognize. She had only just been brought into the game when I was leaving. *Lyla*. I look back at the carcass. The straw-like blonde hair is a dirtier shade than the one in the image.

My phone begins to buzz, and I check the name. *Henry.*

There's nobody here, so I turn to leave and stumble on a near-empty bottle of liquor. It draws my attention to the used needle on the floor beside it.

I lift the phone to my ear. "He's not here. I'm coming out now."

"I know. Because he's back in the city."

I don't know why, but Henry's words make my blood run cold.

"Where is he now?" I ask.

"He's at the bar you're scheduled to meet Honey at in an hour."

Rage engulfs me truer than any emotion I've ever allowed myself to feel before.

Making a move on my empire is a mistake.

Approaching my woman is a death sentence.

CHAPTER 54
Honey

"Is someone sitting here?" a man asks, interrupting as I take notes of the property Daphne pointed out. I look up from my tablet to a man wearing black shades so dark I can't see his eyes.

I shake my head and offer it to him before diligently adding notes again. There's an unsettling smell coming from him, but I try to ignore it.

"It's a nice restaurant," he says charmingly, looking up at the beautiful décor on the ceiling.

"It is," I reply distractedly. I don't know why, but an unsettling feeling comes over me. I look over my shoulder at the bodyguard who's been casually flicking through a paper with an untouched meal in front of him since I sat down.

"Can I ask you a question?" he asks.

"I'm quite busy right now. And I'm waiting for someone," I say as politely as possible.

"Dawson?" he asks.

I look at him now, really look at him. "You know Dawson?"

He nods his head enthusiastically. "Yeah. We go way back." It's then that I notice the tremor that ripples through him and the slight slur of his words. I flick another glance to my bodyguard but realize this man has had his back to him the whole time.

"Uh-uh," he says, shaking his finger. "I wouldn't cause a scene." He pulls back his jacket slightly. The motherfucker has a gun. "I'm not opposed to shooting that wailing child over there before I shoot you if you make any sudden movements."

My screen lights up, and I realize Dawson is calling. It's the fifth time he's called. I'd been so enthralled in my research I hadn't even noticed. "What do you want?" I ask.

He seems taken aback by that question. "What do I want?" He considers as the bartender offers him the drink he ordered earlier. His finger circles the rim thoughtfully. "What I want, I can't have." There's no emotion in his tone. "I've lied, cheated, killed, and fucked, all under the pretense of being charming. And it got me nowhere. And yet, Dawson gets everything he wants. Money. Power. Reputation. A pretty girl."

My back is straight, and if anyone were looking, they might think of this as a business transaction. I've dealt with half-assed power plays before, but not someone sitting beside me with a gun, threatening not only me but others around me. The man is clearly not in his right mind.

"And what do you want from me?" I ask.

He chuckles. It has a velvety tone, a honed craft for pleasure. Was he an escort? Not that it matters, I have to get him away from these people.

"Your boyfriend can't buy his way out of this one," he sneers.

I realize then that he is so focused on Dawson that he has no idea who I am. He tracked me here, sure. But no one smart enough would come after me so boldly if they know who my father is. Unless, of course, they're already a dead man walking.

I slowly pick up my glass and take a sip.

He watches the movement before he throws back his own drink. "You're going to walk toward the bathroom, but instead, you're going to cut through the kitchen and out the back."

I let out a breath. "Let me guess, an alleyway?" I say tiredly.

It's always a fucking alleyway.

"I don't think you understand the severity of this situation," he snaps under his breath, and I try my best not to be affected by it. I quickly glance around at the people in the room. How many could he shoot before my bodyguard stands and shoots him? Three, maybe four? If he shoots the bodyguard first, it might be a free-for-all.

"I understand," I say and carefully press against the bar counter. "Out the back. I'm going now."

He pockets my phone as I leave. When I turn the corner for the bathroom, I sense he's only a few steps behind me. And more than likely, my bodyguard is following him. At least this will be taken elsewhere and take away the danger for the other patrons in the bar. My body shakes as I walk through the kitchen like I own the place. It's not necessarily fear but a buzz, perhaps of adrenaline. Uncertainty. The kitchen staff offer peculiar looks but say nothing.

The cold air hits me as I step into the alley with the psycho right on my heels.

CHAPTER 55
Dawson

She finally picks up her phone as I frantically burst into the restaurant. Plates flying into the air as I run into a waiter.

"Honey?" I say into the phone.

For the first time in my life, I experience very real, living, livid panic.

"Not quite," a man's voice replies on the other end. *Bang!* The gunshot rings through the phone and from the back of the restaurant.

My entire body runs cold as my legs take me through the kitchen, a blur of screams and staff as I burst through the back door.

She can't be.

No.

She's not.

Timothy has his arm wrapped around Honey's shoulder, a gun pressed to her head. One of Crue's men rolls on the ground, moaning, having taken a bullet to the shoulder.

Timothy licks his lips. "Frisky little thing, this one. I had a clear aim before she interfered."

I slowly take a step down into the gravelly alley. My gaze is locked with Honey, my heart pounding. Despite the situation, she looks pissed off, and she blows the hair out of her eyes with a puff. *What the fuck?*

My heart is pounding, yet her attitude, everything about her, reminds me she's a Ricci. And with that, I calm down and collect myself.

"Lose the gun, Dawson," Timothy says, licking his lips.

I ease the tension in my body, trying to see past the red overtaking my vision. Slowly, I pull the gun out and place it on the ground.

"Are you okay?" I ask Honey.

She nods and all but growls in response.

"Eyes on me, Mr. Bigshot," Timothy snarls.

My gaze immediately goes to him. "How many calling cards did I have to leave to get your attention? My God! You took so long to find me." He laughs hysterically, and I know it's a combination of the liquor and whatever was in that needle.

"Let Honey go. This has nothing to do with her. This is between us."

"On the contrary. Why do you get to have everything when we both came from nothing? Why do you get to have her?" he questions loudly.

He presses the gun harder to the side of her head, his hand shaking. Panic tries to grip me again as I look at Honey, who is completely calm. As soon as we make eye contact, she mouths, *Drop.*

I only have a split second to act, but, as do I, so does she. The trust is unyielding.

I roll to the side, and in a quick move, she pushes his arm into the air. The gun goes off again, and she throws him over her shoulder, the gun dragging against the ground as she pushes her heel into his throat.

He tries to scratch at her leg, but she steps down harder until he gasps.

Honey is dangerous and beautiful.

Lethal and sickly sweet.

I'm by her side within seconds, the gun in my hand and pointed at his head.

"You—" he tries to rasp, but I put a bullet straight between his eyes.

Honey looks away as she slowly lifts her heel from his throat and steps back.

"I just bought this fucking suit," she seethes.

My heart is pounding with everything that's just happened. And I'm mad. Fucking furious. Beyond enraged.

I grab her face. "Why would you come out here with him?" I demand.

She seems wary. All that lethalness edging away with her adrenaline levels to reveal the Honey I know. "There were children inside."

"But you could've—" I am a desperate and wild mess. I've never known fear. But today, I felt it like a noose around my neck.

"Dawson, I'm here," she reminds me, cupping my cheeks in her soft hands. "I know how to kick ass, remember?"

And for the first and only time in my life, I'm grateful for her father. That he forced her to learn how to defend herself when I couldn't.

I can't breathe.

I can't stop staring at her.

"I failed," I say miserably.

"Hey." She slaps me hard across the face, and it's shocking. "We did that together. That blood is on both of our hands. I'm not a damsel in distress, Dawson. We do this together. Everything together going forward. Do you understand?"

It's a cold, hard dose of reality as I stare into the eyes of this unsuspectingly dangerous woman.

A click of a gun being cocked grabs our attention from the direction of the door. "Fuck me."

CHAPTER 56
Honey

A wild, voracious storm burns in his eyes as he stares at me. Admiration and surprise. I've never been a sweet thing. Maybe on the outside, but on the inside, I've always been able to look after myself, and they would have known that had I been let a little off my leash.

"Family is everything, and to defy the head deplorable." Those words were ingrained into us as small children.

That is, of course, until my father points a gun at the man I love.

Before I can react, Dawson shoves me back and raises his own gun.

"Papa!" I scream. There's a wild, fierce creature who wants to claw her way out of me. I suddenly understand everything that Dawson's gaze expresses to me without words. "Papa!" I scream again, and my voice doesn't even sound like my own.

Dawson raises his hand to me. "Stay back, Honey."

"You actually have the nerve to raise a gun at me, you little fucker?" my father sneers.

No, not my father.

The man people fear.

He steps out into the alley, two of his guards following with their guns raised.

My mother shouts at him from behind, but he doesn't hear her. Or me. I'm scared that if I move, my father will pull the trigger. But I'm scared if I don't stand in front of Dawson, he will do so as well.

Dawson offers a half smile before throwing his gun to the side in the opposite direction of me. Probably because he knows I'll raise it against my own father.

"You put my daughter in danger," my father snarls.

"I love your daughter," Dawson yells. "And I would do anything to protect her." My father steps up to him, pressing the edge of the gun to his head.

"Papa, no, *please*," I beg. My voice is hoarse, my legs shaky. "Please, Papa. *Please*."

All of my worst nightmares are coming to fruition.

My father is going to kill my first love.

"Not that your daughter needs protecting," Dawson adds, suddenly calm as he looks at me with a small smile. Tears stream down my face, and I can't look away. "But I agree that she shouldn't be following strange men into alleyways."

Is he fucking joking? How could he make light of this situation? But it is one of the reasons I love him.

I feel my father's gaze bouncing between us. I don't want to look away from Dawson, but I must look at the other man I love. The one who finally has to let me go.

I turn to my father. "Please, Papa," I beg. "He's a good man."

My father's gaze is ruthless. This side of him has never been pointed toward me, but I will *not* back down. This time, I fight.

The rage slowly leaves his eyes as he lowers his gun.

"He's a fucking American," my father says, disappointed.

My breath comes out shaky as I run to Dawson. My need to touch, kiss, and claim him again is a very serious thing.

He claims me equally.

Desperately and unapologetically.

We stay like that for several moments before Rya's voice echoes in the alley, "What the actual fuck? We come back from our honeymoon for... what exactly is this?"

"A clean-up job," Crue says as he pushes past my father and looks at the dead man on the ground. "You gave me the wrong address," he says to Dawson.

"Things changed." Dawson shrugs.

"And how the fuck do you think you're going to cover up this one?" Rya asks with hands on hips.

Crue looks at her, almost confused. "Well, firstly, I own this restaurant and everyone who works here, and secondly, it turns out I have a sexy criminal lawyer for a wife as backup."

She chokes out a laugh. "Backup?" And I can tell honeymoon sex has come to an end.

I can't help but laugh as the atmosphere of today's events lightens. The very world I had been ignorant of, yet still a part of, crashed into Dawson's world.

Men stride into the alley and efficiently wrap the body.

I watch them, my head resting on Dawson's shoulder. He's observing them carefully, his expression hard. His polished mask is firmly back in place.

My father approaches us, and I freeze, unsure if he's reconsidered what he most likely thinks of as his "generosity."

"I don't know how you Americans do it, but we usually prefer our killings a little less obvious."

Rya gives a pointed look at our father because the truth is, Crue is anything but discreet. He point-blank shot Rya's boss at her thirtieth birthday party in a room full of people.

"I'll keep it in mind, Mr. Ricci," Dawson says with his arm around my waist.

My father harrumphs at him. "But if you look after my daughter, you do it right. Traditionally."

My heart floods at his approval.

Finally.

I jump at my father, my hug surprising him. "Thank you, Papa."

"I still don't like him. Pretty Boy," he mumbles, but I can tell his opinion of Dawson has changed. I let go of Father and take my rightful place beside Dawson.

It's a bizarre way to get my father's approval, but then I wonder if anyone could have done it any other way.

"Why did you throw away the gun?" I ask Dawson. "My father was going to kill you."

He smiles as if it's the most obvious answer in the world. "I know you love your family, Honey. And their approval is important to you. I have no reason to be in this world if I can't be by your side."

I slap him on the shoulder, a blush heating my cheeks. I love his answer, but it's humiliating and always only for me to hear.

Dawson has a reputation to uphold, after all.

M y heart is pounding as they finish the signage. It's taken me six months to build this from scratch.

The stylish sign reads 'Honey and Bear.' And in two days, we're officially opening.

"You did good," Rya says, putting her hand on my shoulder in approval. Her other hand rests on her stomach, which has only begun showing in the last few weeks.

After their official honeymoon, Rya was greeted with a surprise. More specifically, a bun in the oven. Not so surprisingly, she's come around to the idea of being a mother. And as ruthless as Crue might be, he has been ridiculously cautious of anything that might harm the unborn child, including an entire renovation of one of the wings to the penthouse. And Rya's going slightly mad in the process.

I receive a text message from Dawson and open it

immediately. There are numerous images of toys and lingerie in his new store called 'Honey,' and legally, I own half. I went in as a partner, but Dawson credited his inspiration to his "darling fiancée" as he announced to the press.

I stare down at the giant rock on my finger. It should feel strange being a soon-to-be wife, but it doesn't.

Not when it's with the right person.

Even if he is the most desirable man in all of America.

He's all mine.

Forever.

Always.

For as long as he quenches my sexual curiosity.

I'm starting to think my soon-to-be husband might have bitten off more than he can chew.

But I'm not at all surprised when I feel heat behind my ear. "Do you like the merchandise?" Dawson asks. I roll my eyes, very familiar with his ability to sneak up behind me. Rya has found interest within the store. Obviously, I was more immersed in the images of toys he sent through.

"Hmm," I purr as I wrap my arms around his neck and look into his bluer-than-blue eyes. "It depends if the user knows how to use them. I hope they know how to please me."

His smile promises promiscuous things.

"Dawson." A woman's Russian accent demands his attention.

We both turn to face a beautiful woman with two bodyguards flanking her.

"Anya, what are you doing here?" Dawson asks and stands in front of me protectively.

"I'm trying to find the whereabouts of my brother. We need to talk."

A cold chill runs up my spine. This woman is ruthless and cruel, and in the same light I've seen others around my father. But this woman is willing to flip the world over. Dawson politely smiles and glances inside at Rya, who is watching. Her guards are close.

"Perhaps we should speak privately," he politely asks, then turns his back on her to face me. "Go inside for a little bit. Nothing will happen."

"Who is she?" I question.

There are no secrets between us.

"Anya Ivanov. You could say a business partner of sorts. I'll be inside shortly, Honey."

I eye the woman over his shoulder, who stares at me with little curiosity. She is breathtakingly beautiful, the type where you know her beauty would cut you deep.

I sigh, but I understand this is also one of those partnerships with which Dawson wants me to have no association. I kiss his cheek and walk into the café. Rya is watching through the window when I join her.

"Pretty," Rya comments on Anya as she rubs her belly.

"Violent," I add. All types of power and force ooze from Anya as she speaks feverishly with Dawson.

But as quickly as she arrived, she nods in appreciation and steps back into the chic black car.

Dawson walks into the café, the little bell on top of the door ringing as he blows out a breath.

"Is everything okay?" I ask, suddenly wanting to knead some dough or take my fiancé into the back room.

"No. New York is about to be flipped on its head," he casually says. "But it won't affect us."

He walks up, quickly throwing me over his shoulder as I squeal. "Dawson!"

"Now, I'm due to be away for two nights, but we have some things to make up for before then."

"And I'll let myself out," Rya drawls.

"I might have brought a certain little toy you've been begging to try," Dawson promises as he slaps my ass. "I wouldn't want my fiancée getting promiscuous while I'm out of town."

"I like the sound of that," I tell him, leaning into him.

I can't help but think about that supply closet, where it all started.

And how proud I am of little old me and how far I have come.

And the man who is set to make me his wife...

... of my choosing.

What more could a girl ask for?

Also by T.L. Smith

Black (Black #1)

Red (Black #2)

White (Black #3)

Green (Black #4)

Kandiland

Pure Punishment (Standalone)

Antagonize Me (Standalone)

Degrade (Flawed #1)

Twisted (Flawed #2)

Distrust (Smirnov Bratva #1) FREE

Disbelief (Smirnov Bratva #2)

Defiance (Smirnov Bratva #3)

Dismissed (Smirnov Bratva #4)

Lovesick (Standalone)

Lotus (Standalone)

Savage Collision (A Savage Love Duet book 1)

Savage Reckoning (A Savage Love Duet book 2)

Buried in Lies

Distorted Love (Dark Intentions Duet 1)

Sinister Love (Dark Intentions Duet 2)

Cavalier (Crimson Elite #1)

Anguished (Crimson Elite #2)

Conceited (Crimson Elite #3)

Insolent (Crimson Elite #4)

Playette

Love Drunk

Hate Sober

Heartbreak Me (Duet #1)

Heartbreak You (Duet #2)

My Beautiful Poison

My Wicked Heart

My Cruel Lover

Chained Hands

Locked Hearts

Sinful Hands

Shackled Hearts

Reckless Hands

Arranged Hearts

Unlikely Queen

A Villain's Kiss

A Villain's Lies

Moments of Malevolence

Moments of Madness

Connect with T.L Smith by tlsmithauthor.com

Also by Kia Carrington Russell

Mine for the Night, New York Nights Book 1

Us for the Night, New York Nights Book 2

Stranded for the Night, New York Nights Book 3

Token Huntress, Token Huntress Book 1

Token Vampire, Token Huntress Book 2

Token Wolf, Token Huntress Book 3

Token Phantom, Token Huntress Book 4

Token Darkness, Token Huntress Book 5

Token Kingdom, Token Huntress Book 6

The Shadow Minds Journal

T.L. Smith

USA Today Best Selling Author T.L. Smith loves to write her characters with flaws so beautiful and dark you can't turn away. Her books have been translated into several languages. If you don't catch up with her in her home state of Queensland, Australia you can usually find her travelling the world, either sitting on a beach in Bali or exploring Alcatraz in San Francisco or walking the streets of New York.

Connect with me tlsmithauthor.com

Kia Carrington-Russell

Australian Author, Kia Carrington-Russell is known for her recognizable style of kick a$$ heroines, fast-paced action, enemies to lovers and romance that dances from light to dark in multiple genres including Fantasy, Dark and Contemporary Romance.

Obsessed with all things coffee, food and travel, Kia is always seeking out her next adventure internationally. Now back in her home country of Australia, she takes her Cavoodle, Sia along morning walks on beautiful coastline beaches, building worlds in the sea breezes and contemplating which deliciously haunting story to write next.